Tara Moss is a bestselling author, human rights activist, documentary host, and model. Her novels have been published in nineteen countries and thirteen languages, and her memoir *The Fictional Woman* was a #1 national bestseller. She is a UNICEF Goodwill Ambassador and has received the Edna Ryan Award for her significant contributions to feminist debate and for speaking out for women and children, and in 2017 she was recognised as one of the Global Top 50 Diversity Figures in Public Life. She is a PhD Candidate at the University of Sydney, and has earned her private investigator credentials (Cert III) from the Australian Security Academy. *The Cobra Queen* is her thirteenth book and fourth Pandora English novel.

Also by Tara Moss

FICTION

The Pandora English series

The Blood Countess

The Spider Goddess

The Skeleton Key

The Cobra Queen

The Makedde Vanderwall series

Fetish

Split

Covet

Hit

Siren

Assassin

The Billie Walker series

Dead Man Switch (The War Widow)

NON-FICTION

The Fictional Woman

Speaking Out

TARA MOSS

echo

echo

Echo Publishing
An imprint of Bonnier Books UK
80-81 Wimpole Street
London W1G 9RE
www.echopublishing.com.au
www.bonnierbooks.co.uk

First published 2020

Cover design by Lisa Brewster
Page design and typesetting by Shaun Jury

Typeset in Baskerville

Printed in Australia at Griffin Press.
Only wood grown from sustainable regrowth forests is used in the manufacture of paper found in this book.

NATIONAL LIBRARY OF AUSTRALIA

A catalogue record for this book is available from the National Library of Australia
ISBN: 9781760686260 (paperback)
ISBN: 9781760686512 (ebook)

echopublishingau
echo_publishing
echo_publishing

For Berndt

Chapter One

What is a spirit guide?

I typed my query into the search engine on my work computer and glanced furtively around the open-plan office. On finding that I was unobserved, I sat down low in my chair and pressed enter. This was no mere work query. This was, well, *personal.*

It was only four o'clock in the afternoon on a Tuesday, and I was at the boutique New York fashion magazine where I work. Despite our shared name, my only actual connection with the magazine is my unglamorous position as assistant to the editor. But I do look deceptively important on my business card: *Pandora English, Pandora Magazine*. I wasn't above milking that coincidence when I needed to, short of lying, of course. I'm no good at lying. I don't have a lot of work experience, but I know it's frowned upon to surf the Internet during paid work hours. Thing is, I don't have a computer at home and I don't have the Internet either.

Nervously, I chewed the inside of my lip and clicked on the first search result that came up: *A spirit guide is defined as an entity that remains a disincarnate spirit in order to act as a guide or protector to a living incarnated human being.*

Disincarnate? Lieutenant Luke wasn't always disincarnate.

Sometimes he was really quite carnate indeed. He was very handsome and attentive, and, well, the thought of his carnate moments made my cheeks hot. We had a very special date in just two nights, on the Blue Moon. I'd been looking forward to it all month. I licked my upper lip, which had suddenly become dry, and continued reading: *Spirit guide can also refer to totems, angels, guardian angels*.

Hmm. I guess I could think of Lieutenant Luke as a guardian angel. I liked that idea, actually. Still, what did that mean exactly? That he would push me out of the way of speeding trains or stop me from stepping off cliffs? He'd come to my aid in the past, and mine to his, for that matter. But why did I have a spirit guide at all? What were the rules of engagement here? Is it ethically okay to *date* your guardian angel? Was that done? I had a serious crush on my spirit guide and I didn't know what to do about it for a bunch of reasons – not least was that I had something like a boyfriend already. His name was Jay Rockwell, and he was nice and rather handsome and tall, if a bit embarrassingly wealthy. Oh, and sometimes he didn't remember me (paranormal 'erasure', long story), but by regular-world standards he was what people commonly called 'a catch'. Plus, you know, he was *alive.* The whole issue of dating two men at once was awkward, when only one knew about the other, and only one was living, and ... My life was complicated.

The door opened behind me and I closed the search browser so fast you couldn't even see my hand move.

'Pepper,' I declared and stood bolt upright.

Pepper Smith was the editor of *Pandora*, and my boss. She

was bright, fashionably thin and highly caffeinated, and today she wore her ice-blonde hair in a severe bun right on the top of her head. I think fashion-types called it a 'top knot'. Her lightweight blazer was a striking emerald green, and she wore dark denim finished with a matching green stitch. She was wearing black platform boots with cut outs that showed off fuchsia, pedicured toenails. I was pretty sure I'd never seen Pepper in the same thing twice and today was no exception.

I stood to attention in front of her and she raised a pale sculpted eyebrow at me. 'What's up with you?'

'Sorry … Nothing,' I said and leaned back against the edge of my cubicle, faux casual.

She eyed me suspiciously. 'You are a strange girl.'

There was no comeback for that, really.

'Can you work late tonight?' she asked.

'Tonight?' I found myself nodding automatically, though I suspected I would be exhausted by nightfall. I'd been up late with my … well, my spirit guide slash guardian angel slash sometime other boyfriend. (Can you tell I am feeling guilty?) It had become a bit heated – his lips were like sweet mist and when he kissed me I felt like I was floating … Don't get me started. Suffice to say, sleep was a thing of the past since I'd moved to New York.

'Certainly I can work late,' I replied.

'The fashion shoot has moved. We're shooting at the Temple of Dendur but we can't get in until after dark,' my boss explained.

'Oh.' I blinked. The Temple of Dendur was quite familiar, though I'd never seen it in person.

'For the Egyptian-themed shoot,' my boss said with a hint of impatience.

'Yes,' I replied, because I knew precisely which shoot she meant and why the Temple of Dendur would be the perfect location. This summer would apparently be all about ancient Egyptian-themed fashion – Cleopatra and the like – and we were devoting most of an issue to the look, which included chunky gold jewellery, winged eye makeup, sandals worn with long dresses that draped luxuriously, or skin-tight 'mummy' bandage dresses for the body-con types. (That was an important fashion term now – 'body-con', as in conscious. I'd been regarded as somewhat clueless when I'd asked what it meant.) The big shoot had been organised for Thursday at a studio nearby in SoHo, and I knew when and where because I had organised it on Pepper's behalf. But since then, it seemed she'd had a favour come through and everything had changed. 'That's good then. Isn't it?' I ventured, wondering how we could fit in a planned eight-hour shoot in one night.

'Of course it's good,' she replied. 'But time is short now.'

The Metropolitan Museum of Art's Temple of Dendur. The Met had a famous Egyptology section, including a temple for Isis and Osiris, the gods of resurrection and the afterlife. The more I thought about it, the more a strange cocktail of delight and fear took hold of me. I knew about the place. My mother had talked about it.

'What time am I to be there?'

'We have an eight thirty start time for the first look, after the sun goes down,' my boss informed me. 'You'll arrive at seven and start the set-up with the photographer. There's a lot of glass in there. Astrid will have to put up backdrops.'

I had yet to attend a photo shoot that took less than four hours and I knew for a fact that we had a lot of looks to shoot. Oh, it *would* be a late night then. Another one, but this time with no Lieutenant Luke as an inducement. Still, I'd always wanted to see the Temple of Dendur in person – since I was a kid, actually – and, more importantly, I could use the extra pay. Pepper was good about things like paying overtime, though her predecessor, Skye DeVille, had not been. (Skye had sure pushed the boundaries of proper employer conduct on a few occasions, and that was even before she'd become a bloodsucker.)

'Can Morticia come?' I blurted.

The receptionist, Morticia, is my friend. In fact, she is my only truly normal girlfriend in New York, though you wouldn't think so with a name like that. I didn't particularly like the idea of hanging around late at night at the Met, which is at the corner of Central Park. I hoped I didn't need to explain why. It wasn't the threat of muggers, actually, but I was happy for Pepper to think that.

My boss hesitated. Her pale, steely eyes took in the front desk for a moment. 'Well, that is a good idea, I suppose. We could use an extra set of hands if we plan to get out of there by midnight.'

Yes.

I relaxed a touch.

'Seven o'clock sharp at the main entrance to the Met on 82nd and Fifth,' Pepper said.

She turned around and walked back into her office. Just before she closed the door behind her, she gave me another curious look. I thought she was going to say something, but she just looked me up and down and then disappeared, the door making a faint clink behind her.

Strange girl, I could imagine her thinking.

She didn't know the half of it.

It was just past five as I descended the stairwell from the office, pushed the heavy street door open and stepped out on to the Manhattan sidewalk.

SoHo's Spring Street was busy, as always, and after growing up in sleepy Gretchenville (population 3999 with my recent departure) I was not quite used to the pace of Manhattan yet. It was hardly the biggest change I'd had to get used to since moving to the Big Apple, but there was something about the constant noise and movement of pedestrians and cars that took adjustment. Even in my great-aunt's mansion in Spektor, which was far uptown and curiously quiet, you could often hear the distant sounds of sirens late into the night. It wasn't for nothing that they called New York the city that never sleeps. The sky was still bright, which was a nice change after my first Manhattan winter, and on this particular warm late-spring afternoon the business people and arty types who pushed past me on the sidewalk wore suits with the jackets off, or short-sleeved T-shirts or dresses. The days were already longer and gloriously ... *alive*. I wondered how long the sun would shine and the people of Manhattan would remain oblivious to the supernatural trouble that was stirring.

And it *was* stirring. I had no doubt of it anymore.

I looked up into the sky, half expecting to see the creature who had taken me up there one night.

'It's going to be nice out tonight,' came a voice behind me, and I whirled around.

It was my friend, the receptionist Morticia. She was standing in front of the Evolution store, next to the full-sized medical-grade skeleton that guarded their door. The skeleton was holding a sale sign, and the wind caught it, making the plastic bones rattle.

I took a breath, pushing aside all the things I couldn't tell my friend, all the things that now, conjured by the sight of those bones, flitted around my head like unwelcome shadows.

'Did you buy something?' I asked.

The Evolution store had some real human skulls, along with the medical-grade replicas. The shop window was lined with Venus flytraps and dead butterflies in frames. A stuffed warthog stared at me through the window with lifeless glass eyes. It was an unusual shop and Morticia was often drawn to it. I was too, though these days I'd had my fill of the dark and weird.

'Nope. Just, uh, looking,' she said and joined me on the sidewalk, though I could have sworn she had a large book behind her back that she slid into her satchel. She seemed not to want to share the tome with me, so I didn't ask about it.

I folded my arms, suddenly cold. 'Hey, is it okay that I roped you into coming tonight? I would have totally understood if you'd said no. I kind of volunteered you without even asking. Sorry if it was the wrong call.'

'Are you kidding me? You know I've always wanted to be on

one of the shoots. Plus I *love* the Met.' Morticia drew out the 'o' in love, gesticulating dramatically with both hands to make her point. 'It is the most awesome place ever!'

Though Morticia had rather a penchant for exaggeration, we had a fair number of similarities, all things considered: she was about my age and height, and neither of us had a lot of friends or much of a relationship with our parents. The reasons were quite different – she was on bad terms with her folks, whereas mine were dead. (Dead-dead, not undead. And there is a big difference, let me tell you.) Also, we were both alive – which is a category I've begun to pay attention to lately – but the similarities probably ended there. She was a bit of a goth and she had a tattoo, and though I had never dyed my light-brown hair, she changed her colour a lot. At the moment her shaggy hair was dyed a stark raven black so black it was almost blue. Last month it had been the colour of red food dye.

I tended to wear vintage hand-me-downs from my great-aunt, who'd been a designer in the forties and fifties, whereas Morticia always seemed to wear the same black dress, striped tights and Doc Martens. With her panda-black eye makeup and gangly, Olive Oyl build, she was the antithesis of pretty much everyone else who worked at *Pandora*. I liked that about her. And her name was deceiving. She'd changed it from 'Bea' to Morticia, probably to spite her parents, but she was just a normal young woman living in Jersey and working the front desk at *Pandora*. Meanwhile, I had the slightly less odd name of Pandora, having evidently been named after the woman in Greek mythology who opened a box and let all the evil into the world, yet I lived in a strange suburb on Addams Avenue, a street named for Charles Addams, the Addams Family creator and creator of Morticia's chosen namesake. I hadn't yet told Morticia about that. Nor had I mentioned to her that Mr Addams himself was a resident of the suburb I lived in. And by resident, I mean that he buys his newspaper from the same store I do. No matter that he passed away in the late eighties.

'I thought you might enjoy it,' I said, looking down at my scuffed ballet flats. 'I remembered you saying that you'd never been on one of the fashion shoots before, and you wanted to.'

'I was always keen but Skye never asked me,' she admitted.

Even hearing my previous boss's name made me sneer a little.

'Are you heading home to eat or change or anything?' I asked, though I imagined her wardrobe consisted of identical black dresses and striped stockings.

She shook her head.

Right.

I was wearing a forties shirtwaist day dress belonging to my great-aunt, and I had a vintage cardigan in my leather satchel for when it cooled. Technically I didn't really need to go home and change, and taking Morticia to my new home was something I'd often considered but ruled out for a range of reasons. It wouldn't take someone long to figure out things were, well, different in Spektor. Maybe we could go for dinner near the museum, I thought, and I wouldn't need to rush home at all?

'Do you want to . . . meet up at the museum, or . . .?' Morticia said, clearly fishing, and perhaps thinking the same thing. We always talked about catching up outside of work but we never did. My strange life in Spektor tended to see to that.

'Well, why don't we just . . .' I began, trying to think of the best place to eat on a budget, but I trailed off as a familiar figure stepped out of the sea of pedestrians right behind her and I was rather abruptly at a loss for words.

There he was.

My guardian angel.

My heart stopped for a moment, then resumed at quite a pace, and I felt my cheeks grow warm.

Second Lieutenant Luke Thomas appeared and stood only a couple of feet away, watching me with that irresistibly tender look of his, square jaw clenched and brow knitted with concern. As always, he wore his leather riding boots and a long frock coat with bright gold buttons done up to the collar. The blue Union soldier cap sat at an angle on his longish blond hair, the cap emblazoned with a crest of two gold cavalry swords. His own ghostly cavalry sword hung from the weathered leather belt that was cinched tight over his trim waist. In the early evening light he was translucent and faded, like a dashing hero in an old film, washed out by the sunlight. Lieutenant Luke had the brightest, most beautiful blue eyes I'd ever seen, and now those eyes drank me in longingly, turned inquisitively to Morticia, then looked at me again with a silent question. *Shall I go?* he was wondering. He'd expected me to be alone.

My breath caught in my throat, I licked my lips and considered my options.

'Are you okay?' my friend asked.

Why does the most perfect man I've ever met have to be dead? Why?

'I'm ... I'm fine. We have to be at the Met on 82nd by seven for the fashion shoot. We could maybe ...' I said after a moment, in an exaggerated voice, trying to convey the situation to my spirit guide. He would have expected me to be free tonight. Of course, *I* had expected I'd be free, until the news from Pepper.

'Grab something to eat?' Morticia said, finishing my sentence for me. Her head was cocked to one side, shaggy black hair falling into her eyes.

'Yes. No. I mean ... *You don't have to go*,' I said a little loudly.

Gosh, I wasn't doing this well at all.

'Are you okay? Why are you talking funny?' Morticia asked.

Good question.

'*Am I* talking funny?' I fidgeted with my satchel. *Of course you are talking funny, Pandora. You are trying to talk to a living woman and a ghost at the same time.*

I'd last seen Lieutenant Luke at about two in the morning. We'd started out talking and then at some point we'd been entangled on my bed, and I'd been in that gentle embrace of his, and his lips ... well. Now I found I couldn't think straight with him standing there so close to us. It wasn't just his presence, of course, it was the fact that Morticia was there too, just a few feet away from him, each of them part of very different worlds. I was not yet accustomed to seeing Luke outside the confines of the mansion in Spektor – this was a fairly new ability for him, the ability to get out at all, as he'd previously been cursed to remain in the building. The idea of going out for dinner with Morticia and somehow ignoring Luke's presence seemed a hopeless proposition. I had considered telling her about him, but she'd almost certainly think me mad.

I took a breath, steadied myself. 'Hey,' I finally managed. 'I'd love to grab a bite to eat some other time, but have something to do right now. Why don't I meet you at the steps of the museum. I think they want us at the 82nd Street entrance. Say ten to seven?' I suggested to Morticia. It seemed a small miracle that I'd been able to string a couple of sentences together.

'Okay,' Morticia said and nodded, though I might have detected some hurt in her voice. 'Are you okay?' she asked me, for perhaps the first time giving me a strange look. I was pretty used to being looked at that way by nearly everyone else. Those kinds of looks had started before I was ten, to be perfectly frank. But Morticia had never seemed to think I was odd. Until now.

'I'm fine,' I replied unconvincingly. 'I would like to grab dinner another night though. Sorry I have to rush off. So, I'll see you just before seven, okay?' I called out, backing up on the sidewalk, moving in the direction of the subway station. 'On the steps? Is that okay?'

'Okay,' I heard her say again. She stood still, watching me, the satchel at her side.

As we parted ways I felt a touch guilty, but I didn't know what else to do. I turned away and began my commute home to prepare for the evening ahead. In seconds Lieutenant Luke caught up with me and slid his spectral hand into mine, the bodies of the commuters passing through his as if he didn't exist. His touch was intoxicating and I shuddered.

Yup. My life sure was complicated.

It was forty minutes later when I stepped out of the elevator on the top floor of my Great-Aunt Celia's vast, neo-Gothic Victorian mansion in Spektor, and walked towards the glossy midnight-blue penthouse door with the spirit of the Civil War Second Lieutenant Luke Thomas lingering behind me. Dust swirled in the air with my footsteps. It didn't seem to matter how much I tried to tidy the place up, the cobwebs always came back.

'Miss Pandora, I'm awfully sorry I surprised you,' Lieutenant Luke told me again.

I stopped and turned to touch his beautiful, ghostly face. It felt cool and misty. And those eyes of his, those bright blue eyes were looking right into mine.

We hadn't had much chance to talk on the way to Spektor. What with him being invisible to other subway commuters, I tended to get a bit shy when I knew that other people would think I was talking to myself. I guess I shouldn't have cared what others thought of me, but I was still human. (Even if he wasn't.) I kept my mouth shut for most of the journey but if anyone had looked carefully, they might have noticed the way I kept looking lovingly to the space next to me, or the way my hand was resting in the position of someone who was holding hands with another.

'Really, it's fine,' I told Luke, taking his hand again. Now we were just outside Celia's penthouse door, Luke's body just inches from mine. 'I like seeing you. You know I do,' I said and leaned forward until my lips touched his.

Oooohhhhhh.

Kissing Lieutenant Luke was like ... It was like ...

My mind turned to mush again for a moment.

Kissing Lieutenant Luke wasn't like anything I'd experienced before. It was as if all gravity left the world and I was floating, body weightless, my lips warm and my insides turned to melted honey. After a time our lips parted and I took a moment to regain my senses. 'I like surprises,' I further explained when I'd found the power of speech. 'I just ... Well, I'm not used to seeing you like that.'

Like *outside the house.* Now that Luke was no longer cursed to be trapped in this mansion, our relationship had begun to get serious. There was no longer a neat separation between my life here in Spektor and the broader world outside the ring of mist that surrounded it, and increasingly, my feelings for Luke were no longer so contained either, thoughts of him spilled over into my days.

'I was unprepared, that's all.'

Luke had no immediate reply to this, and looking into his eyes – or at his mouth – did little to help my concentration or to keep my evening on schedule, so I took a breath and – as per my arrangement with my great-aunt – knocked on the door, unlocked it with the key and we stepped inside. Not that Luke really needed the door opened to enter. And not that he needed the elevator, either. I thought it was sweet that he made such an effort not to walk through walls when we were together. I shut the door behind us.

'Great-Aunt Celia, I'm ... *we're* home,' I announced.

My great-aunt's penthouse is spectacular, I should tell you.

Full of elegant and exciting curiosities, and feeling more like a museum or Victorian library than a mere living space, this place still had the power to inspire awe, even after months of living here.

And unlike the rest of the mansion, it was spotless. No dust here. No chandeliers falling at odd angles. Instead, a sparkling chandelier drew the eye to a domed centre of the penthouse's high ceiling, glittering above hardwood floors that reflected its dazzling lights, illuminating a rich space scented with candle wax and incense. Celia's open lounge room boasted large, arched windows looking out over the city, curtains pulled back to let in the night. The room was decorated with antiques, stained-glass lamps and dark portraits of unsmiling nobility; the walls lined with bookcases bursting with elegantly bound tomes, and glass-fronted sideboards containing curious artefacts and objets d'art – some of art deco design, or Edwardian, or Victorian, like the mansion itself; and others seemingly of ancient origin, including small objects and figures of the type my mother once removed from Egyptian tombs at the behest of international museums. One item, however, was new enough to be placed there myself – an elaborate vivarium created to look like a tiny castle, turrets and all. It housed a black widow spider. As a rule spiders did not scare me, but this particular one made me shudder.

My great-aunt was in her usual spot in the reading nook, no doubt absorbed in some giant tome. I could see her elegant slippers lined up next to the chair, and the edge of her elbow, encased in a lace sleeve. I let my work satchel drop to the floor and slipped my shoes off.

'I only have a few minutes to grab some food and change.' It wasn't so far to the museum because it was in Central Park, and the tunnel to Spektor entered on to the upper end of the park. But still, I didn't want to be late for Morticia. To get there when I'd promised gave me perhaps twenty minutes at home, max. That meant not being distracted by Luke's lips.

'Lieutenant Luke is here,' I added, as my great-aunt did not have the gift of seeing the dead.

'Well now,' came her voice, and that elbow moved. I heard the sound of a book closing. One pale, elegant hand appeared around the corner of the nook and she moved the slippers. I heard the chair creak as she rose, and in moments she had her slippers on and had stepped out into the living room, backlit by the Manhattan skyline. She looked at us. Or more accurately, at me.

'I can't see him this evening,' she said, looking right through Luke. 'Two more nights.' She knew full well how the magick worked, probably far better than I did. Perhaps Great-Aunt Celia wanted to remind me that Luke was different, that he was not human, not living, but I could hardly have missed that, especially this evening with his unexpected arrival outside my place of work. I always found any crossover between my regular-girl world and the supernatural word especially unsettling. Increasingly that unsettling reality was hard to avoid, however.

Two more nights. Two nights until the full Blue Moon. My body thrilled at the thought. The moon's strength varied, but it gave us at least one special night together, and sometimes more.

The spectacular nature of my great-aunt's penthouse suited its owner well. She was herself quite something to behold, and she was a mysterious woman, worldly and wise. She should be close to ninety years old, by my guess, but you'd certainly never know it from looking at her. This evening she wore a long, black lace dress, cinched at the waist with a velvet belt in fetching burgundy, adorned with a small bejewelled circular clasp made up of several multi-coloured gems. She wore her widow's veil, as always, obscuring her eyes and the upper part of her porcelain features. Her lips were blood red. Her skin was luminous and peculiarly wrinkle-free.

'You look really ... well. Amazing actually,' I told her, staring a bit. The lace dress was spectacular, even by Celia's rather high standards. As a former designer to the stars of Hollywood's Golden Age she knew a lot more about style than most, and certainly more than I did. She called it 'style' not fashion, because fashion was 'about trends and manufacturing need for sales', as she put it, and style was about something more 'individual and timeless'. Considering my inexperience in the area, it was rather ironic I was the one working at a fashion magazine.

I walked up to her, noting that Luke stayed near the doorway. 'Are you going somewhere?' I asked. Looking so dressed up, she'd have to be meeting Deus, I figured. He was someone (*something?*) who made me feel conflicted. Among other things, he scared me, but he'd also saved my life.

'We are both going somewhere, aren't we?' she said, giving me not one shred of information.

'Yes, I have to be at the Met museum in another forty-five minutes or so. Just grabbing some dinner. There's plenty of leftover roast in the fridge if ...'

She shook her head gently. No, she didn't want any of my paltry leftovers. I never did see her eat, but then she did sleep odd hours. And Luke didn't need to eat. So, dinner for one then. Again.

'Well, I'd better get busy,' I said, blowing a kiss to Luke, who faded out of the room until he was invisible to me. Where he went when he wasn't with me, I did not know. I'd asked but he couldn't articulate it. Something about 'supernatural rules'. There were a fair few of those, I was discovering.

I was about to start towards the kitchen when my great-aunt startled me by placing one cool hand on my shoulder. I went still under her touch.

'Pandora, dear, Vlad has informed me there is a package for you. It seems it may be important.' Her dark, wide-set eyes flickered beneath the mesh of her veil.

'A package? What kind of package?'

'He'll bring it this evening.'

'I won't be here,' I said, frowning. 'Well, not until late.'

'Don't fret. I'll hang on to it for you.' She continued to watch me and I wondered if she was reading my mind. Mind-reading was one of her gifts. If she was reading mine, she'd be disappointed because I didn't know anything about any package.

'Okay,' I said simply.

'You'd better get ready for tonight.'

'Yes, you're right.' I turned around, strode to the kitchen and set about fixing my meal.

I rushed through heating up the leftovers, and ate it a little too fast, my mind racing over several things – Luke's newly freed presence, my feelings for him, my mortal boyfriend, Jay, who I hadn't seen much of lately, things at *Pandora* magazine, and Morticia. *Poor Morticia,* I thought as I washed my plate. She must have thought I'd brushed her off. I'd try to be extra friendly at the museum so that she knew it wasn't about my not wanting to spend time with her. We kept talking about catching up but I never followed through. That was about supernatural problems, not her. But how could I explain?

I hung the drying towel over the rack, decided not to change my dress after all, grabbed a jacket from my room as an extra layer and slipped my shoes back on. 'Well, I have to go. I don't know how late I'll be getting home,' I explained in a loud voice as I sprinted out the door, jacket over my arm and the vintage cardigan on over my dress, so I wouldn't get cold. (Plus the pocket had some rice grains in it. Just in case. Long story.)

'Good luck,' my great-aunt called back, though I could not see where she was.

I locked the door after me, called the elevator and when I stepped inside it, Lieutenant Luke appeared through the closed doors.

'Miss Pandora, may I escort you?'

I thrilled at his presence and began to reach for his hands, but held myself back. 'Sorry … Um, I'd like that, Luke, but, well, I don't think it's a good idea,' I said awkwardly.

I wanted to kiss him, but that was exactly the problem.

Now that he could move around freely, things were very different. In fact, he could move more freely than even I could, because he could pass through both worlds – the spaces of the living and the dead. I was really pleased for him, and pleased I could see him more often, but I felt uncertain about his presence at the shoot. There was the question of how well I could concentrate on work with him nearby. Not well, I suspected.

'You do not wish for my presence this evening.' If ever a ghost's face fell, his did. Luke looked wounded.

'It's not that I don't want to see you. You know that,' I told him. 'But I don't think I'd handle it well if you were around my work tonight. I'll have to concentrate, and well, pretend that I'm normal. When you are around I don't feel normal at all,' I explained, then bit my lip. I wasn't sure if that came out right.

It was all well and good to find you had some kind of special supernatural significance, but that didn't stop the world turning. I had to work like other human beings. I had to earn my crust. I had to eat – even if Luke did not, and even Celia seemed untroubled by the need for three square meals a day. I had to somehow be human, and do the daily human things humans had to do, while also being more, being 'chosen', and dealing with colossally important supernatural issues I did not even understand yet.

The elevator had not moved. We stood face to face, his ghostly and mine screwed up with uncertainty.

'As you wish, Miss Pandora,' Lieutenant Luke said, and with that he bowed his head and vanished.

No! I opened my mouth to speak but I was alone, and for the second time in only a couple of hours, I felt distinctly guilty. I'd let a friend down. Again. I hadn't wanted our conversation to end like that. I'd wanted to tell him that on the Blue Moon, in just two nights, we could spend hours together and I was planning something special. But I didn't get the chance. There would be another opportunity, but still.

Night was coming, and I would have to head to the museum now if I was to be on time. Frowning, I hit the elevator button and began my descent.

Chapter Two

I stood near the Fifth Avenue and 82nd Street main entrance of the Metropolitan Museum of Art, on the second set of steps, panting a little and trying to reconcile the odd mix of excitement and trepidation I felt at the thought of going inside the place. The sun was getting low in the sky now, the clouds turning warm pink and gold. I'd arrived just in time, by my watch, and though I felt lingering guilt about how Luke and I had parted, I felt relieved to be arriving at work without the distraction of his presence. Being here and focusing on work would be quite enough, without trying to pretend my invisible friend wasn't watching.

I looked around me, and not spotting Morticia, I found myself absorbed in the architecture of the imposing building. It was all arches and pillars, a Beaux Arts design that was apparently a facade to cover what had originally been built. The museum building was erected in the 1870s in red brick and stone 'mausoleum' style. Hideous, according to contemporary reports, but additions to the unpopular building eventually engulfed it until almost nothing could be seen of the original High Gothic design, at least not from here. Now this was America's largest museum, one of the most frequented museums in the world, and the tall main doors welcomed millions of visitors each year, but not me. Not until tonight.

My late mother, Oriel, an archaeologist, had been very interested in the Met's collections and early twentieth century excavation work at ancient sites. My bedtime reading had often been taken up with heavy hardcover books bursting with colour images from its archives and grand exhibitions. They had tens of thousands of Egyptian artefacts dating from the Palaeolithic era through to Roman times, showcased in some forty different Egyptian galleries, the pinnacle of which was, arguably, the famous Temple of Dendur exhibit, a place that had featured regularly in my dreams of Manhattan. How peculiar that I had been in this city for months now and never been inside the museum. And tonight I would help out on a photo shoot involving the temple itself.

Had I consciously avoided this place?

As I stood riveted at the sight of the famous building, its grand facade dwarfing me, I realised that this museum, my mother and her career were all deeply interlinked in my mind. She'd told me about it so many times I'd always assumed I would visit it with her one day. But it wasn't to be. I was here and she was gone. That reality stung. The same deep passion for archaeology that had fuelled her interest in the Met had also taken her work to Egypt, where she and my father had been fatally wounded in a 'freak accident' at one of her digs when I was eleven years old. It was a trip I'd had a great foreboding about. But who listens to kids when they ask you not to go on a work trip? Who listens when they are warned of a danger that standard logic cannot account for anyone possibly knowing? They got on that plane and never came back. In some ways archaeology – and by extension, this place – had taken my parents from me.

I looked at the sprawling and stately neoclassical building and swallowed back a lump in my throat.

'Are you okay?'

I pulled myself from the morass of my conflicted emotions. It was Morticia, of course. She stood at the top of the museum's stairs, appearing from behind another couple. She was still in the same black dress and striped tights.

'You made it,' I said and joined her. We sat down together on the stairs and I noticed a sandwich wrap balled up next to her. She'd eaten alone. Again, I felt some guilt at having left her to come alone. 'Hey, I'm sorry about before. I had something I had to do.' I shifted. 'Have you been here before?' I asked, briskly changing the subject. I smiled a bright, false smile, and hugged my knees. The stairs felt cool through the fabric of my dress.

'Oh yeah, it's really awesome. The Egyptian section is amazing!' Morticia responded animatedly. 'I haven't seen it in years, but they have this whole temple, moved from Egypt. I think that's where we're shooting.'

'Yes. The Temple of Dendur. After the building of the Aswan High Dam it was dismantled by the Egyptian authorities to save it from rising waters,' I said. 'It was given to the US in the sixties or seventies, I think.'

My colleague raised one dramatic, pencilled eyebrow. 'Wow. It's amazing how you know all this stuff.'

'I learned it all from my mother.'

The ancient world had been dinner conversation when

I was growing up. It was in the books I'd had as a child, the old tomes about human history and mythology I'd learned to read from while other kids read Dick and Jane books. And everything I'd read was in there still, stored away, like my head was one big filing cabinet – myths, gods, goddesses, pharaohs, spirits, ghost stories. Some of that knowledge was from books, and it had been added to in my recent months in Spektor. Some days I wished I knew somewhat less than I did.

'I haven't been inside before,' I confessed and swallowed. Morticia cocked her head, watching me, her big eyes seeming to get even larger. 'I don't know if I ever told you this, but my mother was an archaeologist,' I said by way of explanation.

'That is so cool.' Morticia smiled and swivelled to face me.

'It was.'

'I wish my parents were that interesting,' she said, then added, 'I'm sorry.' She knew that I was an orphan. 'I'm sorry about your mom. And your dad.'

I took in the sight of the lines of traffic on Fifth Avenue, and the bustling sidewalk filled with pedestrians. 'You know, I think maybe my mom would be proud of me for moving here, for getting out of Gretchenville. I think she would be happy about that,' I said cautiously. I hoped it was true. She was always travelling and adventuring. She'd have wanted that for me too.

'I'm *sure* she would be proud of you. Are you kidding! You've only just moved to New York and already you're doing exciting things.'

'Am I?'

'You're an assistant to an editor, and you get to interview

designers like Laurie Smith, and go on photo shoots and go to big parties.'

As receptionist, Morticia didn't get asked to do any of those things.

'And you're dating one of the most eligible bachelors in New York,' she added.

Jay Rockwell. High flying. Tall. Human. Living.

'You're right,' I told her. 'I am pretty lucky.'

I meant it, but Morticia didn't know the half of it. I was lucky to be alive, really. I'd faced terrors in the previous few months that she simply would not believe, and although we were friends she didn't know that I was 'The Seventh'. The Seventh Lucasta Daughter. (That whole famous 'Seventh Son of a Seventh Son' thing wasn't such a big deal, apparently. It was all about the daughters.) I was still getting used to that title, myself, so how could she understand? Supposedly, being The Seventh means I am a chosen one who comes along once every 150 years or so, every seven generations, to perform some mysterious yet vitally important supernatural role. I didn't understand it all, and I'd yet to be presented with any kind of handbook to answer my many questions. Being The Seventh was huge in the supernatural world, but normal living people didn't know a thing about it. Also, normal living people didn't know that the dead were planning to rise up and take over the living. Which is kind of a big deal, if you ask me. Perhaps ignorance is bliss until your town is overtaken by zombies. I had to tread carefully in our friendship and not let any of that pressing knowledge slip. Imagine how that would go down at work? And yet it bothered me that Morticia didn't know.

I wasn't sure how to approach that ethical quandary.

A double life is a lot of work.

'Well ... the photographer should be arriving any second. We'd better get inside,' I said and stood up, smoothing down my dress, keeping on task and pushing the rest of my swirling thoughts and worries away. Being The Seventh was many things but it wasn't a meal ticket. I needed this job.

Through the main doors of the museum I could see that the lights were on, but when we walked up and pulled on the handle of one of the three big doors it was locked. I tried another and leaned in and cupped my hands around my face to peer through the glass. I could see a museum shop to the right, currently closed, and a security guard or staff member inside at a big desk several metres away. I knocked and waved, but she didn't take any notice.

'I think they close at five thirty. I wonder why they wanted us here so late?' Morticia asked.

'I think it has to do with the light.' I stepped back and peered up at the darkening sky. The Manhattan sunset was blooming. Within an hour it would be dark. 'I guess there is a lot of glass in the Egyptian wing, around the temple. They'll have to erect backdrops and things for the lighting so they don't get reflections.'

Frowning, I tried the handle on the third door, and on finding it was also locked, I banged on the glass with a little more vigour. The woman in uniform looked over in our direction and scowled, but she did finally come to the main doors, if only to tell us to go away.

'We're closed,' the woman said, her voice muffled through

the door. She pointed at her watch to illustrate her point, her tight, afro-textured curls bouncing slightly.

'We're here for the shoot,' I said through the glass, mouthing my words in an exaggerated fashion. I fished around for my business card and pressed it against the glass. 'We're with *Pandora* magazine.'

'If she doesn't let us in we'll be late and Pepper will get cross with us,' Morticia said under her breath, but after only a minute the same woman walked over with a set of keys. They rattled against the glass as she unlocked the door and let us in.

'Thank you,' Morticia and I both said, as if reading from the same script.

'I need you to sign in,' the woman said and led us away from the doors. 'And I need to see some ID.'

'Of course,' I said, and we both began fishing around for our identification.

I was totally unprepared for the grandeur of the Met's Great Hall. Above us were three spectacular, high domes with round skylights, now reflecting the museum lights against the darkening sky, and several large arches. We stood on a marble mosaic floor that echoed eerily with our footsteps. It was such a grand space, and so quiet and empty after hours, though I thought I could detect voices somewhere further off in the vast building. We were signed in and given security passes at the large reception desk and then a bored-looking, middle-aged man in a uniform introduced himself and told us he would take us through. He was about my height, portly and for some reason seemed not to like us. I noticed with some unease that he was carrying a torch on his belt. Where was he taking us, exactly? Surely they still had *electricity* after dark?

He led us past a bank of brochures and maps, and asked us to wait in the Great Hall. He needed to speak with someone, apparently.

Morticia picked up a brochure and I saw her eyes widen.

'Look, they have ghost tours,' she said in a hushed squeal of delight.

'Do they?' I replied, wincing. *I bet I won't need a tour guide to find out what ghosts are here,* I thought.

Rather than being something I'd sought out on a 'ghost tour', contact with the departed had always occurred organically. It was something that couldn't be avoided, and it had always caused me problems. I'd seen cemeteries bustling with centuries-old departed. I had certain 'gifts' and responsibilities as The Seventh – well, my Great-Aunt Celia called them gifts but honestly my ability to chat with the deceased had felt rather more like a curse when I was growing up. After the local butcher was killed (something I'd known would happen) and I told everyone I chatted with him afterwards, the 'weird kid' label was thrust on me and our family was ostracised. I was perhaps nine at the time. My 'gift' had done my family no favours, and had done me no favours when I was younger. But a decade later I was starting to get that this was about something bigger than chatting with small town Gretchenville's dead. Since moving in with my great-aunt I'd learned a great deal. And I'd met Lieutenant Luke. I had no problem at all with being able to see and speak to Luke, of course. But I wasn't sure how I felt about meeting the Met's dead.

'I've always wanted to do a ghost tour,' Morticia told me. 'Look, it says here they use EMF meters, dowsing rods and night vision. What is an EMF meter?'

Now I was intrigued. 'It measures electro-magnetic fields, I think. And dowsing rods are sometimes called "witching willows" or "willow witching" or something. I'm not sure I believe in those,' I replied.

Funny that people used equipment to search out ghosts when I was stuck with the ability to see them, and for them to reach out to me. In fact, I was a kind of beacon for ghosts and supernatural activity. As was Spektor and my great-aunt's mansion (among other things we had the late architect Edmund Barrett to thank for that). I wasn't sure the Met was a beacon, though. There were certainly a lot of fascinating objects here, objects with a history, objects that might retain something of their owners.

The guard was back, his frown still in place. The man had a resting grump face if I ever saw it. 'Okay, come on,' he said, and led the way out of the Great Hall.

To my surprise, most of the Egyptian wing of the Met appeared to be closed off by white boards. This was puzzling as it seemed like a lot of cordoning off for our shoot, considering that it was after hours for the museum, and the general public weren't about to wander in on our photo session. From what I knew the Egyptian section was quite large as well, and the temple was only one part of it, albeit a famous one.

'Is this area under construction?' I ventured, hoping it wasn't. If most of the Temple of Dendur wasn't on view it certainly wouldn't be the shoot Pepper was hoping for. I had visions of the photographer nestled up against scaffolding trying to get a clear shot.

'They are installing the new major exhibition,' the guard informed me in a tone that said I should have already known this. Only after he spoke did I spot a banner announcing the coming exhibition he spoke of. In a large font that mimicked the ancient Egyptian hieroglyphs surrounding it, the banner said:

HATSHEPSUT
Coming soon

The guard escorted us inside a rope barrier, unsmiling, and we followed him through a tradesperson's door in the flimsy wooden boards that cordoned off a large section of the Egyptian wing from the public. Once on the other side, we could see that the installation process was already well underway. He shut the door behind us and urged us on.

Museum staff were milling about, talking and pointing at walls, or lugging large boards around that I assumed were to be used with displays. They were still going after hours. These were the voices we'd heard from the Great Hall. It must be a big job. One fully assembled area we could see looked like a faux pyramid with an entry doorway in it for visitors to walk through, presently inaccessible to the public, of course. I wanted to walk through it, but naturally the security guard led us away from it and the activity. I craned my neck to catch a glimpse of a large area beyond the faux pyramid, full of objects, some still under wraps. It looked like this special exhibition would be quite spectacular when it was finished, yet my gut felt funny when I saw all those boxes. It made my stomach feel cold.

'What is this exhibition, exactly? Is it for Hatshepsut herself or for a bunch of different pharaohs?' I hadn't spotted the names of any other pharaohs. No Ramesses or Akhenaten or Khufu or Tutankhamun.

'What?' the guard grumbled absentmindedly, then it seemed to click. 'Yeah, the one you mentioned,' he said, perhaps unwilling to give a try at pronouncing the name. 'It's the first time she's, uh, travelled outside of the Cairo museum.'

'The first time *what* has travelled outside Cairo . . .?' I began, and we passed a large display sign, already erected. This time the royal name *Hatshepsut* was presented as a backdrop to the pharaoh's likeness, which was carved into an impressive sandstone bust of some considerable size.

'Don't touch it,' the guard warned. 'It arrived from Berlin last week.'

Morticia's hand sprang back. She'd evidently been drawn to it like a kid to a cookie jar.

This was a true piece of antiquity, roughly 3500 years old, and touching it might subtly damage the stone, and would probably set off an alarm – that was, if the museum alarms were already rigged up. I recognised the name Hatshepsut. It struck a chord. My mother had been quite interested in her. In the bust, she was shown wearing the distinctive traditional Nemes striped headdress of a pharaoh, and atop the headdress was the uraeus – the ancient Egyptian representation of the sacred serpent known as Wadjet, a powerful protective deity. The uraeus on the headdress, or crown, indicated that it was worn by an ancient Egyptian deity or royal sovereign. But while the uraeus and Nemes were customary in depictions of pharaohs, the false beard Hatshepsut was shown to be wearing was something of particular interest to her story.

'Hatshepsut was the famous female pharaoh,' I remarked. 'The queen who made herself into a king.' Yes, I remembered some stories about her. She was quite extraordinary among Egyptian leaders. The Met already had an impressive collection relating to her reign, as I understood it, including thousands of fragments of smashed sculptures that were excavated at her temple in Deir el-Bahri in the twenties and painstakingly reassembled.

'A queen who made herself into a king? Gender-bending, you mean?' Morticia said, gawking at the bust.

'Well, sort of. She certainly toppled the gender norms of the time, though the fact she is shown with a beard in this bust doesn't necessarily mean she literally wore one in regular life. It was custom in ancient Egypt to depict the pharaoh as he – or in this case she – was meant to be seen, not necessarily as they were. Depictions were strictly idealised,' I said. 'I think most scholars agree that her depictions as a male were less about her personal identification or preference, and more about, well, her being portrayed as male so her rule could be accepted by the public. Though who knows where the truth lies.'

'Far out,' my friend said.

As we passed another maze of boards in our journey through the partially erected exhibition, I noted another of the exhibition's displays bearing the same ancient name. In front of it was a large object of some type, currently covered in a sheet. I felt the urge to lift it up. Perhaps Morticia wasn't the only one compelled to touch. 'It says here that Howard Carter discovered her tomb in 1903. He's the guy who found Tutankhamun. But Hatshepsut's mummy was missing and her tomb had been robbed,' I recalled. This was often given for a reason why she was not as widely known in modern times – no impressive gold treasures, no mummy. That and the fact that after her death a new pharaoh tried to wipe out any trace of her. What was the story with that again? I squinted, trying to recall.

'Come on, this way,' the impatient guard said and took me by the shoulder. I tried to shrug him off, but his grip stayed right on me. Reluctantly, I was steered away from the display, the sign and tantalising room of half-unpacked objects falling from view. We passed ancient objects that were part of the museum's permanent Egyptian displays, all separated from us by glass – Arts Under the Ptolemies 1 (were those two mummies?), Art of the Early Fourth Century BC, and the entrance to something called a Study Gallery. To our disappointment, our grumpy escort seemed keen to shuttle us through as quickly as possible to get back to his desk. I'd finally made it to the museum and I couldn't look at all those marvellous artefacts. Not on this visit, anyway.

As the guard led us around a corner to the Sackler Wing, I thought hard on that ancient name. *Hatshepsut.* It was familiar to me not just because of her significance in ancient history – and the thought of an ancient princess who made herself king was certainly compelling – but also because of something my mother was working on as part of her last dig in the Valley of the Kings. That final dig. That final work trip from which she and my father had never returned. I could never forget, of course, but I'd blocked so much of that time from my memory that specific things were difficult to recall. Memories were fragmented, many of them too intensely emotional to be clear. Could it be that I was mixing things up? I had only been eleven, after all. Hatshepsut was a major figure for Egyptologists, even if she wasn't half as famous to the modern public as King Tut, thanks to his nearly intact tomb and that magnificent gold funerary mask. Still, she'd been a figure of interest to my mother, I was sure of it.

'I've always wanted to see a mummy,' Morticia exclaimed, and I pictured her again outside the Evolution store, with that skeleton standing next to her and the collection of skulls in the window seeming to halo her, like a goddess of death. Morta perhaps, or Hel. 'When I came here with my parents they wouldn't let me look. Pandora, do you think this female pharaoh's mummy ...?' she began.

'Oh, no, I don't think ...' I said, shaking my head. I didn't think Hatshepsut's mummy had been found. But what if ...? Gooseflesh came up on my arms at the thought. What if Hatshepsut's mummy was here, to be viewed in New York? I'd met ghosts from all walks of life, but ancient Egyptians had strongly believed in an afterlife, had taken many steps to ensure their afterlives. Their bodies had to be preserved – mummified – to ensure their passage into the next life. What if their bodies retained something of them, thousands of years later? If an ancient pharaoh was still present in some way, if their spirit was retained, how would that spirit feel about having their remains viewed like that? Remains they had intended to be left undisturbed and intact for their resurrection and afterlife? Would they feel … angry?

Resurrection was a deeply troubling idea to me at the moment. And ancient Egyptians had believed strongly in resurrection. One of their best-known gods, Osiris, was a resurrected, mummified deity. Everyone had a right to an afterlife, whether they haunted this world or did not. But to be resurrected, to be on the earthly plane among the living? Wasn't that what the Revolution of the Dead was about? The dead reclaiming the spaces inhabited by the living?

I did not understand it all and was frustratingly under-supplied with clear answers, considering I was to somehow play a pivotal supernatural role in it all, but yes, resurrection was a key element. And I'd seen resurrection before, albeit on a smaller scale. But the necromancer was gone, I reminded myself. Celia and I had destroyed him. He – or it – was no longer a threat.

What about other necromancers? What about the Agitation? That period when everything was supposedly in chaos, the boundaries between the living and dead breaking down …

The guard was none too impressed with me. I'd stopped again, my mind whirling with troubling thoughts, not even aware that I was looking back in the direction of the exhibition that was being assembled. Having lost his patience, he took me firmly by the shoulder again and led me away. 'You can wait until it opens like everyone else.'

'When does it open?' I managed.

'The big launch is on Saturday.'

I swallowed. No wonder they were working after hours.

The guard had a large flashlight hanging on his belt, and now he took it in his hand and switched it on. We were about to enter the Sackler Wing. 'Some pieces are late,' the man commented of the exhibition. 'There's a lot of bother about it. Come on. Through here,' he said gruffly. He ushered us through the door ahead of him, and for a moment we stepped into near darkness. Then we looked up and saw it.

The Temple of Dendur.

'Wow,' Morticia exclaimed. 'It looks awesome at night!'

For decades now the temple had been situated here in the Sackler Wing of the museum: a large, purpose-built modernist space with slanted glass taking up one full side from end to end and from floor to very high ceiling. During daylight hours, the sky illuminated the temple with natural light, much as it would have been lit in its original location on the west bank of the Nile River in the Nubian region of southern Egypt. At night it was illuminated with museum floodlights. As we stopped by the doorway the shimmering 'pool of reflection' – a design meant to represent the Nile – separated us from the temple. I stood and gaped.

'Come on,' the guard said and led us around to the left, shining the torch on the ground to light our path.

I kept my eyes on the temple, nearly tripping. The photographer and crew for our *Pandora* magazine fashion shoot had already taken over the space, I noticed. Their lighting equipment fanned out around the sandstone temple, and large black sheets were being erected on mobile frames, so they blacked out sections of the room. Meanwhile the temple itself was spectacularly spotlit. It was quite something to behold, perhaps especially with the associations I had about the museum. Egypt. My mother. That dig.

The Temple of Dendur was dedicated to two of ancient Egypt's best-known deities, Isis and Osiris – Isis being the great mother goddess with the powers of healing and regeneration, a personification of magick and medicine; and Osiris, being her husband, the judge of the deceased, ruling over Duat, the place between this world and the next, where every soul must pass him and face his judgement. A powerful figure of resurrection and the afterlife, Osiris was always represented in mummified form. There was a famous story about him, wherein his brother, Set, kills the living King Osiris to gain the throne, and his wife Isis restores him and they go on to conceive the god Horus.

Resurrection.

We walked past the edge of the water and came into the circle of lights by the temple. 'Thank you,' I told the guard, tearing my eyes from the beauty of the temple, but he was already striding away to get back to the front desk, light bouncing around the ground in front of his feet.

'Is this temple one of Hatshe … Hatchet sut's? Morticia asked, staring around her.

'No. This wasn't Hatshepsut's. It was built more than a thousand years after her reign.' The sandstone temple had been built around 15 BC. I recalled something of the gifting of it to the US by Egyptian authorities in the sixties.

'Oh.' She paused. 'I do know the name Howard Carter,' she said of the boards we'd read in the other room. 'Is he the one who died from Tutankhamen's curse?'

I shook my head. 'Actually, he was the one who *didn't* die. He died of natural causes long after opening the tomb. His death is normally used to explain that there was no real curse. But the others … well, a fair few came to untimely ends.'

Again, those already large eyes seemed to grow larger. 'It's so cool how you know this stuff,' Morticia said.

I knew more than I could tell her, and it wasn't all about ancient curses. In fact, it was the current ones that concerned me.

She frowned, her darkly painted lips pursing. 'Do you believe in curses, Pandora?'

'What an interesting question. I think I do,' I said after a pause, feeling my stomach squirm. 'Yes, I think I do.'

'Pandora!' Astrid called, spotting us. The photographer was a petite woman with a trendy, pastel-coloured pixie haircut and ripped jeans. She wore sneakers and a T-shirt – the very antithesis of Pepper, the unfailingly high-heeled magazine editor who had hired her. She was busy directing a couple of lighting assistants who were covering a section in front of the glass under the watchful eyes of the museum staff. I hadn't even seen them in the dark, dazzled as I was by the ancient, spotlit temple.

'Can you give me a hand with this? Bring your friend,' she said, and we set to work helping to make the space ready for our shoot.

The season's designer offerings were Egyptian-themed, or at least that was what the stylist Amelia had pulled, and to showcase them, we had two models, each in their late teens, like me. They were quite gorgeous, in that slim, almost alien style that was in this season. (The vampiric look was *so* last season. Thank goddess.) I'd seen their portfolios before the shoot, yet they'd been unrecognisable when they'd arrived in casual clothes, their hair in ponytails, and without a scrap of makeup. They'd looked like two young, plain schoolgirls, almost like someone I'd know. But once the hair and makeup artists had done their magic, those perfect bone structures and wide-set eyes were set off and they were untouchable, almost a different species. One was platinum-haired and pale, and the other had shining dark skin and jet black locks, and now that they were both in full regalia and the shoot was underway, they were like twin versions of Claudette Colbert's slinky and sensuous *Cleopatra,* or perhaps Elizabeth Taylor's – but under different lenses: one light, one dark. For the moment the decadently dressed pair stood by the columns of the Temple of Dendur ('Don't touch the sandstone!' I'd heard a museum supervisor shout). They twisted and bent their lithe bodies on the photographer's instructions while the stylist dashed in from time to time to adjust a strap or the fall of an elaborate pendant.

About an hour in, my boss Pepper appeared in a black body-con dress and stylish shawl, a beautiful necklace glittering at her throat. Her arrival was announced by the echoing of her platform patent heels. She had a look around, scanned some of the shots on the technician's computer set-up, chatted with Astrid for a few minutes and, satisfied, left us to resume whatever her evening involved. Something glamorous, by the looks of it. She was the boss, so she had that option. Clearly her confidence in us, in the photographer and the crew, the stylist and the models was enough that she didn't feel the need to stick around. She didn't bother speaking to me, much less to Morticia, though I did warrant a distracted nod of her perfectly coiffed head.

Hours passed, our night in the museum's Sackler Wing wearing on in stretched silences punctuated by shouted directions in the dark and echoing space. With the floodlights off, the Temple of Dendur was illuminated only by the photographer's stark bulbs and the effect added a surreal spookiness to the already evocative scene. The erected blackouts meant the ancient temple seemed aloft in deep darkness, as if there was nothing at all around us – like we'd been pulled into a black hole, or the kind of alternate dimension H P Lovecraft wrote about. The sandstone columns and walls threw freakish, hard shadows on the floors that seemed to move. Time and again I thought I saw movement in my periphery, but when I looked there was nothing but the darkness of shadow and black screens, the room around us evidently quiet and still.

I tried to stay on task and push back the disquieting darkness. I was on the job, after all. This wasn't the time for The Seventh, but just little Pandora English of the fashionable magazine that a small number of people in the living human world read from time to time. (How important that had once seemed!) But while the space around me was decidedly riveting – if somehow unsettling – the process of the shoot itself was not.

Perhaps this was one reason why, given the option, our boss didn't stick around.

Fashion shoots are not as glamorous as the end result suggests, I'd found. In small town Gretchenville I had pored over fashion magazines and dreamed of a more cosmopolitan and glamorous life, but now that I was in Manhattan and working for one, I found the reality was very different. Yes, the models were pretty and some of the clothes were exquisite, but the process of photographing it all was long and repetitive, almost mechanised; nothing like the dreamy artistic experience I'd imagined when I was younger. Being in the industry now, after all those years of admiration from afar, was a bit like peeking behind the curtain and discovering that there was no Wizard of Oz, only a sophisticated system of smoke and mirrors – and airbrushing. The setting tonight was magnificent, yet it was ultimately just a shoot. A job. After the first hour, I longed to wander off down the corridors of the museum and see the exhibits; in particular what was being set up next door where we'd come in.

The models especially appeared bored – though that did seem to be part of the 'look', an affectation of the trade. Their work looked uncomfortable, bending their bodies into strange contortions that somehow looked natural on camera – hips pushed out, stomach in, chest up, chin tilted at an unnatural angle – and they wore one of two expressions: pout or scowl. These models did fashionable disdain like pros, and though the end product would look somehow effortless, I could see it was hard for them, leaning over sandstone blocks while somehow not touching them, and wearing heavy gold jewellery, tight

Herve Leger bandage dresses and platform shoes that were two sizes too small. I could hardly blame them if they were waiting to get home. Every few minutes the hairdresser or the makeup artist or the stylist fussed over them, pushing and pulling at hems, or unruly locks of hair, and adding a bit more kohl to their matching dark lids and winged eyeliner, all of which they tolerated without comment, like the directions from the photographer to move a limb here, turn the gaze there.

Don't get me wrong, it was glamorous, *very glamorous.* And yet, not. It was a fantasy we were creating, but the reality was increasingly dull as it grew late and the girls became tired and the outfits and poses blurred together.

Morticia, however, seemed quite absorbed with the experience, even enraptured. She gladly took instruction and helped move lights or white foam reflector boards, all the while eyes wide, making her look even more like Olive Oyl than usual.

Once things were in full swing, and most of the rack of clothes had been shot, I saw I couldn't be of much further help, and finally took the opportunity to wander around the edges of the Sackler Wing that enclosed us. Pepper wasn't there to judge what I did and I figured Astrid would call out for me if she required anything further. My eyes took a while to adjust to the darkness beyond the photographic lights, but adjust they did, and that was when I noticed we were being watched. The gruff security guard was there, watching, flashlight off and standing by the pool as one of the models worked with a particularly tight and revealing dress. Funny that.

I let the guard be, deciding it wasn't worth pointing out the creepiness of having him there in the shadows – of course he was doing his job, he would argue, and that might be true. I continued my stroll. Just outside our shoot area was a large sphinx, that most iconic of ancient Egyptian creatures. Somehow, despite its size, I had not really noticed it, perhaps because it had not been lit up like the temple when we walked in. I approached the sphinx and marvelled at it in the low light. She had the muscular body of a lion, seated and stretched out, and a human head wearing the traditional Nemes headdress and royal beard. After some inspection I noted that it was, once again, a figure of Pharaoh Hatshepsut, one of many the museum had recovered and reassembled. I noted the female pharaoh's high cheekbones and slightly rounded features. She'd been looking back at us the whole time, watching our shoot from the shadows. While it was fairly easy to imagine what the guard might be thinking as he watched, I could not fathom what this royal sphinx would think of the loose interpretation or appropriation of ancient Egyptian culture, the use of the space, or, indeed, what she would think of being there in New York, so far from the region of her birth.

Hatshepsut.

Odd.

A feeling in my hand broke my concentration. I was wearing the obsidian ring my Great-Aunt Celia had given me. It had once belonged to Madame Aurora, my great-great-grandmother – a gifted psychic, as Celia told it. The ring tended to heat up in the presence of supernatural activity. And it was doing just that now. Why? I closed my eyes and a vision flooded my mind, a vision of snakes, cobras at night, in darkness. I heard a hissing . . .

'Hey!' someone said.

The hissing sound disappeared as quickly and suddenly as it had come. I shook myself and looked again at the ring on my finger. What did the warmth of the obsidian mean, here, in this place? What had that vision been? A communication? Often my visions were premonitions, but not always, I reminded myself. Not always. I turned and walked over to the technician who had spoken, doing my best to hide my unease. It was his job to sit at a computer set up on a trolley, and check the images as they came through to see that they were sharp and in focus, and even to sometimes alter them with Photoshop so Astrid could see how the results could look. I walked up to the screen and squinted, looking over his shoulder. Something peculiar had come up in the latest image fed back from the camera.

'Weird, right?' the technician said. He announced loudly, 'We seem to have some kind of reflection.'

The clicking of Astrid's camera came to a halt. The model stood straight, having been in the process of contorting her body for the lens. Now that the photographer had stopped shooting she bent forward, stretching her back and hamstrings like an athlete.

'What?' Astrid shouted back, her voice echoing in the darkness around us.

'Reflection. I think there's a reflection,' he told her again.

I cocked my head and looked closer as he flicked through some of the digital images on the screen. *That is no reflection*, I thought. Behind the model was a ghostly green shape, like a tall figure, lingering just next to one of the ancient pillars. The sight gave me a chill.

No one else can see this?

'Dammit.' Astrid locked her camera to the tripod, strode up to the model and told her she could take a break. She walked out of the bright lights and joined the other model who was lounging in a folding chair, using her mobile phone. I noticed the stylist run towards the model, gesticulating wildly and demanding she remove the couture before sitting down. The young model was pulled aside to change into a terry cloth robe before the precious garment hit the chair, causing a wrinkle or worse.

Astrid stood on the cleared set and looked over the space where she had been shooting, waving her arms to see how the shadows fell. She bent down in her ripped jeans, kneeling on the cool floor and waving her arms again, looking for changes in the light. She shook her head and stood. 'Pandora, can you snap a frame,' she called out.

I walked up to her camera. 'Um, just click here?' I asked, unfamiliar with her set-up. 'Okay, here goes ...' I depressed the button and heard a click. I looked to the photo technician and he nodded. A new image had come up on the screen.

'Looks good,' he called back in a bored voice. He then pulled back from the computer, shook his head and adjusted his glasses. 'No, wait ... I think there might be something there.'

'Dammit!' Astrid exclaimed. 'Pandora, can you grab some more of the black-outs?'

Morticia raised her hand. 'I can help.'

'Yes, both of you, please.'

We got to work hanging the black cloth over mobile frames brought for the purpose. It didn't seem to matter where we placed them, however, the shapes kept coming up in the images, along with a faint green cast. Or at least they seemed to, but it depended how you looked. It was like seeing something in your periphery. I thought I could spot what was there, but when I really looked at the figures and tried to focus they seemed to vanish.

'We're running out of time,' Astrid said, looking at her watch. It was past ten. 'If we're going to wrap by midnight we need to sort this problem out.'

It was just on the stroke of midnight when the *Pandora* fashion shoot wrapped and the process of packing down began – a remarkably quick shoot considering the number of pages in the spread and the issue with the reflections, which kept coming up despite our best efforts. Finally the hot photography lights were turned off and the usual museum spotlights were switched back on to illuminate the large space. The two models carefully pulled off the designer clothes, handing them to the stylist, and used wet wipes to remove their extravagant makeup, returning to their mortal, wholesome, natural appearance in just a few minutes. It was quite a transformation. Some of the eeriness and magic of the space seemed to dissipate.

Gosh, I was keen to get home.

I was bent over a gigantic black drop cloth, folding it with Morticia's help, when I heard the voice. It was a male voice and it sounded like ... Well, it sounded like ...

'Hey, Pandora!' came the voice again.

I stood up and turned my head, and blinked as my eyes were

met with the vision of the tall and handsome New Yorker I sometimes called my boyfriend. But Jay Rockwell had absolutely no reason to be here at the Metropolitan Museum on a Tuesday night after hours. He had absolutely no reason to even know I was here. In fact, he hadn't returned my messages in a week.

'Jay?' I said, not even attempting to hide my shock. I'd dropped my end of the heavy dark cloth. I stood up and wiped the dust off my vintage dress.

Jay stepped forward into a patch of light and, being totally unprepared for his unannounced arrival on a work set, I was struck with a mixture of delight and embarrassment at the sight of him. He was six foot six and still built like a rower after years of college competition. He's what you'd call ruggedly good-looking, there was no denying it. He always looked a bit like he belonged on a yacht or in a cologne ad or something. Tonight his dark hair was cropped short, he was clean-shaven, and he wore jeans and his usual leather jacket. As always he managed to look effortlessly urbane and practically edible. Jay was the first man I'd gone on a date with in New York. The only man, really, if you discounted Lieutenant Luke on account of his non-livingness. I'd wanted to talk with him about our, well, dating status. We hadn't consummated things (well, I hadn't consummated with anyone before, so to speak) and our on-again off-again time together had begun to feel like the wrong thing. Jay was hard to pin down, and more pressingly, I found I wasn't sure how I felt about seeing him anymore. There'd been a shift in my relationship with Luke now that he was free from the mansion and I was also growing more used to my supernatural life. That would be a difficult one to explain.

Looking at Jay now, I wasn't sure how to react.

'I heard you'd be here,' he said with a smirk as if there were some inside joke, then flashed a charming smile. He had a distinctive New Yorker accent that still sounded sophisticated to my small town ears. My heart felt funny as he neared. My stomach too. Was I doubting my as-of-yet unvoiced decision to part? He was, after all, my main tie with the normal world.

'How did you know I'd be here?' I asked.

'I know a few people at the Met,' he boasted and threw an arm around me. I got a whiff of the lovely leather smell of his jacket before I slid out of his arms again. 'My dad is one of the major patrons,' he continued. 'You could say I made sure you guys could get access tonight for your shoot.'

Oh, you are kidding me.

He was the one who had pulled the favour for my boss? Had the favour been for her benefit, or for mine? I'd thought maybe they'd been in some kind of a romantic relationship at some point, Jay and Pepper, though I didn't know the details, and I knew they were friendly. So it was because of Jay Rockwell that the shoot had changed location? *Well, well.* I shouldn't have been surprised. Jay was often helpful, but in ways that seemed designed to remind me, or really to remind everyone, of his influence – influence being a quality I did not possess at all (in the regular world).

'That was awfully nice of you,' I told him, aware I was slipping back into my Gretchenville way of speaking, all politeness and nerves. 'It's been interesting to be here for the shoot. It's a beautiful temple. I can't believe I haven't visited the museum before tonight.'

I couldn't believe, also, that I hadn't heard back from Jay in a week and suddenly here he was, on set unannounced while I was packing up a shoot he'd evidently had a hand in organising.

I noticed that Morticia was staring at us – well, staring at Jay – with open admiration. She'd remarked many times about how well-built he was and I suppose he looked pretty impressive as I tried to shrink away under his arm. He was certainly muscular, there was no doubt about that, but I bet Morticia wouldn't believe that I'd saved his life once, when a bunch of ill-tempered vampire – uh, *Sanguine*, sorry – supermodels were trying to neck him. (Sanguine is the politically correct term. From the Latin *sanguineus*, of blood.) Of course Jay had no idea I'd saved his life because he'd been 'erased'. That was how the supernatural world kept its secrets – erasing the memories of normal folks when they came in contact with supernatural occurrences.

How will the supernatural world keep its secrets once the dead rise up and take over the earth? I wondered. The prospect had pushed at my mind near constantly since I'd heard of the Revolution of the Dead. *Or perhaps then all those secrets won't matter anymore . . .*

'It's good to see you,' I managed, and resisted asking if he'd got my last phone message.

'You too. You look lovely,' he said.

'Do I? Um, have you met Morticia?' I asked awkwardly, and she scurried over a little too quickly. 'Jay, meet Morticia. Morticia, meet Jay.'

'Unusual name. I hope you're a fan of the Addams Family,' he said.

She nodded enthusiastically. She was.

'I need to help with some packing up here,' I said.

'I know you're working. I thought I could drive you home when you're done.' He looked at his expensive watch. 'It's already after midnight. I don't want you walking around Central Park alone at this hour.'

I bit my lip. 'That is really nice, but ...' What excuse could I give? 'I already have a ... a car picking me up,' I said, not entirely truthfully. 'So there is no need for you to drive me.'

His brows pulled together and he seemed temporarily at a loss for words. 'Are you trying to make me jealous?' he said.

'Me? Make you jealous? No. It's just that I already have a ride. My great-aunt has a chauffeur.'

That was true, but I didn't know if Vlad would show. I rarely knew, in fact. I could hardly explain to Jay that I was trying to avoid his driving into Spektor, the neighbourhood I called home, the neighbourhood that didn't appear on maps, because it did not particularly welcome folk like him.

Jay cocked his head, considering things. 'Well, why don't I wait until you get picked up? That way I'll know you're safe,' he said.

I reluctantly agreed, for lack of a better option. This was a pretty normal-world thing to do, I supposed, but the irony was that I'd saved his life before, not the other way around, and here he was coming up all saviour-like. So, he'd probably end up driving me into Spektor again. It wouldn't be the first time.

That was two guys who'd showed up unannounced today, one living, one dead. My life was so weird. Life really liked to keep me on my toes.

Chapter Three

At nearly one in the morning I found myself in Jay's flashy silver Ferrari, the streets of Spektor welcoming me, but not my driver.

'Jay, could you pull over here, please?' I said.

Jay Rockwell – highly influential human in natural New York who had absolutely no influence in supernatural New York – smiled softly and pulled his impressive car over to the kerb. I took a breath and looked at the man beside me, his handsome face, his attractive lips, and saw that his eyes were a touch glazed. I tilted my head one way, then the other, and he didn't move. I blinked. He didn't. The effect of this place on him seemed to be getting worse.

Maybe this wasn't the best time to have *that* conversation.

When we'd dropped Morticia off at the subway Jay had seemed absolutely himself, absolutely in control. Now we were on the main street of Spektor and though it was one in the morning, practically rush hour, nothing was stirring. Even Harold's Grocer looked closed. This was both because it was a sleepy neighbourhood, but also because Jay was there, I knew. He'd driven me as far as it was helpful to and it was best to get out of the car and send him on his way. Had he been himself he might have insisted on walking me to my door, but he was not himself. And he would not remember any details in the morning, if previous experience with him was anything to go by. He'd driven me home before and always forgotten it the next day. I wondered whether, if pressed, he would have a recollection of it? Was it like when people drank too much, or like when something really exciting or dangerous happened and they only remembered bits and pieces? Was it like a blur or a dream? Would he remember the fog, for instance? Did he have any recollection of that? Or any recollection of those Sanguine supermodels who'd nearly killed him that night before he'd been erased so fully that he hadn't even remembered we'd met? Did he ever get flashes of the 'erased' times we'd spent together?

I looked at his beautiful, blank eyes, and found no answers. In any event, Spektor was doing its thing, remaining closed to Jay's relatively closed mind.

'I wanted to talk with you about something,' I said.

'Mmmm.'

But not now. Not like this. It was better to part for now. 'Call me, okay. I want to chat, when it's … um, convenient.' I held my hand up in the sign for telephone. 'And thanks for driving me,' I said.

He smiled a little dreamily. 'I wanted to make sure you got home okay.'

'Thank you, Jay. That's kind.'

That faraway look stayed in place, hardly an expression he wore during normal daylight hours. 'My pleasure,' he said. It seemed like sort of an autopilot thing. Jay was smooth in conversation. Maybe that was why he could continue it now. Sort of.

'You turn around now and drive back out the way we came, okay?' I instructed, watching him carefully and pointing the way. Some part of me almost wanted to kiss him, or at least thought I *ought to* want to kiss him. It was nice kissing him, a human man, with warm lips and a heart that beat under that broad chest, a beat I could even feel with my hand. But in this state that would almost feel like taking advantage. And besides, I was trying to make some tough decisions here about our future, and I was increasingly feeling like we had no future. How could we? There was too much between us, too many obstacles to any kind of real connection. But boy, the Pandora from Gretchenville would have been impressed by him and this damn car and the whole thing. The Pandora from Gretchenville *had* been impressed. But maybe I wasn't really Pandora from Gretchenville anymore. Maybe I was becoming something else.

Jay nodded dreamily at my instructions, and with that the door of his low slung silver Ferrari opened up like a bird raising one wing and I pulled myself up from the luxurious leather seat and stepped on to the quiet streets with my satchel, the mist enveloping me like an old friend. The supernatural mist smelled faintly of old books, I thought, and I always liked that. I stood on the sidewalk and watched with mixed feelings as the door of Jay's luxurious and expensive car closed and he turned around and drove away. I hoped he would get in touch soon so we could chat under more normal circumstances. But I'd noticed he often liked to be the one making the moves, making the decisions. Or at least thinking he was.

Once Jay Rockwell and his car had disappeared into the mist, I took a deep breath, pulled my jacket closer around me and began to cross the street and make my way to Celia's door.

I had learned pretty quickly that my life in Manhattan was nothing like it had been in sleepy Gretchenville. The past few months had been a rollercoaster. Among other complications, here I needed to keep my wits about me and carry certain items for precautionary reasons. Not the pepper spray one might imagine, but rice – handfuls of uncooked rice. There are some residents of Spektor with arithmomania issues. Sanguine – well, just the Fledgling ones – need to count rice. It was a peculiar and very real compulsion of the undead, and not just a folk myth (or *Sesame Street's* Count Dracula). So yes, though I had grown to feel some affection for the mist, I'd not grown to like all the other things here, and with that in mind I dug my hands into the pocket of my cardigan, touching the rice as a kind of security as I walked the misty street, feeling tired and hoping I would not run into my former boss, Skye DeVille, or the fanged gang she had recently joined, led by my nemesis, Athanasia. (She was an undead supermodel. I figured she kept Skye around for the clothes. Fashion editors, and former fashion editors, tended to have some good threads. There wasn't much else to recommend her.)

Despite the fear of running into unwanted Sanguine company I did enjoy being in Spektor. It had begun to feel like home. Perhaps I even felt more at home here after just a few months than I had in Gretchenville living with my aunt for all those years. Maybe that was the thing with Jay. He was the kind of guy I'd dreamt of in Gretchenville. In fact, I would have thought he was too good for the likes of little old me. But now Spektor was my home and I was The Seventh, my perspective was changing. I wasn't normal. I'd always known that. But I was starting to realise I really had a lot more in me.

Something moved in my peripheral vision. Not the Sanguine I feared, thankfully. It was Lieutenant Luke. I could see his ghostly form as he floated along the tops of the houses, moving from one roof to the next in his sharp uniform. He was earnestly watching over me, watching over Spektor. He often did this now he was able to leave the confines of the mansion.

I smiled and waved. Luke gave a sombre nod in return.

Did this mean Luke had just seen me get out of Jay Rockwell's fancy silver car? Of course he had. It could have been worse. I could have kissed Jay instead of just getting out and sending him on his way. How would that have made Luke feel? He was always telling me I should get out and date living men, that he wanted that for me, that he wasn't enough for me, but it was one thing to say it, and quite another to see it, I imagined. The sooner I spoke to Jay about things the better.

Before I reached the ironwork outside Celia's mansion door I caught my spirit guide's attention and put my hands beside my cheek in the sign for sleep. I needed to get some rest, I figured. We could talk tomorrow. No romantic stroll through the cemetery tonight. No intimate conversations in my room. I needed alone time, and rest. Luke nodded that he understood, but I felt his gentle longing. In truth, it was a longing that was returned. I made our sign for talk and then 'next day' – raising my right index finger for the number one, and then rolling it through the air, as if rolling over the calendar day. I couldn't recall exactly when we'd started to exchange these little codes with each other but we had a few now. I imagined signals were familiar to him from his time as a Union soldier, though he preferred not to use military signs or talk much about those times. It was a language we were creating for each other.

Luke noted my signal with an unreadable nod, and his eyes flashed blue.

Oh Luke . . .

I wished I could find something online about having a crush on a spirit guide. My feelings troubled me.

Now I was outside my great-aunt's mansion at Number One Addams Avenue, my beautiful spirit guide perched on a gargoyle far above me, watching over me. The mansion was built in neo-Gothic style with a series of stone arches, turrets and spikes stretching up towards the night sky. The heavily embellished windows on the middle two floors were boarded up, because this place served as a kind of halfway house for vagrant vamps, for reasons that I was yet to fully comprehend. Something to do with Celia's friend Deus, I suspected. It was all very complicated.

There's no place like home, I thought, not without some irony, and walked past the open gates. 'Please let me in,' I whispered to the immense front door, and the house welcomed me. The heavy wooden door opened easily under my hands and a gust of air pushed up the ubiquitous dust in the foyer, sending it swirling. 'The chandelier in the centre foyer was finally straight. I was still getting used to it, and looking at it I felt a stab of sadness thinking of the heartbroken woman who had taken her life there. Hauling my sorry self inside, I felt the instant drop in temperature that always characterised the lower floors of the house, and I was about to head towards the old lift when a tall figure startled me.

A man stood but one metre away from me wearing a pair of dark sunglasses, silent and seemingly unbreathing. My own breath caught in my throat.

'Um, hi, Vlad.'

My great-aunt's chauffeur stood on the tiled floor, unsmiling. He hadn't picked me up from the shoot, but then I hadn't really expected him to. In my experience, Vlad never spoke so it did not surprise me that my greeting went unanswered. In the four months I'd been here I had only ever seen Vlad inside the house a few times before, most notably that time he was carrying a large and rather frightening axe. (A door needed chopping down. Long story.) Though Vlad hardly needed an axe to appear intimidating. He was tall and curiously pale, and obviously quite strong. Like a casting central version of a funeral director, if he could bench press you and was a wee bit undead. Not that Vlad is actually undead. He got around by day, which wasn't the sort of thing Sanguine types did. I didn't quite have him figured out.

Vlad nodded his head and moved past me with his usual lumbering walk. I took the lift up to the penthouse, watching the cobwebbed floors pass, and got out. Of course, any normal great-aunt would be asleep at this time of the morning. Not my Great-Aunt Celia.

'Great-Aunt Celia, I'm home,' I declared after knocking and entering. I stepped into her entryway and closed the door behind me.

'Late for a shoot,' her voice came back. I heard her but could not see her, until she turned her head to the side and leaned out of her reading nook to address me. That was her usual spot, where she could be found nearly every evening. 'You've had an exciting night. What is it that troubles you?' she asked. She had a way of knowing things.

What troubles me? Where to begin? First, there were all these unsettling thoughts of my mother and the museum. Plus the eerie 'reflections' at the Temple of Dendur, and that vision of snakes. And the weirdness with Jay Rockwell. And what should I do about my feelings for Lieutenant Luke? Oh, and was it really the Agitation yet? I knew it was supposed to be happening *now*, though I couldn't see it. The Agitation was supposed to mean that the veil between the living and the dead was thin, thinner than usual, but it was hard to know how my experiences this month compared with the last. Things had been pretty intense since I'd moved to Spektor, as far as paranormal activity went. Was there a sliding scale?

A lot of things troubled me.

'Yes, it is late and my evening at the museum has been … exciting.' I slipped my ballet flats off and unburdened myself of my work satchel and cardigan. I padded over to see Celia, resplendent in her stunning black satin skirt and cap-sleeved jacket, her calves encased in fine black stockings. Her stockinged feet were up on the leather hassock, and now she swung them down and slid her toes into the delicate slippers on the floor beside her.

'The ancient Egyptian theme,' she said in a distant voice.

I nodded. 'Yes. And there is a new exhibition coming. Hatshepsut, the pharaoh.'

Celia nodded, her thoughts unreadable behind her ever-present mesh veil.

'Hey, I saw Vlad in the foyer. Is everything okay?'

'Perfectly, darling Pandora. Vlad brought this from the post. Harold held it for you.'

'Vlad brought what?' I noticed the large parcel next to her. It was wrapped in plain brown paper and covered in stamps.

'I spoke with your aunt,' Great-Aunt Celia informed me, by way of an answer. This was supposed to ring a bell, perhaps, but it did not.

'You spoke with Aunt Georgia? What about?' I paused. 'You don't have a phone,' I added. I just couldn't imagine my great-aunt finding herself a telephone box somewhere and using it to call my aunt in Gretchenville.

'We correspond by post,' she clarified. Harold at Harold's Grocer sometimes posted things for her, because I didn't know of any actual post office in Spektor.

'Of course,' I said, surprised somehow by the idea of them corresponding at all. Aunt Georgia, for all her good qualities, was rather conservative and, well, nothing like my great-aunt, who was about fifty times more exciting, deeply fashionable, deeply wise and many other things besides.

'There is a box you were to have been given when you turned eighteen,' Celia declared, sweeping a pale, manicured hand through the air over the parcel. 'Your aunt failed to give it to you.'

Failed?

I was gobsmacked. 'Really? Something I was supposed to have been given? What is it? Why wasn't it sent?'

She gestured to the parcel. 'It is from your mother,' she said then, and my heart seemed to stop.

I could not speak.

My great-aunt could see I was speechless. 'It should have been given to you before, but it's here now,' she said gently, and though she surely meant the parcel and whatever it contained, it also seemed to mean that this signalled the arrival of something I'd been trying to push back. The subject of my late mother had just waltzed into the room, again. And only hours earlier I'd had to face the fact that I'd avoided the Met museum for no other reason than my mother had so often spoken about their Egyptian collection before her death. My Aunt Georgia had taken many of my mother's favourite books on mythology away after she died, but I'd also attempted, in my own way, to distance myself from memories of her, to push it all back. An impossible task, of course. And now I knew the exhibition was on Hatshepsut, of all the ancient Egyptian rulers they could have chosen. The Hatshepsut I'm sure my mother had told me about, though I could not recall the details.

Celia rose elegantly from her chair and picked up the parcel. 'It is heavy,' she warned as she handed it to me.

It was heavier than I expected, heavier than any great-aunt might be expected to lift so effortlessly. I held the enormous parcel in my arms, hands gripping the corners, knowing that my eyes had welled up, and even blinking would bring tears cascading down. Celia patted me on the shoulder and offered me a pre-emptive handkerchief.

'I'm sorry for your loss, Pandora,' she said. 'It shouldn't have been this way.'

I nodded, accepting her kindness, but I still could not speak. Here was something of my mother's. I had so little of hers. Only her suitcase. That wedding photo. I had so little of both of them. And here in my arms was something my mother intended me to have. The emotion was almost too much. Before the first tear spilled I thanked Celia and made for my bedroom. Though she said nothing further, I felt my great-aunt's support. She let me go, to process this new development in private.

Pandora's Box, I thought and shook my head. I'm really opening it.

I used a sharp letter opener from the desk in my room to open the parcel at the sides. This first layer was fresh. New packaging. Inside was a stiff cardboard box, sealed with tape that – unlike the outer layer – had yellowed with time. Frowning, I used the opener to split the old tape and pull the edges back.

I didn't know what to expect, but I certainly did not expect what I was seeing. The box seemed to be filled with my mother's old clothes.

Mom.

The tears flowed freely now. For a moment I let them fall, not able to progress further, not able to pull out the clothing and sort through it. I put a hand into the fabrics inside and felt that there was a shoebox in there, and who knew what else. Her clothes. My late mother had worn these. I ran a hand over my face. *I can't do this tonight,* I thought. *I can't.* Through teary eyes I looked at my clock. It would soon be two in the morning. I had to be up for work in a few hours, had to keep myself together. After Luke showing up at work, the museum shoot and Jay arriving out of nowhere and everything, I needed rest.

Slowly, deliberately, I placed my hand on top of the clothes, and shut my eyes. When I was thirteen I'd thought my mother had visited me. My Aunt Georgia hadn't believed me, hadn't listened, had refused to entertain the idea that I could have been right. She'd been cross that I could say such a thing. She'd been disappointed. Now, knowing what I did since moving to Spektor, I *knew* I was right. That had been my mother, not my imagination. I had not seen her for six years. It seemed cruel somehow, that I could see the spirits of so many strangers, but not those of my own parents.

'I love you, Mom,' I said softly to her and to what had once been her possessions, feeling almost that the fabrics spoke back, albeit not in words. And then, with lingering regret, my hand retreated and I closed the box and put it under my bed.

I went about preparing for bed, and before I closed my eyes to sleep they lit upon a small portrait in a silver frame on the antique writing desk under the window. It was a portrait of a young man and woman, affectionately clutching one another, broad grins across their faces. The man wore a white suit and tie. The woman's beautiful face was haloed by her white wedding veil. Increasingly I recognised myself in that face – the features. It was my late mother and father on their wedding day. Strange to think that I did not yet exist when the photo was taken, and now I was here and they were gone.

Grief doesn't really go away. It changes, but it never ends. I could never stop loving those I'd lost, could never stop missing them, longing for them. I would face whatever my mother had sent me after work. For now, it was time to finally sleep.

Chapter Four

I woke with a start in the darkness of my bedroom, the covers and delicate lace pillows thrown off the four-poster bed and the night air chilling my bare legs. Feeling exposed, I sat up and pulled my white cotton nightgown back down over my knees. I'd been dreaming of snakes, I realised with a shiver. Thousands and thousands of snakes. I wrapped my arms tightly around myself, wondering what it was that had so violently woken me from my nightmare.

Screeeeeech.

Something was scratching against the glass pane of one of two narrow, arched gothic windows. I squinted through the darkness, and to my horror saw that something was there, beyond the mist – a shape – a human-like shape, but inverted. A pale white face sat against the glass, grinning at me upside down.

I gasped and covered my mouth.

It was Deus. The ancient Sanguine. At my window.

Don't open the window, I thought. *Don't!* Yet despite all ideas of self-preservation, I swung my legs over the side of the bed and my arms reached out towards the window, as if animated by an outside force. I noticed that the latch was undone. He could have easily pushed himself inside already, but he had not. He was just there, floating outside my window. I pulled the window open and regarded the ancient Kathakano, face to inverted face. He continued to smile at me despite what appeared to be a lustful thirst. His fangs were fully extended. They were such big fangs, I thought. So fascinating to look at. I'd only seen them once before and that had not been a good moment at all. Now it was like looking at two shining tusks – surreal and beautiful.

Am I still dreaming? I wondered.

I thought I could feel the night air on my face. I thought I could feel myself standing on the hardwood floor. These sensations *felt* real but this simply could not be happening because I was somehow not alarmed by this predator at my window, and the sight of his enormous, thirsty fangs comforted and fascinated me.

'Deus,' I said in a voice that did not sound like mine.

'Pandora English, The Seventh,' he replied.

'Please come in,' I said before I could stop myself from speaking those three vital, unwise words. Sanguine were not invited into the main penthouse. He could not enter without my permission and somehow, for some reason, those words had just fallen from my lips, as natural and necessary as exhaling. 'I am still dreaming, aren't I?' I said aloud as he drifted in my open window and turned in the air until he was the right way up, standing on the floor of my bedroom in his black suit, his black, collared shirt open to show a hint of pale, smooth chest.

His fangs. Just *look* at them.

'Come,' Deus said, and led me to my four-poster bed as casually as if he had done it a thousand times.

He will bite me now, won't he? I thought. That is what he does. Deus is a vampire, a killer. Somehow, though, I was relaxed about the proposition, as if I too had done this a thousand times, as if there was nothing at all to fear. It felt as if I was watching myself from a great, comforting distance. The frustratingly magnetic, smiling creature seated himself on the edge of my bed, ignoring its dishevelled state, and I sat next to him. Now I was smiling, and I thought, *Yes, this is a dream,* as the ancient vampire lifted his wrist to his mouth and tore it open with those white fangs. I did not flinch at the sight of his spilled blood. He offered his wrist to me, and I bent over his lap like an automaton, and suckled happily from his bleeding wrist like a hungry child. I could feel the blood dripping down my throat, and my chin, warm and sweet.

Ahhhhh …

The blood. It transported me.

And now I was back in the familiar realm of that hilltop in my dreams, my white nightgown billowing out in the wind. I was in the company of a great and beautiful ancient tree, the two of us basking in the wholesome rays of the sun, my arms outstretched like the great tree. Softly, something fell upon my head, and I saw that the green leaves upon the tree's branches had begun to wither and darken, turning brown with the season and preparing for death. One by one, the browning leaves floated down at my feet and shrivelled there, until, in decay, they joined the earth itself. I licked my lips and they tasted of warm, salty blood.

Time passed, the sun rotating across the great sky and the leaves rotting and the tree bending with the wind as she shed her leaves and stood bare. The skies turned red then and the rays of the moon broke through, a crimson moon taking the sun's place. And still, I stood. Waiting. Waiting for something.

He is come.

On the horizon, a figure appeared. My soldier. This was a familiar part of my dream, and some distant part of my mind recognised it – acknowledged that I was indeed dreaming. *Lieutenant Luke,* I thought with some relief. But as he approached I could see that he was not himself. His mouth was fearsome and misshapen, his jaws stretched downward and his teeth pointed like a shark's. His flesh seemed to rot on his bones.

There was a rumble of hooves as his horse approached, and the tree at my back began to shrink into the ground, as if out of fear.

And then came the hissing. A terrible hissing.

Snakes. The tree was not a tree at all. It was a mass of snakes. *Thousands of cobras.*

I woke with a start. The early morning sun shone rays across my bed. I was tucked in safe and tight, the sheets up to my neck.

Instinctively, I sat up and looked at my shaking hands. No blood. With panic I felt my smooth neck on both sides. It was intact. No wounds. No blood on the sheets or on me. I closed my eyes and took a slow breath, steadying myself.

What a vivid dream. Snakes. Always the snakes.

I swallowed and shook my head. Perhaps I shouldn't be surprised that my nightmares were worsening as the Agitation was supposedly underway, and the Revolution was nearing. I felt refreshed, at least. I seemed to have got enough sleep despite the late night, but now I had to get to work.

Before I left for the day, I looked at the corner of the box waiting under my bed, and found myself pulling it out and placing a hand on top of it. In a whisper, I promised my mother that when I returned home from work I would go through everything she'd seen fit to give me.

I left for work with a lump in my throat.

'Hello, Jay. It's Pandora here ...'

It was an afternoon break from the grind of work at *Pandora* magazine when I called Jay Rockwell's number. As usual of late, he wasn't answering.

'Thanks, um, for the lift last night,' I said, thinking uneasily of that dazed look on his face when we entered Spektor and he fell under its spell. 'I need to speak with you. Can you give me a call back when you can? It would be good to have a chat,' I said and hung up.

'Damn,' I whispered under my breath and did a quick scan of the open-plan office around me. Light was streaming in. One of my colleagues, Ben, was over by the printer in his crisp business shirt and suit pants, light-brown hair styled to perfection. Morticia was in her usual black, bent over and busy with something at the reception desk. Others were away from their desks. It seemed no one was watching me, though if they were, I suppose I could pretend that what I was going to do next was something to do with the Egyptian-themed shoot, which, loosely speaking, it was. I leaned over my computer, brought up the search engine and entered my terms:

Who was Hatshepsut?

I pressed enter and took a sip of my water.

Hatshepsut's name brought up several results, and I quickly found that I recalled much of her story from what my mother had told me. Yes, she was known as a 'princess who became a king', the daughter of Queen Ahmose and the pharaoh Tutmosis I – also spelled Thutmose I or Thutmosis I, depending on the source. Her name meant 'foremost of women'. She was described as an eighteenth dynasty pharaoh who ruled for twenty-two years in the fifteenth century BC, and passed away in 1482 BC.

I scanned through the results some more, opening short write-ups from *National Geographic* and the British Museum, which showed pieced-together statues and busts of her. She had been very young, probably about twelve, when her father Tutmosis I died and she married the heir to her father's throne, her half-brother Tutmosis II. Marrying within the royal bloodline was the done thing back then, as was marrying young. I wondered what that must have been like for her?

Her husband, Pharaoh Tutmosis II, had been older and when he died after fifteen years as pharaoh, kingship was passed on to his only son, borne by one of his 'lesser wives' (ouch), Isis or Iset. But he was just a baby and so Queen Hatshepsut acted as the young king's regent. In time she began to identify as Egypt's pharaoh – or king – and that's when things started to get interesting. A woman identifying herself as king? It wasn't unheard of for women, and for that matter female deities, to be portrayed alongside males in Egyptian society, and Egyptian women did have many rights that women in comparative ancient cultures didn't have at the time, but still, pharaohs were supposed to be male and the title passed to male heirs, not female.

Hatshepsut would have been about thirty by some estimates when she began leading the country, with a lifetime spent at court and many years as queen, so she was certainly qualified to be king, if such a thing mattered to how these titles fell. She must have been a good politician and had support from the court and advisors because she reigned successfully and peacefully for twenty-two years, during which time official documents increasingly referred to Hatshepsut as 'he' and showed her wearing the crown and artificial beard we'd seen on the bust in the museum. Pharaohs were supposed to be male so she was portrayed as male. How she regarded herself is another question.

Where is Hatshepsut's mummy? I dared to type in next. I swallowed back a lump in my throat.

If Hatshepsut's life was complicated, her afterlife was even more so. Twenty years after Hatshepsut died, her co-regent and successor Pharaoh Tutmosis III seems to have taken every possible step to erase all traces of her rule, destroying statues, defacing obelisks and monuments and scratching her name from records in what archaeologists now believe was an attempt to remove evidence of female interruption in the male Tutmosis royal lineage.

What a royal jerk, I thought.

It seems to have been politically motivated, as there may have been challenges to his legitimacy as ruler, because Hatshepsut was born female. So they just tried to rewrite history without her in it, it seemed.

I read on. British archaeologist Howard Carter discovered Hatshepsut's sarcophagus in the tomb, known as KV20, in 1903 but it was empty and Hatshepsut's whereabouts were a mystery. He also found tomb KV60, which had been ransacked and held some badly damaged grave goods and two mummies. An unidentified female mummy, KV60A, was found there, but regarded as too unimportant to investigate or move as she had no clothes on, no royal headdress or jewellery and none of the treasures of a royal, let alone the famous treasures that had been provided for the relatively minor pharaoh, Tutankhamun. The unidentified mummy was not even in a coffin. But it seemed that this mummy ...

'Whatcha looking at?'

I was startled by the voice and immediately closed the search window and turned around. Thank goddess it was only Morticia. My friend had her head cocked, dark shaggy hair spilling into her large, black-lined eyes.

'Hey, you look guilty of something,' she added, smiling slyly with purple-painted lips. 'What were you doing?'

'Oh nothing, really,' I said, and bit my lip. 'I was just interested in that exhibition they were setting up at the Met.'

'The one about the woman who was king?'

I nodded. 'Exactly.'

'What does it say about her?'

'Well, it's a bit confusing. It looks like her mummy was

missing. It was quite the mystery to archaeologists.' I wondered again about my mother's work. How had she been involved with Hatshepsut, exactly? I was only eleven when they left on that fateful trip to Egypt's Valley of the Kings, and there wasn't much I remembered clearly after all these years and so much heartache and loss, but Hatshepsut's name kept coming to mind. Could my mother have gone there to Hatshepsut's tomb, KV20? Or to the other one, KV60? I had a good memory for the historical figures, gods and goddesses my mother told me about, but the name Hatshepsut brought a different level of recognition. She'd been significant to my mother, I was sure of it.

I reopened the online page I'd been reading and Morticia bent over my desk to look. 'An Egyptologist named Elizabeth Thomas thought the unidentified mummy that had been found in KV60 without a coffin or royal goods was Hatshepsut, but passed away before she was able to prove it,' I explained to her. 'And it looks like she was right. Now it's supposedly been proved with a CT scan and a matching tooth known to be hers, from a Canopic box bearing Hatshepsut's name and also containing a liver and spleen. The tooth fits the mummy and Egypt's Supreme Council of Antiquities has claimed this proves the unidentified mummy – uh, KV60A, the mummy found in the sixtieth tomb discovered at the Valley of the Kings – is that of Pharaoh Hatshepsut. So that solves the mystery, I guess. Though of course scholars always disagree with each other,' I added. There were evidently some who remained unconvinced.

'Wow,' Morticia said. 'It's so weird, the Canopic thing,' she remarked, looking at the photograph of Hatshepsut's ancient Canopic box. 'All the organs taken out.'

During the mummification process organs were removed and placed in decorative Canopic jars, or in this case a Canopic box, and buried with the mummy. *Most* organs, anyway. Ancient Egyptians believed the centre for thinking was the heart, not the brain, which was why other organs were kept, but the brain was commonly destroyed with a whisk-like motion using a sharp instrument like a knitting needle, and then disposed of once it leaked through the nose.

'So gross,' Morticia commented, nodding, then added, 'Cool ...' as if the two things went hand in hand.

'So Hatshepsut's mummy has been identified. Well, it seems so anyway.' I paused. 'She was definitely important to my mother or her work,' I added, increasingly sure.

The Met was already known for their Egyptian digs in the twenties and thirties, and having pieced together a lot of ancient fragments from Hatshepsut's reign. Their permanent Egyptian collection was huge, so it followed that a special exhibition would be, too. I went to look up more information at the Met museum site when Pepper's office door opened.

On instinct I closed the search window and stared at a random spreadsheet on my screen, not wanting to be seen googling on company time.

'Ben ... Pandora,' Pepper said, indicating with a nod of her head that she wanted us in her office. I had on my most innocent face when my name was called, and smiled and nodded when addressed.

Today my boss had a fashionably severe ponytail with

dead-straight, ice-blonde hair falling down the back of her head. As usual not a single hair was out of place. Her jacket had shoulder pads – the eighties had evidently come round yet again – and her skinny jeans were worn with high heels and showed off a trim, fit physique that seemed to be made of something as firm as steel. She was a pretty good boss, a great improvement on the previous editor, but I found her intimidating and I wasn't really sure what she thought of me. That was my problem, I supposed. I felt unfashionable and almost a different species next to her, and I supposed you could argue that, technically, I was. Still, insecurity was something I'd been grappling with since leaving Gretchenville and I did my best to quiet the self-doubt I felt and to just stay positive and do my job. You could tie yourself in knots trying to double guess what people thought of you.

'The images are up,' Pepper told us, and I relaxed a touch, knowing she hadn't come out to ask me why I was (again) using office time to search the Internet. She was hardly going to understand that I couldn't get Wi-fi in Spektor because it seemed to exist in a different plane, or within some kind of supernatural bubble. She had two mobile phones on her person at all times, and probably had an array of screens at home.

'Great,' Ben said eagerly, walking over from the printer with a folder under his arm. He grabbed a pad of paper and a pen from his cubicle and marched inside our boss's office. I followed his lead and did the same. There had been a rush on the images, and the photographer had evidently come through. She must have worked through the night, I thought.

'Can I see, too?' Morticia asked. She was standing near an

abandoned cubicle, hands folded in front of her. Pepper paused for a moment, looked her over then nodded her assent. Skye had always been so rigidly opposed to Morticia's involvement in much of anything, I allowed myself a quiet smile.

Pepper had three computers in her office – in other words three more than were in Celia's whole building – and the largest of them was the desktop kind with a big screen on it for viewing digital images. 'That damn reflection,' she cursed, her brow creased into a deep frown.

I leaned in and looked at the photographs from the previous night's shoot, and with a rush of nausea remembered the figures I'd seen. Not only had they not been my imagination, but the camera lens had actually captured them. Spirits had really surrounded us in that big museum, there was no doubt about it. With everything else happening, I'd momentarily forgotten.

'I thought we'd sorted the glass reflections thing out. How is it still there?' she demanded, looking from one of us to the other.

Ben shrugged. He hadn't been there, so could hardly be blamed. I wondered if the photographer, Astrid, would get a talking to, or me.

'We did try several different things, and sometimes it seemed to work, but this did come up periodically,' I noted, being my most professional self and pointing at the shapes on screen as if I wasn't absolutely certain that it was the ancient dead somehow making themselves visible.

There was a moment of tense silence in the office.

'We can colour-correct the green. The shots are beautiful,'

Ben offered, breaking the quiet, and he was right. The two models looked exotic and mysterious in the images – they really were pros on camera, despite seeming bored between takes – the Temple of Dendur rising up in refined lines behind them, petal-like carved shapes at the top of the pillars, ancient sandstone providing an infinitely more compelling backdrop than any studio wall. The large slanted windows of the Sackler Wing had been blacked out in sections and some of the erected frames and the tape to secure the drop sheets could be seen out of focus in the background. Nothing a bit of Photoshop couldn't cure. That was to be expected. But the 'reflections' were something different. They dominated a number of the images, despite all our attempts. One image in particular made my stomach clench. Behind the two models it looked as if a figure with the ghostly head of Medusa, snakes spiralling out from her head, was standing there.

'Don't you think this one looks a bit like ... a figure?' I ventured, unwisely stating what I thought was obvious. I almost covered my mouth when the words slipped out, so keen was I to avoid this clashing of my normal and paranormal lives.

My observation seemed to excite Morticia. 'Yeah, it does. Oh my god! Like King Tut was there to haunt us!'

'Not Tutankhamen,' I replied under my breath before I could help myself. King Tut always seemed to come to mind when people spoke of pharaohs, but we often forgot that he was a fairly minor pharaoh in Egyptian history – the 'boy king' buried in a small chamber with a fraction of what Seti the Great or Ramesses II's much larger and more elaborate tombs would have held before they were robbed in antiquity.

Hatshepsut reigned for much longer and had many more achievements and monuments to her name, despite all attempts to erase her from history. She'd been relegated to a common tomb, no sarcophagus, no clothing, no crown. Was that the spirit of Hatshepsut caught in our images? Or some of her servants or protectors?

Pepper was looking at me strangely, I realised. I plastered that smile on again.

'I only mean to say that … Well, they say that the curse of King Tut is made up,' I managed, somewhat awkwardly. Pepper, Ben and Morticia looked away. The faux-disbeliever stance seemed to take the focus off me immediately. I was relieved. Because I'd almost made a point – at work – that there was a lot of supernatural activity at the museum and while Tutankhamen was unlikely to be present there, it was quite likely that some other spirits were. That one image was particularly disturbing, while the figures were less distinct in others, causing blurs at the edges of the frame, almost like sun flares, though there had been no sun to speak of in the dark museum wing.

'Perhaps we make it part of the look,' I suggested. Pepper ignored my suggestion, and I shrank back once more. I'd said enough. Almost too much.

My colleague Ben leaned in. 'I think it's beautiful. We can make it look intentional,' he announced, and our boss Pepper began nodding.

'That's a great idea, Ben,' she said, and I blinked. Hadn't I just said the same thing?

'We could play on the idea of the mummy being there.

You know, *the pharaoh herself*,' he added, and I wondered how that would fit with the two models posing in modern clothes at a temple which was built centuries after her death. 'You know, the new exhibition they have opening soon. What's her name?'

'Hatshepsut,' I mouthed, my voice too faint to be noticed.

'They'd like that, yes,' Pepper agreed. 'I did promise to mention the exhibition.'

'Well, that's perfect then,' I said. Pepper looked at me for a moment. I realised I was still smiling, and she looked away. My smile dropped.

'I printed off some information,' Ben said, all business. 'Some information on pharaohs and the iconography.' He spread some printed sheets out across the desk and put his hands in his suit pants' pockets.

I sure had a lot to learn about work ambition, I thought, watching Ben and Pepper converse. But with everything else going on in my world(s) I didn't have the energy to be terribly ambitious at the office. The prospect of being responsible for all of humankind seemed enough for now.

I moved over to stand beside Morticia and gave her a silent smile, which she returned, the two 'odd ones out' in the room. Once more I reminded myself that the Gretchenville custom of smiling to show camaraderie and friendliness did not serve me so well in Manhattan, not when it came to fashion circles. When it came to the two of us, Morticia and I could smile all we liked, but with Pepper and Ben and the like I had to practise a more neutral expression, preferably aloof. And I had to work on my clothes, I reminded myself again, seeing how well

Pepper and Ben were put together. It was as if every thread, every hair, every inch of them were manicured. I couldn't keep up with that, but I had to accept that I was judged here on my appearance and my sartorial senses needed honing. Celia knew a thing or two about that. She'd helped me when I'd first arrived. Maybe she could help me again, help me to 'step it up', so to speak.

I pulled my gaze from my boss's perfect manicure to one of Ben's printouts from the Encyclopaedia Britannica Online, and my eyes lit on one paragraph in particular: *'The pharaoh's divine status was portrayed in allegorical terms: his uraeus (the snake on his crown) spat flames at his enemies; he was able to trample thousands of the enemy on the battlefield; and he was all-powerful, knowing everything and controlling nature and fertility,'* it read.

Right. All those ancient guys controlling fertility and trampling thousands. I shivered. Modern leaders seemed to have remarkably similar obsessions, even if they didn't wear crowns that spat flames.

'Um, I can bring in some books on the subject, if you like,' I offered. It would be easy enough to get them from the library, or to search Celia's collections. These printouts were from superficial online write-ups, I could see. Still, it was clever of him. Instead, I would bring in some fascinating tomes on the subject, weighty books with images and reproductions of paintings and scrolls, the kind of books I grew up with. That would provide a lot more inspiration for the typesetting and layout.

'That won't be necessary,' Pepper said without looking at me, and I closed my mouth again. Not everyone was interested in old books, I reminded myself. 'Pandora, can you get me a skim latte?'

'Sure thing,' I said.

'I'm very disappointed with these reflections,' my boss added. 'You'd better make it work, Ben. It was a real coup we could get in there to shoot. I wish you'd been able to join us.' The last line was cutting. Clearly she'd expected him to change his plans at the last minute and he had not.

'I'm sorry, I . . .' he began apologetically, and in that moment I felt perfectly happy to be ignored.

There were many other things going on in my world(s) but at least as far as the *Pandora* magazine Egyptian-themed spread went, I wasn't the one under pressure. And that was just fine with me. I left the office, Morticia trailing behind, and set about fetching my boss her caffeine.

Trying to keep up with the living, the dead and the undead is a 24 hour job.

When I returned to Spektor on Wednesday evening it was uncharacteristically late. Pepper had worked late so I'd worked late, too. I suppose this meant I was moving up in the world of *Pandora* magazine, but it also meant that again I wasn't getting home when I'd planned. After our awkward parting in the lift I wanted to speak with Lieutenant Luke, and I wanted to open that box of my mother's.

I was trapped between worlds.

All the talk of the Met and of ancient Egypt during my day

at work brought me back to my mother and our conversations when I was young. I wished I could remember exactly what she had told me. I wished I could remember everything about her, every moment, every curve and line of her face, but slowly the years had robbed me of that. I had a strong feeling of her, strong love, but the memories themselves were slippery, hard to get hold of with any real clarity.

And my mind had kept circling around that passage from Ben's printout on the crown of the pharaoh: *his uraeus spat flames at his enemies; he was able to trample thousands of the enemy on the battlefield; and he was all-powerful ...*

I found it a deeply unsettling image.

Now it was already after sundown and I just wanted to get home and pull off my shoes and dive into that box. I wasn't as tired as I'd expected to be, but I wanted to use every last ounce of my energy to look through what my late mom had wanted me to have. Perhaps it would enlighten me somehow, and if not, at least I would have something more of her. And then I planned to talk with Luke, and fall into a long, deep sleep. If I wasn't careful, the pace of everything happening in my life would soon take a toll.

So it was with a deep weariness that I noticed I was being followed along the misty footpath to Celia's mansion. Not by Lieutenant Luke – that would have been welcome, even though my mind was fixed on that box waiting for me. No, I could sense, quite unfortunately, that it was someone else. Even with his tendency to look over me as my spirit guide Luke certainly would not stalk behind me like this. The footsteps could barely be heard, just a faint 'click, click, click'. *Heels,* I thought, and decided it was one of the Sanguine. I reached into my pockets to reassure myself with the feel of uncooked rice grains and, not slowing, I looked over my shoulder.

Athanasia. *Oh hell.*

This was worse than I thought. The Sanguine supermodel Athanasia was following a few metres behind me, like a prowling cat, and her being there couldn't be coincidental. You have to understand, Athanasia is perhaps the most terrifyingly beautiful woman in the world, though of course she is no longer a woman, strictly speaking. Thanks to my mother's books I knew 'Athanasia' meant immortal, which just told me that there wasn't as much chance and coincidence in the world as people liked to imagine. Athanasia was a top model, or had been, and she still looked the part – willowy and stylish, with even features and full, pouting lips, presently painted an unnerving red. Tonight her hair looked as dark as a raven's wing and just as glossy, though it had been a kind of dark auburn once, I thought. Her face was perfectly formed, skin gleamingly pale, eyes glamorously painted under arched eyebrows but black and terrible within, her pupils filled with a glittering malevolence. I'd felt that malevolence when she was behind me.

I looked again. Yes, those black eyes were fixed on me.

I had feared Athanasia for months and for good reason. When last I'd seen her, I hadn't been aware that she was trying to kill me. That was, until the elevator in Celia's building fell out from under me. I'd narrowly escaped with my life, though I didn't suppose that was good enough for her. She was probably a bit sore about that time I staked her. (Unsuccessfully. I'd been unaware that with Sanguine the staking part was just step one;

decapitation was the important thing. Oops.) And she was probably still torn up about that time I hand-delivered some garlic bread to her face. Celia's friend Deus, who seemed to be a kind of undead leader for the area, had banished Athanasia from the mansion after what she'd done.

You could say we had a bit of history between us.

Tense, I kept my hands in my pockets with those reassuring grains of rice, ready to spill them, and turned to face her.

Athanasia's gaze was unwavering, though the look in her dark eyes was puzzling. Was that hunger? Desire? Fear? She took another step towards me, and I thought, *Hell in heels, she's going to neck me*, and I was just about to spill the rice from my pockets, when to my utter surprise she lowered her gaze and whispered, *'She is The Seventh,'* her voice conveying a kind of awe. And quite suddenly, I found that we were not alone. Three other familiar undead faces appeared from the street corner outside Celia's mansion. They filed over and stood next to Athanasia, four Sanguine all in a row.

Blood buddies.

I stayed tense, fists filled with uncooked rice, unsure of what to do. Why were they gathering like this, on the street? As I watched, my nemesis Athanasia, my undead friend Samantha and the two remaining Sanguine models of Athanasia's lethal posse got down on their pale and slender knees and bowed to me.

That's right. *Bowed.*

To *me*!

On the streets of Spektor.

'The Seventh,' they said in unison.

I could not have been more surprised. Maybe I wouldn't be needing uncooked rice anymore? I thought, and pulled my hands from my pockets. My, how things had changed since they'd seen me suspend Celia's old lift in the air.

They stayed bent over.

I stared.

That had been it, right? The pivotal moment? I'll admit, stopping that lift from smashing on the ground had been something of a feat, albeit an unconscious one. I would have been well and truly dead if my powers of telekinesis had not kicked in to stop the speeding elevator mid-air. The moment I'd realised what I'd done, I'd freaked out (wouldn't you?), and the lift had crashed the rest of the way down, causing quite a bit of damage to the lobby floor but not much damage to me. Vlad had spent weeks and weeks getting the lift going again, though some of the old tile work would never be the same. So this grovelling figure at my feet had expected me to die in that little 'accident' of cut lift cables, and now she was in awe of me, along with her little blood-sucking posse? Life was full of surprises.

I stared at the tops of the four Sanguine heads for a moment, unsure of what to say or do. I couldn't count the number of times these creatures had tried to kill me. Well, the supermodels among them, not so much poor Samantha, though she had deadly impulses too. Some deeply immature part of me found this new behaviour of theirs quite, well ... *satisfying.* I guess I'm not above that. It felt pretty good for a moment, and then I turned and noticed Skye DeVille approaching me from the other side. An ambush?

My former boss at *Pandora* magazine was glaring at me. Petite and stylish in life, she'd really taken her whole undead turn to the next level, wearing an edgy all-black ensemble of vinyl mini and lacy top, and slicking her short, dark hair back from her forehead. Her face was pale and her lips were thin and painted a dark, blood red. It was a regular undead convention here. Was this a … trick? I was surrounded.

'I should, uh, head up to my room,' I said and waved awkwardly at the grovelling Sanguine. I turned around and tried to walk past Skye towards the mansion and the safety of Celia's penthouse. Skye stepped into my path. 'Excuse me,' I said, waiting for her to step aside. She didn't.

'Ugh, look at her, with her pathetic hair and her old clothes,' Skye spat, pointing at my cardigan and slurring slightly as fangs like a panther's slid out from under her lips. She was referring to the vintage clothes I was wearing. They were very nice vintage clothes, as a matter of fact. And there was nothing wrong with my hair. Skye had been rude in life, too. I ignored her insult and tried again to pass her. She stood in my way a second time.

'God, get off your knees. Look at you all!' Skye shouted with evident frustration while her colleagues continued to grovel with their heads down. 'She's nothing!' she shouted, arms in the air. 'She's just some clueless small town hick!'

And then, before I knew what was happening, Skye's white face contorted in shock, eyes bulging, and she flew backwards across the footpath.

Flew!

I blinked. How odd. I realised my arms were extended, and, confused, I brought them to my sides and watched with horror while my former boss, who was someone I was admittedly not exactly fond of, hit the pavement with a sickening thud and sprawled out like a rag doll, her short, black skirt fanning out around her hips. It seemed to happen in slow motion, but I was powerless to intervene. Skye had flown several metres through the air like she'd been shot out of a cannon. Had her black stockings been torn beforehand? I couldn't recall, but they looked bad now. That must have really hurt.

'Oh my! Are you okay?' I exclaimed, running forward to see if she was all right, as if I finally had control of my body once more. None of the others got up, I noticed. They would not go near her. Or was it me? Yes, it was me they would not go near. They stayed down, knees and palms on the pavement, watching silently, heads still partially bowed.

I did that, didn't I?

What had come over me?

'Sorry,' I said, realising. I offered Skye a hand to help her up. She just stared at me, wide-eyed. Her fangs had disappeared. She didn't move.

'She is The Seventh,' I heard the others say in creepy unison, as I collected myself and sprinted away, holding my satchel. *'She is The Seventh.'* I hauled open the heavy front door of Celia's mansion and shut it behind me, sliding down the inside of the door, the cold lobby a comfort in contrast to the confusion outside.

I ran a trembling hand down my face.

What just happened?

'And then *what* happened, you say?'

I had arrived in Celia's penthouse buzzing with adrenaline, any ideas of a long sleep put aside for the moment, and my great-aunt, a perpetually astute observer, insisted I take tea with her. Her tea was always strengthening. After her careful preparations, during which I paced back and forth by her tall windows, running over events in my head, Celia had calmly pulled a chair out for me and taken the seat in her book-lined alcove. As usual I was drawn to her stunning ensemble, which seemed like something for a night out – a long black taffeta dress with a sweetheart neckline and a belted waist, the fabric of which caught the light – but I did not attempt to grill her about where she was going. I knew she wouldn't tell me. Over sips of tea, I told her about Athanasia and all the Sanguine on their knees on the streets of Spektor, and then my former boss Skye flying through the air.

'Great-Aunt Celia, I threw her through the air!' I repeated in shock. 'I hadn't even touched her, but my arms were out like this,' I said, standing up to demonstrate, 'and she flew through the air and hit the pavement hard. I mean she just *flew*!'

My great-aunt tilted her head and nodded sagely. 'Well done, Pandora. That will teach her.'

'What do you mean, well done? I didn't even know I was doing it!' I said, still standing, and now throwing my arms in the air with frustration.

Celia's red lips curved into a subtle smile. She stroked her albino cat, Freyja, who meowed softly, then picked up her teacup again. 'You do need to keep them in line, you know, show your authority,' she said. 'You can't take insults like that without reprimanding them. I'm sure Deus would approve.' She crossed one elegant leg over the other and leaned back into her alcove. 'And you are getting stronger, aren't you? This is as it should be.'

I resumed pacing, agitated.

'Your mind movement skills are proving quite expert,' my great-aunt added after a minute. 'Think of the Janus coin, and how important your talent proved when you raised it in that crucial moment, or the elevator, and how stopping it from plummeting saved your life. You already know this telekinesis is a gift of yours. What surprises you then?'

I didn't know what to say to that, so I continued to pace around the sitting room, and then stopped and looked out over the Manhattan skyline. 'I guess I just don't think it's my place to throw people around for insulting my clothes,' I finally said.

'She insulted your clothes?' she asked.

It wasn't my first time unconsciously enacting telekinesis. But it was my first time doing it for a reason other than real self-defence. 'I think maybe she hit a nerve,' I admitted. 'But who cares what she thinks? It's so silly . . .'

'Go on.'

I came back from the window, took a breath and sat down again. 'Maybe that's part of what's bothering me so much – that something so trivial would set me off. It's just . . . sometimes I feel so uncool,' I confessed, adjusting my sleeves. 'At work, I mean. My boss is trendy and self-assured. She always looks perfect. I don't think I've seen her come into the office in the same outfit twice.'

My great-aunt frowned. 'A person who can't wear the same thing twice is rarely self-assured, Pandora.'

'Do you think so?'

'No woman need change their entire style every day, or even every three months, though the magazines and the dress shops will certainly encourage you to. First it's a round toe shoe, then pointed,' she said, making a dismissive gesture to her elegant slippers. 'Flared jeans, then skinny. Short hems then long. Don't buy into it, Pandora. The marriage of these disparate, ever-changing elements seldom works, and so it necessitates a whole new look. It is that way by design – not the design of clothes, the design of the market.'

Celia would know what she was talking about, having been a designer for so long, though I didn't think the term 'dress shop' was used a lot anymore. 'What do you mean by disparate elements?' I asked.

'The fashions today change too rapidly. In my day they spent years – even the better part of a decade – perfecting certain looks,' she explained. 'It was refined over time, the changes being subtle. A different expression here, an original interpretation there. True, there may not have been as many dresses or fabrics to choose from as there are today, but there were a lot of exciting designs and different ways to wear them – with scarves, capes, hats, gloves, different hairstyles. You could have innovation and this excitement of the new without changing everything. The shoes and hems, colours and cuts worked together. It was harmonious. You didn't have to change your whole wardrobe to suit a pair of shoes or a new jacket.'

'Do you mean there was a kind of … style synchronicity?' I ventured.

'Proportions went together, and you made or bought what suited you best, and altered it as you wished. There are some exciting designs today, that's true, but in the forties and fifties people were generally more stylish than they are today,' she said. It was hard to argue she was wrong there. Perhaps that was why she dressed in her own forties style. 'Yet they spent far less on things, Pandora. They bought less. If a woman owned, say, four dresses and two pairs of good shoes, she could make it look different with scarves, with hats, with jewellery. She might get a new dress every few months, or once a year. Now there is constant buying, nothing matches, and few things are made to last.'

I nodded. I was beginning to see her point. Still, I did need to blend in with the fashion world better.

'The fashion world today is driven largely by commercialism, not aesthetics. A few good pieces are all a girl needs. Think of the times during the Second World War, when there were fabric rations. Women – and men – mended and reworked old clothes to keep up to date with the style of the time. Women tried different hairstyles and a new scarf and voila, it was a new look. They looked better than many people in their street clothes today.'

'You are right, of course. But I work at *Pandora*. Don't I need to try to keep up with what is happening in fashion?' I said, thinking of Pepper and Ben and how they seemed in quite a different league.

'No,' she said, to my surprise. 'As I always say, darling

Pandora, fashion changes, but true style is timeless.'

My great-aunt certainly did seem timelessly elegant.

'These clothes suit you well,' she said, patting the fitted shoulders of the dress. 'No, you shouldn't listen to Skye. She has her own issues.'

Like becoming a bloodsucker. She had a point there, or two.

'I know we've talked about this before, but I guess I'm still sensitive about it. I know I'm judged around the office on what I wear. And my boss intimidates me in so many ways, and Skye had put me down before I threw her.' It had, I could now confess, been satisfying.

'You don't need to worry about clothing, Pandora. You have your job and you are doing it well. Don't be afraid to look unique.'

Celia did have a way of making problems seem smaller. We finished our tea and when she placed her cup on her saucer she said, 'You should go through that box you received from your mother. Don't put it off. You'll be fine.'

She was right. And before I knew it Celia was wishing me a good evening and standing to leave, Freyja at her ankles. I thanked her and watched her go, her heeled slippers made faint clicks on the hardwood floor and she was gone.

I ate a late snack alone, as usual, and in time I retreated to my room and changed out of my things, hung my vintage clothes up on the edge of the antique wooden wardrobe to air them (a trick Celia taught me to prolong the life of the clothes and avoid damaging them through over washing), bathed and got into my long white nightie. It was time.

Soon I found myself sitting on the edge of my four-poster bed, absolutely wide awake. The long, warm bath had not done the trick of helping my heart to slow to a normal pace. Not when flashes of what had happened on the street kept flickering across my mind: my arms extended. Skye flying through the air. That sickening thud. The look of shocked terror in her eyes. The Sanguine grovelling and chanting in unison, *She is The Seventh* …

I glanced at my clock. It was nearing ten now. I would do this. I would go through this delayed parcel and savour it. Nothing to fear but memories …

CHAPTER FIVE

I rose, took a breath to steel myself and hauled the mysterious box from my late mother up on to my bed.

I'd been thinking of this box all day, holding out for this moment, yet I found I was daunted by the prospect of opening it. What was I afraid of, exactly? Learning something I didn't want to know? Or perhaps I was afraid of finding that even with a few more of my mother's precious things in my life, I still did not have enough of her, still did not have enough questions answered. The hole left when my parents died was not one that could be adequately filled, I knew.

But why had this box been delayed, if there had been instructions?

My Aunt Georgia had meant well, I was sure, but the older I got the stranger her choices seemed. Why had she taken all the photos of my mother down? Why had she given away so many of my mother's books? She'd effectively cut all tangible links to my mother out of my life. This box, at least, meant that there would be something more of my past to keep. The older I became, the more I realised the importance of keepsakes. Some objects held strong memories and even seemed to retain some essence of their previous owner or experience. That sense of history and belonging could be a comfort to someone with so little living family. This stuff mattered.

And then I realised that something very specific bothered me about receiving this box. This was from my mother, not from my Aunt Georgia. Or at least that was how Celia had described it, and she was not one to be careless about details. A box organised by my mom. Did a lot of parents box up belongings for their kids when they were still so young? My mother had been just thirty-six when she'd died, and my father the same age. They'd not yet been middle-aged. Boxing something up to pass on to younger generations was something a grandparent might logically do, something for those in their late years or those who were unwell and knew they were not long for this world. Although I'd had a day to get used to the fact that my late mother had compiled a box of things for me before she died, a lump formed in my throat just looking at it. *Had my mother somehow known she would die before her time?* How could she know? Did this prove that she knew? I wavered back and forth and realised I was procrastinating once more. I wouldn't know more if I didn't open the box again and get started.

Come on, Pandora.

Barely aware that I was holding my breath, I pulled open the cardboard flaps to see what was waiting for me. I reached in and my fingers soon found white lace. Carefully, I pulled a delicate garment from the box and laid it across the bed.

Lovingly, I smoothed out the wrinkles and flattened the edges. I couldn't see clearly now, the tears were falling too freely, and without thinking I crawled on to the bed and lay on my side, placing my head on the empty bodice of my late mother's beautiful dress. The old lace felt good against my cheek, comforting somehow. I lay there, curled in the foetal position, remembering what I could of the mother I'd lost. My eyes were closed, my hand sitting gently on the dress, and when I finally opened them again my gaze fell on the black-and-white wedding photo of my parents on the antique writing desk a few feet away. There were my mom and dad gripping each other joyfully, my mother's veil pulled back to frame her face like a snowy halo. They both looked so young and carefree. And there was the same white lace wedding dress with its delicate cap sleeves and sweetheart neckline, with my mother inside it. Smiling. Living. She was right there. So close. So near in my thoughts. I felt her presence keenly.

I took a deep breath and closed my eyes again, savouring the feeling of the lace against my cheek. That old photograph had been waiting for me when I arrived from Gretchenville. Great-Aunt Celia had instinctively understood its value, that it would make me feel more at home, not less. I needed my past to cope with my future and there was so much I had not been told about my family history by my own mother. I'd spent so long in the dark. Perhaps I would always be in the dark. Perhaps it would always be like this. My mother so close and yet so far away.

In time I sat up, noticing little damp patches on the lace where my tears had temporarily turned it a faint grey. I wiped my eyes with the backs of my hands, then found a tissue and wiped them some more. And then I forgave myself. I forgave myself my procrastination and my surge of fear. Even if this dress was everything I found in the box, even if that was it, I'd let out a flood of tears on encountering it. It was wonderful and hard to have this gift from her, and there could be no other way. Of course it would be emotional. Of course.

Go on, Pandora.

When I was ready, I reached back into the box, delving more deeply and found heavy books lining the bottom – my mother's big hardcover books, the ones I'd missed. No wonder this parcel had been so heavy. My mother had earmarked some of her favourite books for me, books we'd read together when I was younger.

The Greek and Roman Myths

Ancient Cultures

The Gods and Symbols of Ancient Mexico and the Maya

Celtic Myth and Legend

Ancient African Civilizations

Elementary Treatise of Occult Science: Understanding the Theories and Symbols Used by the Ancients

The Ancient Egyptian Book of the Dead

Hatshepsut: From Queen to Pharaoh

I blinked, pulling the smaller book up out of the cardboard box. So we *had* talked about Hatshepsut at some length when I was younger. I hadn't imagined that. And these were hardly kids' books, I realised, looking them over. Some were more sophisticated than others, but they had all taught me valuable lessons about the belief systems of other cultures and times, with many focusing on the spirit world – a focus that would prove more important than I could have imagined. In the context of world history, the modern rejection of the spirit world was unique. My mother had read these with me, led me through the historical stories and information, but I would probably understand them so much better now than I had as a child. So this was where they'd gone – into a box to be given to me. I'd wondered why Aunt Georgia had cleared them away. It seems I needn't have feared she'd thrown them out. My heart softened a touch at the realisation.

There were a few more pieces of clothing inside the box, and when I reached back in my fingertips found the edges of some smaller box hiding just under a familiar striped shirt. A shoebox? It was on its side after I'd disturbed the books underneath. This would probably be my mother's wedding shoes, I guessed. Perhaps she had hoped that one day I would find a nice young man (a living man, presumably) to settle down with, and that I would marry him in her own wedding ensemble. Lucasta women were always the same size, apparently. (Lucasta – that would have been her last name and mine had surname traditions not been so unswervingly patriarchal.) I took a deep breath once more and reached for the box. *Is that what you hoped for, Mom? That I'd wear this?* It was impossible to know what she'd make of my confusing love triangle with Lieutenant Luke and Jay Rockwell but so far there were certainly no weddings on the horizon.

The old shoebox felt lighter than I'd expected. Perhaps it didn't hold shoes after all. It was sealed with yellowing sticky tape and I peeled the corners back on three sides, then flipped the lid. I was surprised to find myself looking not at delicate wedding shoes, but something wrapped in tissue paper. *How curious.* There was a bit of weight to it. Yes, something was wrapped in there. Something solid. Beneath it, I could see a thick envelope. I picked it up and examined it. The envelope was crinkled and sealed with more of that transparent, yellowing sticky tape. It had been sealed some time ago. Something was written on the outside of the envelope. One word:

Pandora.

My heart sped up in my chest.

This was unmistakably my mother's writing. The way she wrote even those seven letters of my name (I was The Seventh and Pandora was seven letters! I hadn't put that together before) was so familiar that I wasted no time ripping the tape off and opening the seal to see her message for me. I unfolded the pages my mother had written for me and absorbed the sight of her handwriting.

Dear Pandora,

I hope I am sitting next to you, talking with you about this, or at the very least reading you this letter myself. If I am not, and something happened to me before I was able to explain all this, I am sorry I failed you, daughter. As it is your eighteenth birthday it is time to tell you all . . .

But it was not my eighteenth birthday, I thought. That had been over a year and a half ago. Why had Aunt Georgia kept this letter from me if my mother had given instructions? She couldn't have known how important it was, I told myself. Often, when people did the wrong thing it was because they didn't know any different. My aunt, for all her good qualities, had not much approved of the woman her brother had married, and I'd been a burden of sorts – a 'strange girl'. Perhaps she somehow blamed her brother's death on my mother? Could that be? I mean, they would not have been at the Valley of the Kings if not for her. Or perhaps Georgia had simply wanted me to forget my parents and the tragedy of their premature deaths – as if that were possible.

I returned my attention to the letter. It was seven pages long, and I could see at a glance the term 'The Seventh' and also 'the Revolution of the Dead' a few pages in – a term that made me shiver. Here, at long last, was hard proof that my mother knew what I was and wished for me to know when the time was right. She'd decided my eighteenth birthday was the right time, yet it had taken my wise great-aunt to make contact and whisk me away from Gretchenville to the Big Apple when I was nineteen for me to find out. I read on.

There are things you must know, darling daughter. If my instructions have been followed, with this letter, you should have the Babel Pendant.

A pendant? I picked up the small tissue-wrapped bundle that had been in the shoebox and began unwrapping it. After tearing a few sheets off it, to my surprise, a pendant on a chain slid right out of the wrappings and landed in my hand, the stone glowing like a flame for a second before turning dark. I blinked. The shining white gold chain had fallen across my extended fingers in the jagged shape of a single digit: *7*.

I stared at the chain. The tiny hairs on the back of my

neck went up as though I'd touched a Teslacoil. What was this? Now the stone was dark and opaque but it had seemed to glow for a moment. It was oval-shaped, a couple of inches across and neatly held in a simple, elegant setting that seemed not to have tarnished with the years. With trembling hands I placed the pendant on the bed covers next to me, wondering about the coincidence of that chain falling into the symbol of a seven. I wasn't sure I believed in coincidences anymore. I had a distant memory of seeing this piece of jewellery when I was very young. My mother had worn it, hadn't she?

I turned back to the letter and my mother's words:

> *... with this letter, you should have the Babel Pendant. Wear it, and have all languages revealed to you as all languages were revealed to me in my time.*

This pendant had allowed my mother to interpret ancient languages and sites? It had not just been her keen mind and studies, her ability to learn and interpret things, but also a special pendant? How extraordinary. I thought of the legendary Rosetta Stone, rediscovered in 1799 and dating back to around 196 BC, which had the same text in three ancient languages inscribed upon it, allowing scholars to decipher ancient Egyptian hieroglyphs. It was very large, however – certainly not something one could wear on a pendant – and I could see no writing on this one. If this pendant did indeed help reveal language it did so in some other, less direct way. Was it perhaps magical? My mother, Oriel English, was born Oriel Lucasta, and as a Lucasta daughter she must have possessed gifts – we all did, apparently, although as far as I knew she had rarely, if ever, used them. She certainly hid any clearly magickal gifts from me.

Intrigued, I steadied myself and picked up the pendant again, this time by its chain, frowning. The stone in this pendant was some kind of darkly opaque gem I did not recognise. It was a deep red, almost black. Not ruby. Was it a kind of dark-red amber, perhaps? Or something else?

Put it on, I thought. The urge to wear the pendant came on strong and I put the thin chain over my head without needing to unclasp it, and pulled my smooth hair back through it, the stone settling on my chest with a gentle and reassuring weight. Immediately an eerie cool began to descend on the bedroom and my stomach turned to that icy cold feeling that I knew meant death or a visit from the other side. A white mist circled around the wedding dress on my bed, and around the pendant, which seemed to warm on my skin.

'Hello?' I stood up from the edge of the bed and looked around. 'Luke, is that you?'

For a heart-stopping minute I wondered what to expect. A presence was here. Something that had not visited me in this room before. Could it be . . .?

'Who are you?' I ventured. The presence was comforting, not malevolent. 'Mom? Mom, are you here?' I hardly dared to hope.

Slowly, a figure appeared before me, first as a pale and faint outline, barely perceptible, and then in opaque form. Details began to take shape, details I recognised. I began to feel hopeful. *Yes,* I thought. This is my mother, taking form in my bedroom like an imprint on a cloud. She's here. Finally, she's here.

Gradually the details of my mother's familiar features became more defined until she looked as real and present as Lieutenant Luke's spirit when he visited me – real but not real, human but not. My mother's hair was long and wavy, just as I remembered it. She had amber eyes, just like mine, and a slender figure, just as I'd inherited. This could not be my imagination, I thought, as the details were too accurate, too real for something I could conjure. I was struck by how much of my adult appearance I'd inherited from her, now that I was so much older than I had been when I'd last seen her. The angle of her cheekbones and chin. The shape of her nose. The placement of her eyes. The way her mouth moved. And then there were the other things she'd passed on to me, as a Lucasta woman. Things that we hadn't talked about.

'Mom, I've missed you so much!' I cried, feeling emotion well up and unable to hold it back.

Tears had begun streaming down my face. The waterworks were quite involuntary, and instead of being embarrassed by it I allowed the teardrops to fall. I reached out to the figure of my mother and embraced her, tentatively at first, and then with vigour. Yes, it really was her. She felt cool and comforting beneath my touch, like a cloud and yet substantial as well. It was her. For the first time in years I felt warm inside, complete. To say I'd missed her was an understatement. I tried to hold back a little, in case this was all imagined, but found I could not. This was my mother's spirit. This was as close as I'd been to her for nearly a decade. I held on to what I could of her, refusing to let go of her misty form, and she inclined her head into my shoulder. We were almost exactly the same height now that I'd grown.

'My daughter,' I heard her say.

That voice! That familiar voice!

We stood there embracing one another in my bedroom in Celia's penthouse for a long stretch of time. She wrapped her arms around me and I did not let go of my grip on her spirit form. It was an indescribable feeling after so painful a parting. She'd been far too young when she'd died. I had only been eleven, just a girl. I was older now and she had not aged, but she was no longer part of the living world, either, and I sensed that although her visage was unchanged from what I remembered, her spirit was. I felt a deep peace within her, or a knowing calmness one sometimes found in wise elders. My heart was racing. After a while I pulled away and looked at her, still not quite believing that we were reunited.

She looked at me and smiled, then looked to the bed. 'My wedding dress,' she said softly.

'It's beautiful, Mom. It's so beautiful. Thank you for keeping it for me.'

'That was a very happy day. And the day you arrived was the happiest day of my life.'

'I've missed you so, so much,' I repeated and hugged her again. She felt real under my fingers and I could almost imagine we had not been torn apart eight years before.

'I've missed you too, darling daughter,' she replied, and sat on the edge of the bed, making a slight indent in the covers, much the way Lieutenant Luke often did. 'Though I am never far away.'

I sat down next to her and stared at her Otherworldly form, the long, flowing hair, the folds of ghostly fabric in her dress.

'I had hoped that you could live a normal life but I see that was not to be. I'd thought that somehow this could be avoided. I was wrong,' she told me, hands folded in her lap.

I hesitated. This had perplexed me. 'You didn't mention that I was The Seventh,' I pointed out in a small voice. It was kind of a big deal, that.

'I'm sorry, Pandora,' she said and reached out for me, taking my solid, warm hand in her misty and cool one, and looking me in the eyes. 'I have thought on this often, darling daughter. It troubled me to keep this from you, though you were still so young. In my heart I knew it to be so – that you were The Seventh and this burden would be upon you one day – but when I looked on your young face I'd hoped, somehow, that it wasn't inevitable, that these dark times might not come to pass.'

My brows pinched together as I listened.

'I tried to shield you,' she went on. Her ghostly face looked downward, mouth pulled into a frown. 'In doing so I failed you. I was foolish to pit my will against Fate. Instead of changing your future all I did was delay your knowledge.'

I squeezed her ghostly hand. 'It's okay, Mom,' I said, trying to understand. I had flashes of memory then, of my mother so carefully teaching me about ancient myths and cultures, of stories of the Underworld and Hades, of the spirit world, guiding me through those books she'd earmarked for me, and more. She'd given me so much knowledge, knowledge I still held on to; knowledge that had served me in recent months. But she'd kept the critical piece from me. Until I arrived in Spektor I had never heard of the Agitation or the Revolution of the Dead, nor did I know how I fit in to the picture. I'd had no idea I was The Seventh Lucasta Daughter, or what that meant. I could see that her letter explained these things, along with the pendant, but what would I have made of it all had I not already met Celia and learned so much? Or had my mother's spirit not been here to help? It would have been hard to grasp. In many ways it still was.

'And you did not get my letter on your eighteenth birthday. This is late,' she said, frowning again.

I nodded. 'The Agitation has already begun, I'm told.' I hadn't really seen evidence of it, though, at least not since I'd used Luke's sabre to end the hideous necromancer who'd been pulling bodies up in Manhattan and marching his army of the dead to the portal to the Underworld under Celia's mansion. (Did I mention I lived on an entry to the Underworld?)

The Otherworldly necromancer had wanted to open that portal and bring about the Revolution, and it had been a close call, to be sure. Since his death and the breaking of his powerful spell, the portal had remained closed (*or at least I believed so, perhaps I ought to keep checking?*) and I had not seen any evidence of the Agitation and the changes it was said to bring. Things were just as normal as usual – or, um, just as paranormal as usual, if one could even gauge how much paranormal activity was traditional around here.

She absorbed that and looked towards the window, as if wondering what forces might be gathering just beyond the glass. 'You aren't sure if it has begun? You have not seen it for yourself?'

'Sort of,' I said. 'Well, I'm not really sure.' There were many things I was unsure of. 'Lots of strange things have happened since I moved here but I'm not quite sure what to look for, I guess.'

'I'm sorry, Pandora. This is a heavy burden for you and you've had so little time to prepare. You were still so young. I had hoped to tell you myself.'

'Tell me about this pendant. Is it like the Babel Stone, or the Rosetta Stone?' I asked my mother, holding it in one hand and looking down at it. 'How does it translate?'

No, she replied, her lips unmoving. *My darling daughter, it is unlike anything carved by men. As long as you wear it, it will translate for you and you will hear the words in your head as you hear mine now. Wear it and understand all.* She touched the necklace that was around my neck. The red stone gained colour until it shone. *See?*

'Oh! Thank you, Mom.'

'It did me a great service in life. I hope it will do the same for you. I sense that I was only ever its caretaker. I think it always belonged to you, my daughter, The Seventh,' she said.

I put my hand to the pendant and felt its warmth against my chest. 'How long will the Agitation last?' I asked. 'I mean how long do I have before . . .?'

My mother shook her head. 'Not long.'

That wasn't what I wanted to hear.

'Soon the Revolution of the Dead will begin and when it does you must do what only you can. You must be brave.'

'But what does it mean to be The Seventh? What must I do?'

My mother put a cool, ghostly arm around my shoulders. 'I am a Lucasta, but I am not The Seventh, Pandora. I'm sorry. That burden falls to you. I was not told these things, and they are not mine to know. But I believe in you. I believe that when the time comes, you will know what you have to do. You must trust your instincts. You must let The Seventh in you take over.'

You must trust your instincts. My Great-Aunt Celia had been saying that a lot, too.

'How can I let The Seventh take over if I don't know what I have to do? I mean, can't anyone tell me?' I said, my frustration welling up. 'What will happen? What will I be facing, exactly?'

'My darling, you will be facing the possibility of the end of the living world. The dead will inherit the earth, ending all life, or they will remain in the Underworld or Otherworld for another hundred and fifty years until the veil grows thin during the next Agitation and Revolution. You will have the power to influence which way the Revolution falls. You alone. This is the burden of The Seventh Daughter.'

Living world or dead world. No big deal.

I stood up suddenly, and swayed in place for a moment, absorbing that bit of information. Unsteadily, I ran a hand down my face, trying to imagine what that would look like – to have little me, Pandora English, stand against the legions of the dead. Would I suddenly come over with supernatural strength? Would I fight off the demons of the Underworld ten at a time? One hundred at a time? How? I didn't seem terribly suited to such pursuits, I thought, looking down at my skinny arms and my slender frame. I frowned. No one could tell me what I had to do, what I had to expect.

'Mom?' I asked.

'Yes?'

I turned. 'Is Dad . . .' I swallowed. 'Is Dad all right?'

'Yes, dear. He doesn't have the powers I have, or he would be here with you now. He loves you very much. And he understands now.' My father in particular had been uncomfortable with any talk of the mystical or the paranormal. He was a smart, learned man, and a loving father but also a slave to the clear and concise 'logic and reason' he'd been taught to respect above all else. His was the kind of reason that did not allow for mystery or the invisible, let alone ghosts, and he'd been strict about cutting out discussions of anything of the kind. He would have thought it was for my own good, and who could blame him when nearly everyone in the community would agree? No one had taken well to my ability to speak with the dead, not until I came to Spektor and met my great-aunt.

I returned to her side, on the edge of my bed, and listened.

'He understands all of it now. He is sorry he didn't before,' my mother continued. 'He always found it very difficult to accept that I was different, and that . . . well, you are too.' She gave me a sad smile and I saw that she had been torn in life between what she thought she knew and what society could take, what her marriage could take. It was not easy to have special gifts in a world that did not accept them, in a world where you would be thought crazy and dismissed, and where you were made to doubt yourself and your knowledge. She must have battled it for some time, and channelled her special gifts into her work, where it could be hidden beneath layers of discussion of ancient cultures and beliefs and not thrust into stark relief against modern thought.

This brought another question to mind. 'Mom, did you really visit me when I was thirteen?' I had to ask. I'd thought we'd had many conversations that year. Had we talked about archaeology, about ancient myth? Yes, we had – or at least I'd thought so. No one had believed me, of course, least of all my guardian, Aunt Georgia, who forbade me discussing it – not unlike my father, who had forbidden me discussing my visitations when I was younger. I had eventually been more or less convinced that they were right, and these visitations were little more than signs of an 'overactive imagination'. Or if I wasn't exactly *convinced* they were right I was certainly convinced I was 'wrong', literally and figuratively. A 'wrong' child. Strange.

'Oh, darling daughter. You doubted our time together? All those conversations?'

'Really? It did happen?' I felt a rush of relief that made my heart soar. I had been made to doubt myself. 'Why did you not come again?' I then asked, my voice unintentionally tinged with hurt. I had missed her so terribly. Not seeing her for years had gone some way to convincing me it had never happened.

'Pandora, it was not possible,' she said gently, placing a misty hand on my leg. 'I could not blame you, but you became closed. I could not reach you.' *She* could not reach *me*. I was stunned. 'I am always near to you, Pandora. Always.'

This was puzzling to me. There had been times I'd missed her so badly I'd thought I couldn't go on. And all that time she'd been near to me? How had I not known? How had I not felt it?

'There is something else,' my mother said. I still had so many questions for her.

'Yes?' I replied.

'There is an exhibition at the Metropolitan Museum ... an exhibition you are involved with.'

'Yes ...?' I said. 'I mean no. I mean I went to a photo shoot and they were setting up the exhibition. It's in the Egyptian wing ... the one that always fascinated you. I always thought I'd see it with you.'

Her ghostly eyes looked back at me, understanding.

'It's an exhibition of artefacts from Hatshepsut's reign. I think you'd like it, Mom. It looks like it will be quite big.'

'Be careful, my daughter. It seems like more than a coincidence.'

'How?' I glanced to her book on Hatshepsut and her eyes followed.

'My work took me into her world. We were at the site of Hatshepsut's tomb, KV20, when ...' She trailed off.

My eyebrows shot up. 'You *were*? No one told me anything about that!'

My mother only watched me with a pale, ghostly expression of concern. Of course no one had told me which site my mother was working at when the tragedy happened. My Aunt Georgia hadn't much cared for my mother's career, and so she probably wouldn't have known one Egyptian site from another. In fact, details had never been forthcoming. Now it appeared my mother and father had actually been at the site of Hatshepsut's tomb when they died?

'Hatshepsut's tomb? You were there? What happened?'

'I don't know precisely what happened,' she said, brow pinched and a faraway look in her eyes. 'We were in the Valley of the Kings on the west side of the river at Luxor. Hatshepsut's tomb has a very long tunnel going in, roughly dug out, and descending for some six hundred feet into the rock, hundreds of feet below the surface. As an ancient burial site it is odd. For one, it has mysterious corridors running through it. The tomb was also altered after it was first built, because, you see, this had been the burial chamber of Tutmosis I, it is believed, and when Hatshepsut herself became king she wished to be buried with her father, as a true pharaoh would. An extra chamber was cut from Tutmosis's burial chamber, and it is believed that was her tomb. When I first saw it, the site had long since been discovered, having been damaged by looters in antiquity, and explored by Napoleon, Belzoni, Lepsius and Carter, respectively. Howard Carter had done the most well-documented work there, finding smashed funerary furniture and a shabti for Hatshepsut, as well as two significant sarcophagi – one for Tutmosis and one for Hatshepsut, but both empty. The site did not warrant as much attention as it might otherwise because of the looting that had come before. Hatshepsut's treasures, which must once have been vast, were not there. The bodies of the pharaohs were not there. Still, it was a site of significance for my work.

'Looting and flooding had plagued the site and our team were doing further excavations, fine work, mostly. It wasn't considered high risk or ... well, I wouldn't have brought your father in. But he was with me, for the first time in my career. We'd saved up for that trip. It was a proud moment for me,' she said, and her voice faltered. 'I was showing him our work and the . . .' She trailed off, her voice filled with regret. 'The connecting corridor to her chamber must have given way somehow. It was very sudden and unexpected. We were overcome, just your father and me. Pandora, I remember everything coming in on us, and the dust and sand filling my lungs. It was so fast. One minute all was peaceful, and the next there was this rush of sand and rubble bearing down on us. At least we were together in the end, holding on to each other.'

A tear escaped the corner of one eye, then another, and I felt them fall down my cheeks, in sync with my mother's own ghostly tears. In my mind I saw the two of them, my mother and father, locked together in death, like the famed 'Lovers of Valdaro', under the ancient rubble of the Egyptian tomb, the sand of the Valley of the Kings closing in on them. We embraced each other, sitting on my bed in Spektor, and I did everything I could to hold on to her, to my dead mother, to express my love for her, and my sorrow.

After a time we eased our embrace and I searched her face. 'You think Hatshepsut's exhibition is more than a coincidence? How?'

My mother nodded. 'I cannot say. But please be careful, my darling. The dark forces are gathering, and you are the ultimate prize. Much depends on you. If there is no Seventh, the Revolution will be quick.'

I swallowed. The implication was clear.

'Mom, I'm scared,' I admitted. I thought of the battles ahead, and the uncertainty. Was I qualified for this important supernatural role? Was I strong enough?

'You must be brave. Know that I am here for you, even when you don't realise it,' she said, and embraced me. Her ghostly arms felt comforting but not as solid as Luke's. I wanted to squeeze her harder, wanted to grab hold of her and never let go, but I couldn't quite seem to get a grip on her. She was fading, I realised. I had so many more questions, so many things to say.

'I must go,' my mother told me. 'I wish I could do more.' Luke had told me there were 'supernatural rules' and one of them was that the knowledge the dead possessed could not be imparted to the living (uncovering the secrets of the dead had been the aim of much necromancy in the past). Still, I needed so much more from her – more information, more time. 'I love you, Pandora. I'm proud of you. We both are. Wear the Babel Pendant with goodwill and openness. We believe in you.'

She placed a hand on my shoulder and I reached for her again, desperate. Crushingly, my arms went through her. She was fading away from me, fast, and soon there was only the air of my bedroom and not a sign of her presence except for the wedding dress and the pendant she had given me, a half-emptied box and the vision of her imprinted on my mind, standing before me with one arm outstretched.

No.

My mother was gone. I sank down, feeling utterly empty.

Limbs heavy, I lay back on my four-poster bed next to my mother's dress. I stayed in my room an hour after her visit, just holding on to her delicate lace dress and unable to do anything productive, unable to move, unable even to sleep. To finally have contact with her meant so much, but a part of me felt like

I'd lost her once again. There were still so many unanswered questions. I wasn't ready to say goodbye again, not at all. I had seen her ghost only once since she had died, and now that she had visited I feared it could be six years again before I'd see her next. Or would I *ever* see her again?

My head whirling with questions and worries, I lay across my bedcovers holding her wedding dress, the Babel Pendant glowing warmly around my neck. I ignored the thirst in my throat, the ache in my bladder. In time I raised myself up and pored over her letter to me, absorbing everything I could. It seemed not to tell me more than I'd learned in our recent conversation and in my months in Spektor. I suppose Great-Aunt Celia had seen to that. It seemed she'd made sure I knew all it was possible for me to know about my special role as The Seventh. It was just frustrating that no one appeared able to tell me precisely what it all meant, not even Lieutenant Luke, and he was supposed to be my spirit guide. (Thinking of Luke made me realise I was yet to speak with him. As I was still wide awake, I thought I might reach out for him after speaking with Celia.)

Wear this pendant with goodwill and openness. We believe in you …

I had to try to believe in myself. But I didn't quite know how.

I touched the small stone on my chest and it warmed. I felt a part of my mother was in the stone, as though she was not quite gone (perhaps there was a part of all the Lucasta women in this gem?) and this helped, finally, to animate me. I pulled myself up from the bed, stacked my mother's books on the writing desk by the window next to the portrait of my parents on their wedding day, and caught myself lingering on the mental image of them caught in an embrace under the rumble of Hatshepsut's tomb.

Stop it, Pandora. Stop. With deliberate and forced calm, I put the image out of my mind, examined the other clothes in the box my mother had given me, including a striped shirt of hers and a red dress she'd worn on special occasions, and I carefully put them away again. Next, I packed my mother's beautiful wedding dress back into the box, lingering on the feel of the lace, the sense of her presence. I would try on the clothes, wear them with her memory close to me, but for now it was late. Finally, I took my mother's letter, which was spread out on my bed covers, folded it carefully, put it back in its envelope and placed it on the writing desk with the books. There would be an opportunity to pore over it again another time, perhaps even in the morning, and who knew, maybe then I would find more in those pages to answer my many questions. But at least for now I knew I'd been kept in the dark about being The Seventh not so much by choice, but because of my mother's premature death. The unintended result of a tragedy – a tragedy at the plundered tomb of a great pharaoh to be celebrated in the upcoming Met exhibition.

My tears dry, I made my way into Celia's main room, my long white nightie flowing behind me. I was simply too unsettled to slip into peaceful dreams and I had hopes that my great-aunt would be back at her little reading alcove, a calming and sensible force. Perhaps I would feel better if I talked with her for a while or had some of her restoring tea. That had helped so much before.

What would Celia say about my visitor, and the Babel Pendant? Had she heard of it, perhaps?

The magnificent penthouse was quiet and dark, moonlight streaming in through the tall, arched windows. Disappointingly, I could see at a glance that Celia's reading lamp was off and my great-aunt was not back in her usual book-lined alcove. There were no candles lit or soft noises in the room to indicate her presence, or even Freyja's. However, I was immediately distracted from my thoughts by the view outside the windows. The moonlight was very strong tonight, though the full moon was not until tomorrow. (I'd learned to keep track of such things.) I walked through the dark room, right to the glass and stared out. In the far distance, beyond the mist, I could see the Empire State Building – a building that had featured in my dreams of Manhattan as a child, and where I'd since taken Lieutenant Luke once for the view. It was also where I had met the unfortunate Evelyn McHale, the ghost of the young, immaculately dressed bookkeeper trapped in one of the cruellest cycles I'd yet encountered, jumping from the 86th floor observation deck of the giant building and crashing into a ghostly United National Assembly vehicle below, only to re-emerge to play out her suicide again and again. No place in a town as full and vibrant as Manhattan was without its tragedies, or its ghosts.

The imposing Empire State Building, though no longer the tallest building in the world, was always an impressive sight on the Manhattan skyline. But it seemed curiously lit tonight, as if the moon were focused on it like a huge, sea-green spotlight. Perhaps it was a trick of the light?

Pulling my attention from the striking view, I walked over and switched on the sparkling chandelier hanging at the highest point of the domed ceiling, and the room was softly illuminated. Here she had antique glass-fronted sideboards filled with curious artefacts, objets d'art and exotic plants including a Venus flytrap and for a moment I allowed myself to become absorbed in the objects and fading photographs on the shelves – a fertility statue, a figurine carved of bone, strange butterflies and moths displayed in small glass domes, and the castle-shaped vivarium containing a black widow spider of particular importance.

I padded up to the entry to look for Celia's fox stole, and there it was, hanging from the mirrored Edwardian coat stand. In my experience she never left the penthouse without that stole. She must be home then, I reasoned.

'Celia? Great-Aunt Celia?' I ventured.

I looked down the hallway, past the kitchen, and noticed that the door to the antechamber was open. This was unusual, and something about the sight of it caused a ripple of fear in me. For the first couple of months that I had lived here, that door had been locked shut and my great-aunt had expressly forbidden me from exploring what was beyond it. Since I'd acquired the skeleton key for the mansion, which I often wore on a thin gold chain around my neck, much had changed, and Celia allowed me to roam, so long as I followed certain rules. Now I knew this antechamber of hers led not only to her personal quarters but also to a secret door hidden inside a casket in the floor. (Yes, an actual casket, and not one Celia had installed, which begged the question, who had lived here before her and why on earth had that coffin seemed like a good idea to them?) You could reach secret passageways from there, leading down through the mansion or up to the roof.

She probably left the door open on purpose, I thought, though I felt a sense of foreboding as I neared the room.

'Great-Aunt Celia? Are you home?' I said.

'I am here, darling,' came her voice after a minute. Her voice sounded a bit thick, like she had been drinking. I'd never seen her touch a drop of alcohol before.

I pushed the door to the antechamber open, and it creaked. 'I just had the most extraordinary visit from –' I began, and stopped.

Here she was. In the sunken, candlelit room, my great-aunt was draped elegantly across her deep-red velvet chaise, one pale arm propping her head up, the other curled in her lap, holding a dark goblet of wine. One pointed shoe touched the floor and the other was hidden beneath the folds of the long, black taffeta dress she was wearing. Celia still wore her black widow's veil, as always, but now the mesh was pushed back to expose her face from the nose up. Her exquisitely sculpted – and oddly youthful – features had a kind of excited glow about them. In the candlelight of the antechamber, her pale skin was particularly luminescent. Her dark eyes sparkled and her mouth, which was always expertly painted with the deepest red lipstick, hung open in a slight smile. As she regarded me, she sat up and I noticed that her lipstick was smudged across her chin.

Oh boy.

'What are y–you ... drinking?' I stuttered, standing at the

door. She *had* been drinking, but not alcohol, I realised. I took a step back and brought my hand to my mouth.

My great-aunt licked her lips and adjusted her veil. 'I think you know,' she said in a slow drawl.

I swallowed.

I did know.

Blood. Great-Aunt Celia was drinking blood. This was how she stayed so young. I'd never seen her drink blood. Ever. But she wanted me to see this, I thought. She'd left the door open so I would see this. So I would finally know her secret. But we'd talked before and she'd sworn she wasn't Sanguine?

'Yes, you know,' she replied in that strangely languid tone. 'And you didn't seem to mind it yourself, as I recall.' She gave me a steady, unblinking look from beneath her veil. 'Come. Sit with me.'

I stood at the top of the three stone steps, frozen in the frame of the doorway, unsure what to do. 'Are you a vampire?' I finally demanded, unable to hide my fear. My great-aunt, one of two living relatives on the whole planet, was sitting there in front of me casually drinking from a goblet of blood. Was she really a *living* relative, or was she something else? Normal living people didn't go around drinking blood and staying out of the sunlight. I had learned she was a witch, of sorts, or at the very least did some of the things witches could do, but what exactly did that mean in her case? There were many kinds of witches, from what I knew. Whose blood was this, anyway? I thought I knew whose blood, actually, and now I thought I could smell it, sweet and metallic, and . . .

'Language, darling,' Celia scolded. Her face had darkened at my question.

I'd said vampire, I realised. 'Sanguine,' I corrected myself. 'Are you Sanguine?'

It was not the first time I had asked her. I'd thought we'd settled it before but her protest that she was not undead did not explain her youthful appearance or her unique relationship with the ancient Sanguine, Deus. What was between them, exactly? Nor did it explain why she allowed the middle floors of the mansion to be used as a kind of halfway house for wayward bloodsuckers. Or why she was sitting there now, drinking blood.

'No, I am not Sanguine. Are you?' she countered. It wasn't a real question.

I put my hands on my hips, frustrated.

'Sit with me,' she repeated and after another moment of hesitation I walked down the cold steps in my bare feet and sat in one of the two plush antique chairs next to the chaise lounge.

'But I don't understand. Why ...?' I began. 'How ...?' I was not doing well with my interrogation. Here I'd wanted to speak with her about the visit from my mother's spirit, and the pendant, and Hatshepsut's tomb and what I'd learned, and suddenly it all seemed like a conversation for another time. The sight of that goblet in Celia's hand was too much. It was like a flame I could not help but stare at. And when I looked at it my mind seemed to go blank. And I felt ...

Hunger.

'Ichor, darling. We have spoken of this.'

Ichor – the mysterious lifeblood, or 'nectar' of the gods. I had heard of this, even before Celia had spoken of it with me.

I'd known the term from the tale of Talos, the giant bronze man animated by a vein of ichor running through him and stopped like a cork in his back with a giant nail. He was built by the god Hephaestus to protect Crete from invaders, and walked around the island throwing boulders at any enemy ships. This giant bronze protector was a kind of robot imagined before a time of robots. The sorceress Medea pulled the nail out one day and he bled to death, the ichor running out of his body. Of course, as the ancient Greek tales go, Hephaestus also created Pandora, my namesake, who rather infamously opened that box, or urn, depending on the telling, and let all the evil into the world.

Always the women. Eve. Pandora. Medea. Sigh.

'*Hesiod*,' Celia muttered crossly under her breath.

'Pardon?'

Celia looked at me. 'You want to know why the signs of age have not caught up with me,' she said.

I nodded. She'd dodged this question in the past. Celia liked her secrets.

'Yet you know the way the blood affects you. You were saved by it. You looked so radiant,' Celia began.

Had I looked radiant? I guess Morticia had said so a few times, after I'd drunk a few mouthfuls of Deus's blood after being poisoned by a ... well, an arachnid. I would have died if Deus had not given me a bit of his blood. It had some magickal qualities. But that was a couple of months ago now.

'It is a strong restorative, and more. It had quite an effect, ridding your body of the poison. And that was only a couple of mouthfuls, originally,' she finished.

Gross.

I couldn't help it. I winced at the thought of having drunk that blood months before. I didn't want to be reminded.

Celia sighed with disappointment. 'Oh, Pandora, it is not gross,' she said, having read my mind. 'I think you know that.' She leaned forward and caught my eye. 'Deus is delicious.'

I covered my mouth to gag or show shock, but it didn't come. My great-aunt had me there. My mind was rather revolted by what she was saying, but the rest of me knew she was right. He had been delicious and some part of me longed to taste him again. Every time I laid eyes on Deus it was a temptation. *He* was a temptation. In some core part of me, I wanted to know if I could taste him again, if there would be another excuse for just one more sip. *What can I do to get him to feed me again, just one more time* . . .? I actually wanted to taste a vampire's blood. I really did. What was wrong with me?

'This is terrible! I did not want this!' I blurted. 'I never asked to taste that blood!'

'Darling, you would have died and you know it.'

That sunk in. 'I know, and I am grateful for that, but . . .' I trailed off, unsure of what to say.

I was acting ungrateful. I couldn't quite understand why. Deus and Celia had saved my life. I was deeply conflicted, perhaps as deeply as I'd ever felt in my life. *Blood?* My supportive, caring, wise great-aunt drank blood? And some part of me wanted to as well? It was an awful realisation leaving me painfully split – one half of me disturbed to my core by the idea of having drunk vampire blood, of having seen my dear Great-Aunt Celia drink vampire blood; the other half of me understanding the reason and the importance of it. That other half of me was, well, a *different me*. Not something new, exactly, something previously undiscovered. Something latent.

'*This is serious*,' my great-aunt said with emphasis. 'This is a very serious time, Pandora English, The Seventh.'

That snapped me out of it. I was The Seventh and I had to get it together. I was acting fearful and that wouldn't help anyone, myself included.

'I'm sorry,' I said. 'I didn't mean to be so thrown.' I'd seen far stranger things since moving to Spektor. Still …

'I finally opened the box from my mother and she, well, she visited me,' I continued. 'My mom actually came to me. It was wonderful but … I guess I am shaken.'

My great-aunt's expression warmed a little. She got up from her chaise lounge and placed a cool, reassuring hand on my shoulder. 'It's okay. It is normal to be shaken, and that was a big moment for you. But that is not all you are shaken by. You know this to be true.'

I frowned.

'I see she has given you the Babel Pendant. This is good. It belongs with you.'

I put my hand to it, felt its warmth like company, like it was imbued with part of my mother and her mother before her.

'Now Pandora, listen well. Stop resisting. Expand your mind. You must,' she said, still with that peculiar glow. Unshielded by her veil, her eyes were particularly magnetic. And grave. She was trying to tell me something, something important that I wasn't quite grasping. 'Let go of the old obstacles and constraints. Unlearn what you were taught by those teachers and neighbours as a child. Stop holding yourself back. You are strong enough for this.'

Unlearn.

You are strong enough.

So. It is upon us, I thought. This had to be what she meant. It was a serious time because the Agitation was upon us, the slow and steady building of supernatural activity, and soon the Revolution of the Dead would start. It was not just a supernatural folk tale. (And as I'd discovered, many of those 'folks' had known precisely what they were talking about.) It was real. Celia had started to reveal her secrets because I needed to face facts. I could not afford to be squeamish. I had to find my inner strength. How long did I have before the Revolution came? A day? A year? What could I do about it? And where could I learn what was expected of me if even my departed mother had not been able to tell me?

My great-aunt straightened and her gaze flickered behind her, to the shadows behind the casket in the floor that acted as a secret entry. I looked and to my horror, saw that we were not alone. A dark shape waited there in the corner – a shape in the form of a man.

Deus.

I swallowed as the ancient Sanguine stepped into the light of my great-aunt's flickering candles. He was not really handsome, I told myself again, though I stared at his every feature almost like I loved him – his impossibly smooth skin, his sensual mouth, his dark brows and long, black eyelashes, his eyes, which seemed to speak to me …

'Deus,' I said, staring.

'You have been feeding from me for two weeks, Pandora English, The Seventh,' he announced in his ancient accent, grinning that eternal Kathakano smile of his.

I what?

I stood straight up, rigid with shock, knocking my chair over. Involuntarily, I began to shake my head. 'No, no, no ...' I repeated in a low voice that did not even sound like me. I backed up towards the door, my palms up. *Why would Deus say such a thing? What kind of trick is this?* I wondered. Though I sensed that in my heart, I already knew he was telling the truth. He had been coming in through my window each night and I had been feeding on him. Not the other way around – *I* had been feeding on *him*. The opposite of every folk tale I'd heard of. It had not just been in my dreams. All of it had been real.

There was a long silence in the antechamber as I grappled with the clear reality that I'd denied until that moment. I too was a blood-drinker – a drinker of Sanguine blood.

'Have you been here the whole time?' I asked, body shaking.

He nodded and I felt my cheeks redden viciously. He'd heard what I'd said about the blood. *His* blood. That had to be insulting. And now my great-aunt had to hear that I was drinking from the same Sanguine that she was. Was that like ... cheating? I didn't know how all this worked. I was so confused.

I righted my chair. 'I'd thought it was ... I thought I'd been dreaming,' I managed, eyes averted.

'You called me to you.'

'I–I did? *Called you* to me?' I could hardly believe it. How had I done that? Without even knowing? I thought my spirit guide was the only one I could summon?

'Yes.' He nodded, grinning.

Looking at his face, I simply could not believe he was lying. But then, he was Sanguine and they did not seem like a terribly trustworthy species, especially as they generally made humans their prey. I had been feeding off him, but why? Surely he had tricked me into it somehow? I'd been told that the older Sanguine are, the more trickery they have mastered, and Deus was one of the oldest Sanguine in the world.

'Have you bitten me?' I asked, grasping at my throat, panic rising. I'd seen no marks.

'No,' he said plainly, that smile of his unfaltering, as always. 'Would you like me to, Pandora?'

'No!' I cried and put my hands to my neck again, this time to shield it.

I sensed my great-aunt was watching me. When I looked to her I saw a mixture of amusement and disappointment. 'You two have some things to talk about,' Celia said, moving towards the door, and I recalled the way she described Deus's blood as ichor, the blood of the gods. Sustaining. Powerful. I was being childish, and ungrateful, wasn't I? I was better than this. And yet . . .

'I'll speak to you when you come back,' Great-Aunt Celia told me calmly and stepped out of the room, closing the door.

'Come back? No, no. Wait,' I protested, not ready. I did not want to be alone with Deus. I did not trust . . . Well, I didn't trust him. But I also did not trust myself. I didn't even *know* myself, if what he said was true.

'Trust me,' the ancient Sanguine said, unnervingly hitting on the issue at stake. (So to speak.) Despite my protests my great-aunt had abandoned me to his company, shutting the door of the antechamber behind her. I was alone with the magnetic, grinning Kathakano vampire. He held out a cool hand to me. 'Come with me,' he said in his gentlemanly voice. His eyes beckoned.

Good goddess, what have I got myself into?

'Do you want shoes?' he added.

'Why? Where are we going?'

'Where you will not be seen,' Deus told me, adding, 'by the living.'

'I'd better, um, grab some,' I said, pushing down my panic. I sprinted up to the doorway with half a mind to run inside the main penthouse where the undead were forbidden to enter, shut the door behind me and not come back. He couldn't follow me there, could he? But when I opened the door I found my ballet flats waiting for me. The coat Celia had given me was hung over the back of the doorknob. My great-aunt had left them there but she was already gone. With some reluctance, I slipped my shoes and coat on, and turned to face the vampire.

He had the casket in the floor open, and he was standing in it, the lower half of his legs disappearing inside.

'Come Pandora English, The Seventh,' he beckoned.

I did.

I followed my magnetic companion through the secret passageway and stepped through a heavy doorway in a turret on the roof and walked out into the crisp spring night air with the ancient Kathakano at my side. My heart was still skipping along too fast, but I'd found my calm, and conquered, for now, the panic I'd felt earlier.

The rooftop was jagged with spires and sections of dramatically sloping roof, and flanked by gargoyles with long claws and contorted faces. Out of the corner of my eye I thought I saw one of them turn its monstrous head to me and raise an animal-like paw. Again, the sky seemed subtly different, more illuminated tonight. I looked up and marvelled at the way the clouds were lit by the moon with a faint greenish cast. The full Blue Moon wasn't until tomorrow, I had thought, and though there was great power in the moon on the days before and after it was full, it seemed too bright tonight. And more green than blue. Had I made a mistake?

'Young lady,' Deus began in his old-fashioned way. 'Get on me.'

What? I whipped my head back around to look at him. The Sanguine had gone to stand on the edge of a nearby section of roof, the house disappearing in a sheer five-storey drop just behind him. The moon haloed his head and silhouetted his elegant body, the dark slim-fitting suit he always seemed to wear. His hair was perfectly coiffured, I noticed, shining in the moonlight, and his smooth skin almost seemed to glow. I could feel as much as see his darkly magnetic eyes lock on to mine, and a vision of his long dark lashes and sensual mouth came into my mind.

Oh boy.

I hesitated. My cheeks had grown warm, and other parts

of me as well. His proximity made me tingle inside, seemingly on some primal, cellular level, and before I knew it I'd walked right to him without even being aware I was moving. Now I was standing just inches from him, feeling his presence like an electric current. *You really have been drinking his blood, haven't you?* I thought. My physical reaction to him seemed to confirm it. The few sips I'd originally been fed to save my life had affected me, but this was far worse, far more intense. The pull to him was strong and by now I was all too aware that my body wanted to be wrapped around him, to get as close as possible. My mind was not so sure that was such a good idea, though, and I thought for a moment of Lieutenant Luke and how he would feel about this physical attraction to Deus, or the fact I'd been drinking from him. I'd have to tell him the latter, at least. He should know.

'Where are we going?' I asked, the wind rising up to push the edges of my coat back.

'There is something you need to see,' Deus said, evading my question.

Deus had mastered flight. Apparently this was a rare talent among the Sanguine. He was perhaps one thousand years old, one of Crete's traditional race of vampires – the grinning Kathakano – making him one of the oldest in the world. It was not the only talent he'd mastered, I guessed. He had flown me across Manhattan on his back once before, though that time it had been a supernatural emergency. There was not the same level of urgency now, it seemed, though he clearly wanted to show me something. If I hung on tight I should be safe – whatever 'safe' meant when climbing on top of the undead on the edge of a jagged roof, and journeying where the living would not see.

'Okay,' I whispered, with the slightest quaver in my voice, and I resigned myself to climbing on. He was only a few inches taller than me, and I pulled myself up with ease, wrapping my legs around his hips and locking my arms around his strong shoulders. My blood – well it was his too, wasn't it? – seemed to want to be closer, closer to this vampire, and locking on to him felt good, like a magnet finding its match. Deus's body felt cool and as hard as marble. Of course this position not only allowed me the safety necessary to be flown far above the ground, but it brought me into a kind of intimate embrace with the very creature for whom it seemed I suffered an irresistible attraction. Cold, undead and ancient, Deus inspired a dangerous level of interest in me, an interest I'd fought against since first meeting him. It wasn't a cerebral thing at all. If I thought about it, I knew I wasn't really attracted to him. And yet here I was, and the physical pull was undeniable.

Sanguine trickery, I reminded myself. It was the blood.

'Ready?' he asked.

I nodded in response, an answer he could feel, my face tucked into the back of his neck and silky black hair, and in seconds he took off straight into the sky, flying off the edge of the old mansion and through the layer of fog surrounding Spektor while I gasped, adrenaline running through my body like little electrical shocks as I dug my fingers into his hard muscles. Without a word we sped down the length of the island, the tall buildings and grid of streets passing below us in a swift blur. Soon the concrete and glass dropped away and

I found myself looking down at the glittering reflection of lights on water, and when I looked up again, there she was, *Libertas*, the Roman goddess of freedom, better known as Lady Liberty, looming in the fast-approaching distance. The copper figure stood more than three hundred feet over New York Harbour, from the layers of pedestals at her feet to the top of her magnificent torch. Deus flew towards Liberty Island, and before I knew it, we'd landed on the colossal shoulder of the statue. It had all been so fast.

La liberté éclairant le monde.

Liberty enlightening the world.

This was New York's most iconic statue and one of the most famous symbols of freedom and hope in the world. And here we were, perched on her shoulder like tiny birds caught in the beam of lights illuminating her.

Deus reached up and held my hand as I carefully climbed off his back and sat down on a large fold of Lady Liberty's copper robe. Somehow, I did not fear slipping to my death, perhaps because I knew my companion could catch me, and he had plenty of motivation to do so, as I was, according to him, the only hope for the living and therefore, the undead. (Who needed us for, well, *sustenance*.) I placed both hands on the cool shoulder of the giant woman, and thought I could actually feel the heat of her torch above me as she held it aloft – but of course that would have to be my imagination. Though the flame seemed alive at times, it was covered in gold. Above us, her beautiful neo-classical head looked out towards the sea, waiting stoically to welcome new visitors. Below us was the huge tablet she held, displaying the date of American independence in Roman numerals, and beyond her colossal feet and the graduated squares and spikes of her platform and the grass beyond, the lights reflected in the stretch of water between us and the island I called home. Manhattan. I'd dreamed of this place back in Gretchenville. But I never could have imagined this particular moment.

Deus sat down next to me, elegantly folding his legs and looking out. Over the din of the whistling wind, I heard him say, 'Look.' He pointed towards Midtown Manhattan and immediately, I could see why.

Across the sparkling water of New York Harbour, the cityscape of Manhattan was lit up by tiny squares of light, shining from the windows of the countless buildings that were her heart. But there was also another, more unusual source of light on this night. Something very different – and frightening. It was what I'd seen reflected in the clouds above the mansion, and through Celia's tall penthouse windows back in Spektor. Only now it was clear this was not simply an unusual phase of the moon. It was not the moon at all, and in fact, the source of the glow came from *below*, not above. Without the veil of mist I could see what appeared to be swirls of eerie fog drifting up into the sky, and centered at various locations across Manhattan island. Somewhere further up the island the fog was accumulating in a huge, floating ring miles above the streets. This was causing the illumination I'd seen lighting the Empire State Building. It was a supernatural fog, not unlike that around Spektor, yet rather than silvery mist, this was unmistakably virescent. And oddly, as I watched, I noticed the fog was moving quite unlike any fog I'd seen before, supernatural or otherwise. It moved up, like a waterfall falling *upwards*, and it seemed to taper up from the ground to towering points across the city, hundreds of feet in the air; moving, always moving.

In our brief flight I had not seen these accumulations of green fog, looking as I was towards the ground speeding by beneath us, but now from our vantage point on Lady Liberty it appeared so huge, and was so unmistakably a supernatural occurrence, that I marvelled I'd not sensed or seen it clearly from Spektor.

I covered my mouth and stared. But when I blinked, the vision seemed to vanish.

'Wait, it's gone!'

'Has it?' Deus said steadily.

I shook my head, ran a hand over my eyes and looked again. Now the odd vision was back. And it seemed to be growing. We both watched the phenomenon in the clouds for a long stretch of silence, the surreal sight of it making words seem quite pointless for the moment. I had no frame of reference to comprehend what it was. What could you say in the face of such a sight?

'Why does it vanish?' I finally asked.

My undead companion did not answer me.

'You *can* see it, can't you?' I asked. He'd pointed out the phenomenon so surely he could see what I saw. 'Can everyone see it then? Can everyone see this happening?'

Because if they could – if the people of Manhattan looked around them and noticed these giant green waterfalls of fog falling up into the sky – well, there would be absolute mayhem, wouldn't there? There would be widespread panic. Crowds would trample each other to get off the island. The army would be called in. Yet from our vantage point on Liberty Island, it looked like business as usual on the streets of Manhattan. Cars honked, crossing the bridge, pedestrians moved from A to B on their way home from drinks or plays or late work shifts, catching taxis and walking to the subway, and going about their lives as if the world wasn't about to end. It was all so terribly normal, so typically New York, if you didn't notice the disturbing green fog accumulating everywhere.

Maybe just a little panic wasn't such a bad thing? The living had been oblivious for far too long, as far as I was concerned. Surely they had to find out at some point that their entire existence was in jeopardy? That a battle between the dead and the living was nearly upon them? That a battle between them and whatever the heck that was in that fog was inevitable?

'No. They cannot see yet,' Deus said of the humans inhabiting the island. 'The supernatural hides itself. It has always been thus.'

Right. I'd had this explained to me before. Most living humans blocked knowledge of the supernatural. That was why it was children who most often told tales of ghosts and strange happenings, before their natural sensitivity to those realities was punished out of them and they began to block it like everyone else did. How many times had I been told to stop 'making up' stories? To stop being so fanciful? To stop imagining things? As I took in this extraordinary view of Manhattan with an ancient Sanguine at my side, I wondered what my father would say, now that he was on the other side, and understood.

'Pandora, The Seventh?' Deus said. I'd been speechless for a while.

I nodded. 'I'm still here.'

I watched the weird mist swirling dangerously in the sky above Manhattan and thought of the powerful spell of the necromancer I'd faced months earlier, raising the dead and marching them to the portal in Spektor, with the aim of opening it and triggering the Revolution. He had been so powerful he'd raised hundreds of dead, and terrifyingly, he'd been able to command Luke as well. His – or *its* – spell was visible to me, I recalled, and it had looked a bit like a glowing green swirling mist, but no one else had been able to see it, not even Deus with all his powers and his years on this earth. He'd been able to sense it, but not visibly see it. My ability to see it had been something about my being The Seventh, I was told.

'Deus, you can see this, though, can't you?' I asked.

He nodded.

'Yet you could not see the necromancer's spell?' I didn't understand.

'You wonder why?' he said. 'Imagine one thousand necromancers, like the one we encountered, enhanced by the power of the Agitation …'

I certainly didn't want to imagine that.

'… all working to the same end, their individual powers magnified,' the vampire explained. 'You have special gifts that I do not possess. You have a level of sensitivity that I do not share. But I am not blind to such a level of power.' He looked back at the strangely lit Manhattan skyline. 'The Agitation is upon us. It won't be long before the Revolution of the Dead begins. The portals will open and the veil will be lifted, and then no one will be blind to the truth.'

I swallowed. 'What will it take for the … the rest of the living to see this? Why does it come and go?'

'Pandora, it does not. Your vision comes and goes. A tussle between the parts of you, perhaps. The human you and The Seventh.'

I watched the eerie fog move, a lump in my throat.

'It is not easy for me to see even something of this magnitude, but I know it is there,' he said. 'The Agitation does not want to be seen yet, not until the Revolution, not until it is too late. That is why it tries to be invisible, even to you. But do not let it slip from your knowledge, Pandora English. This is important. Do not deny it. You have seen it now. Hold it in your mind.'

My heart was thumping in my chest, and I realised I'd been gripping Lady Liberty's cold robe with white fingers. *Do not let it slip from your knowledge.* I looked back out at the skyline, willing my sight to be clear, and there it was, greater and more terrifying each time.

'How do we stop it?'

The ancient Kathakano shook his head. 'It is inevitable, I believe. This moment comes every one hundred and fifty years, and if the battle is won in favour of the established balance, things continue on. When the time comes you will know what to do.'

'But I don't know what to do! How can I know what to do? I don't know anything. No one will tell me,' I protested, shouting above the sound of the wind. 'You've been around for centuries. If you've seen it before surely you would be better placed to handle this?'

Deus shook his head. 'No, Pandora English, you misunderstand entirely. I have continued through it,' he said, deftly avoiding the term 'lived'. He turned and looked at me with those dark, hypnotic eyes. 'I have not *seen it*, as you put it. Not as The Seventh must. That is not my place, nor really is it my battle. You know more than you realise. The Seventh has been dormant in you until now. You are awakening.'

I am awakening. Or rather, The Seventh is awakening inside me.

This was both a comforting and terrifying thought, as if an alien life form was inside me just waiting to take over when the time was right. Would I even have a say about that? About what I did? Would I just be overtaken somehow? What part of me had thrown Skye? I hadn't had a say when I was drinking from Deus each night, or had I? Was that The Seventh, or me?

'I'm sorry if I seem frustrated,' I said a little sheepishly, and crossed my arms over my chest, hugging myself. 'And that I, um ... I've been drinking your blood.' The thought of it caused a great deal of conflict in me.

'Do not be sorry, Pandora English,' Deus replied, grinning as always. The Kathakano always grinned, and the grin was always mesmerising. It was one of their peculiar traits. 'I am indebted to you,' he said. 'If there is anything I can do to help you prepare for what is to come, I must do it.'

'Is that what it is, do you think?' My brows pinched.

He nodded sagely. 'You are strengthening yourself for the battle to come.'

So, my subconscious self, this Seventh, was preparing for

the Revolution of the Dead by stocking up on ancient, magical Sanguine blood. *Right.* I looked down to the top of the pedestal on which this statue stood, so far below us. I noticed the broken chains at Lady Liberty's feet. *Freedom.* Was that what the dead wanted? Freedom? Was it right to withhold it from them, and if not, where were Luke's allegiances? He was my spirit guide, but he was still a spirit, and so was my mother. How could they truly be on my side – on the side of the living – if they were dead? Deus, for his part, had already showed his hand. He wanted the status quo because without the living the undead could not survive. It was a blunt and brutal logic, but I trusted it. What would a Revolution of the Dead mean for the living? I supposed it meant we would all be dead, if the powers of The Seventh proved inadequate. Not a comforting thought.

There was so much that I did not know or understand.

'Come. There is more,' Deus said, and held out his cool white hand again. He turned his back to me, encouraging me to climb up on to him once more. But how much more could I possibly take tonight? After my mother's visit, Celia's blood-drinking, and the knowledge that necromancers were at work across Manhattan?

Dreading to think what I would see next, I mounted his strong back and held my breath. We sailed off the side of the Statue of Liberty in one breathtaking leap and swooped down over the water. The air felt cool and exhilarating over the harbour, and he moved us quickly and deftly, flying us up over the tall buildings of Lower Manhattan and climbing higher as we approached Midtown, his body hard and capable beneath me. I was almost able to enjoy the feeling of his strength and mastery of the air. So odd, this feeling of physical, almost *cellular* attraction, and the simultaneous feelings of safety and repulsion, calm and fear all mingling together. I shook my head and was glad Deus could not read minds as Celia could. As far as I knew, he felt none of this mix of conflicting feeling for me. He had never attempted to actually seduce or drink from me. His blood was inside me, not the other way around. How did that feel for him? Was he impacted at all by the blood bond?

Stop thinking about it.

Now I could see what Deus wanted to show me, and this took my focus. It was the Metropolitan Museum of Art, and it appeared to be a hive of supernatural activity. We were above it now, where there was a gathering of swirling green mist, like I'd seen in various parts of the island. Below us the view was quite clear. The fog was so odd, the way it rolled upwards, almost billowing, and for a moment I swore I saw snake coils of green moving up into the sky towards me.

'What is *that?* Snakes?'

At first Deus did not answer. 'I do not know what it is,' he finally said, shouting above the wind and shaking his head. 'But I know *why* it is. This is the Agitation, Pandora. You have already pulled great powers to you in Spektor, and to Manhattan, with your very presence. Now, ancient supernatural forces are gathering power. The old rules are fading fast. The Revolution is very near.'

The veil between the living and the dead is wearing thin, I thought with sudden certainty. The old rules. *Soon the veil will break.*

'This is because of me? This gathering of forces?' I asked, disturbed by the idea. I thought of what might happen if I left

Spektor, left this densely populated island. 'What if I ... what if I leave Manhattan?' I could go somewhere else, somewhere like Gretchenville even, where there are fewer people.

'No, Pandora. It is not so simple as that. Without you there would be no one to stand against the dark forces, no one to face the necromancers and the powers that seek to open the portal and unleash the Revolution. The energy is drawn to you, drawn to the entry to the Otherworld, the entry to the place of the dead.'

Drawn to the mansion in Spektor, which was built on a portal to the Underworld. Yes, I knew this.

'There is no undoing this. There is no avoiding what has been foretold. All is as it must be.'

I opened my mouth, unformed questions on my tongue, but for now nothing came out.

'There is more you must see,' Deus told me and glanced upwards. 'But we won't be able to stay up there long.'

'Up there ...?'

'Take a deep breath,' he advised, and before I could say another word he shot upwards like a grinning torpedo and all I could think of, as the air whistled past in a roar and I held the breath in my lungs like a diver without a tank, was that if this was it, if I died right then, embracing this ancient creature at midnight, speeding miles over the city I had dreamed of since I was a child, at least I will have died in one of the most thrilling and exhilarating moments I had ever known.

Death, so close is death ...

Deus slowed and then stopped, and in a move that might have been indecent, but somehow felt safe and welcome, he turned over in my shocked embrace and we were belly to belly suspended next to the clouds, Deus holding me tight so I would not drop to my death if I let go. I wasn't about to let go – in fact, I was holding him so tightly my fingers ached. But I could pass out. Yes, and there was something else, some odd pull to death that came with his presence. We were far, far above Manhattan, so high that I could barely find oxygen. The view was dizzying, surreal.

'Quickly, look Pandora,' he urged me, catching my eye. 'Look in all directions.'

From our vantage point far above the earth I could see that these green swirling maelstroms formed a larger pattern, like three spirals radiating to a centre, each moving clockwise. The twisting fog was spread out across Manhattan in three points, like a kind of moving triangle, at the centre of which was Spektor. My mind seized upon a symbol I'd seen in the past, something with three spirals that I'd only recently been reminded of. I gasped for air, struggling for oxygen, my eyes watering, and just as the great pattern spreading miles in all directions had imprinted itself on my mind, Deus darted downwards again, holding me in his cool, steely grasp. Perhaps sensing my struggle for air, he slowed over upper Central Park and I gasped like a fish out of water until I'd gulped down enough oxygen for my breathing to slow again. I felt myself grow faint, blackness reaching out for me and in a flash I found he'd transported us to a dark and quiet piece of green, and was placing me tenderly on a soft lawn. My feet touched down and I steadied myself before I crumpled, still breathing hard. I looked around me through watering eyes.

The area was unlit. As my eyes came into focus I noticed tombstones.

Of course we're in a cemetery.

'Young lady, are you okay?' the ancient Sanguine asked me.

I nodded, though I was still panting, and blinked several times, wiping the water from the corners of my eyes. I regained control of my wobbly knees and stood firmly once more. This was the Trinity Church Cemetery and Mausoleum, I noticed. It was late at night, just after midnight no doubt, and the gates were probably locked. We would not be bothered here. It was a good choice.

'Now you have seen it – the Agitation,' he said, holding my focus. My eyes had become accustomed to the dark, and I could make out his features, the strong brow and long lashes. Under the lashes his eyes shone like black jewels.

The Agitation. It really was happening. I had known it, even if I'd tried at times to entertain the notion that it was 'just a folk tale'. Now I could no longer deny that the foretold chaos was truly underway, the tensions between the living and the dead becoming too strong to remain quite hidden, at least to some. Everything I thought I knew about the world – about the divisions between the living and the dead – was in turmoil. I thought of the way the green swirls of supernatural activity came and went in my vision. How long could the supernatural world keep knowledge of the Agitation and coming Revolution from the living population? And was it still a good idea that they were kept in the dark? All of this 'erasing' the memories of people who witness supernatural occurrences – I was no longer convinced that it was in the best interests of the living.

It seemed more like it was in the best interests of the undead, to hide their secrets, and the dead, to keep them oblivious to the battle that was coming.

'What was that pattern we saw?' I managed to ask. 'That was familiar, like an old symbol of some kind. It's in one of my mother's books on ancient Celtic myth, I think.'

'Curious, this word "myth",' Deus remarked, and after a beat I knew what he meant. If there was one thing I'd learned since moving here, it was that many so-called myths were simply truths. 'Perhaps you mean the symbol sometimes referred to as the triskele,' he said.

Yes, that's it. It looked a bit like what I knew as an ancient Celtic symbol. But what had that symbol meant? Some said it was the triple goddess, others that it represented the three realms – land, sea and sky. Or hell, earth and heaven; or destroyer, sustainer, creator. Christians had sometimes used it to describe the Holy Trinity. And here we were in the Trinity Church graveyard. It had many meanings.

'We had this symbol on our coins and pottery in Greece long ago,' Deus explained, and it was still shocking to imagine he'd been around to see ancient coins in use. 'The name comes from the Greek for three-legged but this symbol dates back at least to what you would describe as Neolithic times. In most cultures there is something like this described by the elders. Many religions have used it. It is called the triskele, triskelion or triple spiral, but there have been other names.' He paused. 'Are you okay, Pandora English, The Seventh?'

I still seemed to be breathing fast. I hadn't quite recovered from that perilously quick journey into the skies. Or perhaps it was the conversation, or who I was having it with, that quickened my breath. The blood bond was distracting, and I was far from coming to terms with what it meant. 'I didn't get a full breath of oxygen in before we went up there,' I explained, and though that was true, it wasn't the whole explanation for how I felt.

'I am sorry,' Deus told me solemnly. 'I forget what it is like to need to breathe. I will take you home, if you like,' he said, and opened his arms. 'You have seen enough for now.'

Deus stood in the dimly lit cemetery waiting for me to embrace him. For a moment I allowed myself to take him in – his magnetic ivory grin, the smooth, elegant lines of his body in the calming stillness of the old graveyard, moonlit and set against tombs of the dead he outdated by centuries, his dark suit, his outstretched arms and the cross his pose formed, mirroring a crucifix atop a weathered mausoleum behind him. Odd, this was. All of it. My body was distinctly stimulated by his presence, blood pumping, my heart still racing from the nearness of death I'd felt far above the world held in his grasp. And yet the idea of walking into his arms felt like a safe harbour. I did not fear he would drop me or endanger me, or latch on to my neck and drain me of my blood as he surely had done with hundreds or thousands of mortals in his time. Somehow, I trusted him. What was between us was exciting, mystifying perhaps, and yes I felt something physical. I knew somehow that Deus would not attempt to seduce me. Every action of the creature before me seemed at once dangerous and arousing, and yet calming, and I did not understand how that juxtaposition could exist. How could such a dark and capable creature be calming? Perhaps it was because I knew this ancient creature needed me, or at least he believed he did.

For me, Deus was a protector. Though not a giant made of bronze like mythical Talos, he was nonetheless a powerful guardian animated by ichor. He was dangerous, yes. Deeply dangerous. But not to me.

I took a breath, and feeling ready, I walked into the arms of the Kathakano vampire whose blood strengthened mine. He closed his cool embrace around me, held me tight, and we sped up and over the flowering trees of the beautiful cemetery, Manhattan flying past beneath us, and entered the supernatural ring of mist that surrounded my home with my great-aunt.

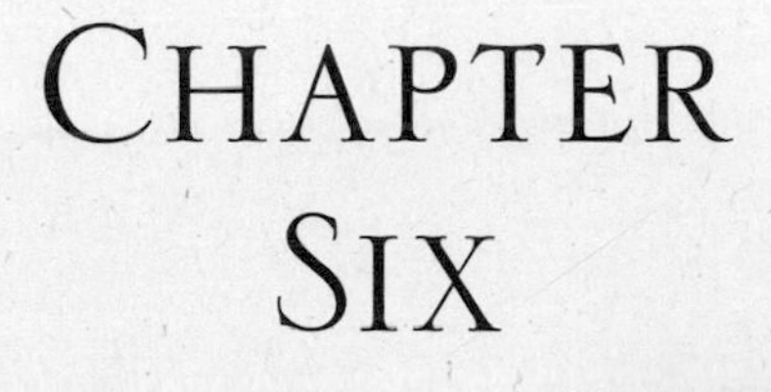

Chapter Six

I woke on Thursday morning before my alarm, feeling surprisingly refreshed despite the excitement of the previous two days and a lack of sleep. Last night had been fantastical, something I could not yet process. I may have dismissed it all as a vivid dream or nightmare if I did not know better. The bizarre dreams I'd had about drinking Deus's blood had been real, too; something else to ponder. Drinking ancient Sanguine blood explained why I was so refreshed and full of vigour despite my lack of rest. But was it a blessing or a curse?

Taking a deep breath, I reached over and turned off my alarm before it started up, then swung out of bed and made my way to my ensuite bathroom, eager to look myself over. The previous night had been intense, and it showed in my amber eyes, though not in the ways one might expect. There was no redness in them, despite the late night. The whites were clear, even extra bright. My amber pupils shone. *Interesting.* My hair was sitting softly at my shoulders, and I pulled it back on both sides and turned my head this way and that. My neck was unmarked. And I couldn't help but notice that my skin was glowing. My complexion was usually pale – a Lucasta trait – but now it was particularly luminous. And

I detected a faint tan on my chest and cheeks. I'd seen this before. This wasn't from sun worship. To the contrary, I'd hardly seen the sun since moving to Spektor. No, this was from drinking Deus's blood. It made a human extra UV sensitive to have vampire blood inside them. I'd have to take to wearing a hat.

Frowning, I leaned towards the mirror and lifted my lips to examine my teeth. All human. No fangs. I wasn't Sanguine, then. Just a blood drinker, I guess?

Mom, what do you think of all this?

I put the Babel Pendant on, the necklace sitting higher than the skeleton key on its longer, thin gold chain, deciding to wear it whenever I could, and I went about getting dressed and ready for the day.

Today wasn't just any day. Tonight would be the full moon, a special time to see my spirit guide Lieutenant Luke, though if I got caught up thinking about that, and him, I'd never get through my work. Before leaving for the *Pandora* magazine offices I tenderly touched the top of the envelope containing my mother's letter, then packed my mother's two books on ancient Egypt into my satchel, including the one on Hatshepsut herself.

I looked to the book that had been beneath them, the one called *Celtic Myth and Legend*, and my eyes widened.

There it was. The triskele.

'Pandora?' came a voice.

I slammed my mother's book shut, the image of the triskele etched in my mind. *Earth, water and sky, spiritual, physical and celestial ...*

It was late afternoon, nearly time to head home. The workday had gone fairly smoothly – so far. I had mostly kept my mind on work, though it was hard with the full moon coming, and with all I'd seen and learned the night before. All day I'd fetched an inordinate number of caffeinated beverages at Pepper's request, typical for when we approached deadlines, and now at her beckoning I pushed the book I'd been peeking at aside, rose from my little cubicle and walked into her office, unsure what to expect next. A request for a skim soy chai latte, perhaps?

(How banal these mortal demands were in the face of those green swirls of mist.)

When I entered her office Pepper had several screens up with images from the Egyptian-themed shoot, and her desk was piled with magazines. As usual, I couldn't help but notice her outfit – pinstriped linen from shoulder pad to fashionable ankle cuff. It was an off-white and beige ensemble that was a play on the masculine suit but softer and more draping for a spring fashion mood. Over the day it had wrinkled somewhat, but so high was the quality of the linen that this did not diminish the look. Perhaps to offset the softness of the linen, Pepper's ice-blonde hair was styled in a tight, high ponytail that fell straight down her back. Every hair had been utterly tamed at some point early in the morning, and I marvelled that nothing had moved since. Did she spray it to death in the toilets when no one was looking? But wait, it was longer than usual, well past the shoulder blades, I noticed. Was this a new look? One with a hairpiece? Those temporary hairpieces were in vogue, I'd heard. I dared not ask, and stood straight as a soldier awaiting her command.

'I have an invitation for you for Saturday night,' Pepper said, much to my surprise, and that dead straight ponytail shifted barely perceptibly. She handed me a printed invitation card embellished in gold hieroglyphs and the name HATSHEPSUT. 'You'll need to take some notes about who is there, and who they are wearing, for the social section,' she explained, not looking at me.

'Of course,' I responded, nodding and gripping the card. I was keen to see the Met exhibit on Hatshepsut, though I was more than a little worried about what my mother had said, and what I'd seen from on high over Manhattan, suspended in Deus's arms. (Even the thought of him made me flush.) 'Good then. Thanks,' I said and something about the way I'd responded made her look up.

Weird girl, I again imagined her thinking as she looked me over.

'It's a plus one invitation. You might like to take Jay,' she suggested, and watched me.

I resisted gulping, though my mouth came over all funny. The way she said his name seemed loaded, and the thought of him did make me feel conflicted. I suppose I should *want* to go to the fancy opening with Jay Rockwell, handsome (living) man about town, but I searched myself and found I did not. Going with my beloved Luke wasn't an option either, or rather, if he attended he wouldn't need a formal invitation.

'I don't think I will,' I eventually responded. 'I have someone else in mind.'

Her already high eyebrows rose. 'Is that so?' It seemed now that her painted brows were somewhere near her tautly pulled hairline.

I nodded.

Pepper cocked her head. I thought I could see some pleasure there, perhaps. I knew she and Jay liked each other. I'd known that even before she became my boss. She shifted on her heels. 'I want the who's who and the basics,' she told me, all business once more. 'There will be a photographer taking official images, so you can concentrate on the rest.'

That was an improvement. I did enjoy photography, but at a social event it was pretty stressful, I'd found, knowing you were on the clock and if you missed an important face or the shots didn't turn out you would be in trouble. And walking up to strangers and asking to take their picture wasn't the easiest. That kind of photography experience was not at all like spending time in the calm graveyards I'd photographed when I was younger, to say the least.

'Would you like a brief piece on the launch event? Say five hundred words?' I queried. Perhaps in amongst the who's who and who's wearing who, I could drop in a well-placed line about Hatshepsut herself and her fascinating history, I thought, but then felt ill at ease. *Oh that's right. You spoke with your dead mother. She died at the site of Hatshepsut's tomb*. A lump formed in my throat.

'Good thinking,' Pepper replied. 'We may only have room

for three hundred or so words, however,' she said, nodding with a flick of her long ponytail. It moved like a whip.

'And I'll get my own byline?' I dared to add.

There was an awkward pause. This had been a problem between us before.

'Yes,' Pepper confirmed, her thin, painted lips barely moving. 'You will have your own byline.'

Good, I thought, and allowed myself a smile at this assurance. It was hardly going to be a groundbreaking piece to cover the social goings on of the Met launch but correct attribution matters. In that moment I realised I'd changed a lot since I'd started working there – I mean in human ways – because the fact is I wouldn't have dared press an issue like that only a couple of months earlier. Perhaps I was gaining confidence, as Celia had suggested. I wouldn't let Pepper grab credit for my work again, and I wouldn't let my previous boss Skye push me around either.

An image flashed into my mind of Skye DeVille flying through the air and hitting the street in Spektor with that sickening sound, and I stifled a shiver. Yes, a lot had changed.

'Thank you,' I said.

'And well done bringing those books in. Ben has copied the relevant sections. I think it will help with the layout.'

'My pleasure.'

'I've been wanting to say, Pandora, that you've been here for a few months now and you shouldn't be afraid to ask for a raise, if you want one,' my boss said.

I blinked. *Well, I'll be.* Pepper was actually encouraging me, thanking me, inviting me to ask for an increase in pay? This was something. It had taken months to hear a single thank you from her and stealing credit for my work on the 'Blood of Youth' story hadn't helped my view of her. ('Additional reporting by Pandora English'. Please!) So either I was moving up at *Pandora*, which seemed to be the case, or she was developing some manners. Maybe it was both. Or maybe, with Skye gone, she was finding her own style of dealing with employees. With everything going on I honestly hadn't even thought about a raise.

'Thank you, Pepper,' I said, feeling genuinely appreciative. 'I will keep it in mind and get back to you soon.'

'Good,' she said, and turned away from me, getting right back to her work. I'd been dismissed, but with a smile on my face, at least.

I gathered my mother's books and packed up for the day, and for a change, it was right on five o'clock when I walked up to the reception on my way out.

'Hey, Morticia, do you have a minute? I wanted to ask you something,' I said, leaning on one arm and propping my heavy satchel up on the corner of the wide reception desk.

My friend looked up and pushed the black, dyed hair out of her eyes. 'Yes?'

'Would you like to go to the Met exhibition opening with me on Saturday?' I asked her. 'I have a plus one.'

At this her darkly painted mouth hung open, and she stood up from behind the desk. 'Me?' she said. 'You want *me* to go?'

I nodded. 'Yes. I'd love you to come with me. Pepper offered me a plus one invitation and I'll have to work a bit, but I thought it might be good to go together. The launch should be ... something else.'

I'd been about to say the launch would be 'fun' but then a visual had popped into my mind of the supernatural green reverse flowing waterfalls spookily hanging around the building, and the snake-like formations I'd seen from the air, and well, I had a new view of the Met. And according to Deus, I shouldn't let it slip from my mind.

I sure hoped nothing bad was going to happen on Saturday night, I thought. I wondered if I should open up to Morticia about what was going on.

I must have looked funny because Morticia tilted her head to one side. 'Are you okay?'

Was I okay? That depended on your definition, I supposed. Was anyone 'okay' with an impending apocalypse? How could I explain the situation to her? Come to think of it, I didn't know enough about the situation to explain it to anybody. But if there was one living human person I wanted to inform about the coming Revolution of the Dead, it was Morticia. But right now in the *Pandora* offices was not the time.

'Yes. I thought if you wanted to go to the exhibition ... Well, there isn't anyone else I'd rather go with,' I said. And I did mean it. 'And I'd like to talk to you about something beforehand. You know, when you have time?' I added.

She nodded. 'Okay. How about tomorrow? Lunch break?' She looked intrigued.

'Friday lunch. That sounds good,' I said. That was a bit more than a day before the opening. But would she be able to hear what I had to say and get back to the rest of her workday?

Gosh . . . I didn't know how to approach this at all, but I could at least try to start the conversation.

'Great. Thanks, Pandora,' Morticia continued. 'I know you asked me to come to the fashion shoot because you know I've always wanted to be on set, and I appreciate this. It's nice of you.' She paused and looked down at her black Doc Martens and dark mesh tights. 'What about Jay, though?' she asked.

I shrugged. 'I'd rather go with you, Morticia. You're my friend. And hey, you had to work on the fashion shoot. It's not like I was doing you any big favour. Let's hope Saturday night isn't too much work,' I said, and smiled at her. I decided I ought to wait to say anything more.

There would be time to tell her at lunch. Maybe I couldn't tell all of it, exactly, but I felt like there had to be a way of preparing Morticia if this whole Revolution of the Dead thing was real. And imminent. And Deus had certainly thought it was, and that view of Manhattan was pretty hard to argue with. I wouldn't be able to forgive myself if I said nothing to Morticia and something happened to her.

I'd have to think of how to approach it before our lunch. We only had half-hour breaks, I remembered. This was going to be hard.

As I walked down the stairs on to the SoHo street just after five, my satchel heavy with my mother's books, I was busy thinking about exactly what to tell Morticia. How does one start that conversation? With my peculiarities? Or 'gifts' as Celia called them? Or with Spektor? Or the prophecy that the living world could end?

'Hi, Pandora.'

In that moment, hearing a man's voice, I was hit with a most disorienting feeling, thinking of Lieutenant Luke waiting for me on the sidewalk but instead finding living, breathing, non-transparent Jay Rockwell.

'Um, Jay? You got my messages?' I said.

'Yeah,' he told me, shifting a little on his feet. Standing taller. His smile faltered, perhaps because my greeting wasn't what he expected. Instead of feeling excited by his presence, his *aliveness*, I felt a surprising stab of disappointment at seeing him. He seemed to sense something was amiss, too.

'I wanted to ask you something,' he said, and my stomach seized up, as if I knew exactly what he was going to say.

'I wanted to speak with you about something, too, actually,' I said. 'It's important. Can we go –'

'Do you want to come with me to the Met opening on Saturday?' Jay said, cutting me off.

I pursed my lips. *Dammit.* 'I'm going with someone else,' I found myself saying flatly. I hadn't meant it to come out so harshly, but I saw his face fall. 'I've been trying to speak with you about something, Jay. Can we go somewhere and talk? Maybe sit down somewhere?'

His mouth opened and closed a couple of times. 'Oh,' he responded. 'There's someone else then.'

It's not like that, I wanted to say, but I realised I'd be lying. There was someone else. There was Luke. I'd mentioned him before, mentioned that there was someone I cared deeply about but he had passed on. But it didn't matter that Lieutenant Luke was dead. Well, it *mattered*, of course, but not like that. I would no longer listen to Luke's encouragement that I should date a living man. I didn't want to.

'Yes, there is,' I told Jay. 'I didn't mean to tell you like this though, standing on the street. I thought we should go somewhere and talk.'

'Well, we're talking now. It's okay, I'm a big boy. I can handle it.'

I walked up to Jay and embraced him. He was so tall. I'd always liked that about him. His size – literally and figuratively – had made me feel safe in a new big city. I'd been swept away. He was a 'big man', an important man in New York, and I'd been fresh off the plane from Gretchenville, totally out of my depth. But I didn't feel I needed a protector like Jay anymore. I was strong enough on my own for the human world now, and for the supernatural world there was Luke, and there was Deus, and there were my own growing powers. So much had changed.

He'd been good to me at times, but it was never going to work between us. We were too different. Sure, we were both living, but there were more important things than that.

I looked up into his hazel eyes. 'Thank you,' I said, and smiled.

I kissed Jay Rockwell on the cheek with affection and walked away while he stared after me.

I arrived in Spektor feeling lighter. Even my satchel, laden with my mother's heavy books, felt easier to carry. The sun was still up, and there was time get some things done before nightfall.

I knew exactly what I wanted to do when the sun went down.

Nearing Celia's mansion on Addams Avenue I could see the hand-painted sign for Harold's Grocer, the old-fashioned shopfront beckoning me. It was in some ways your typical corner store, but it was in Spektor so it was very much not normal. As I neared, I noticed the smell of old books and mothballs.

I looked through the pane of glass in the front door before trying the handle. It was open, and a bell chimed as I entered.

'Miss Pandora, it is a delight to see you.'

'Thank you. And you, Harold. I am planning a special night tonight,' I explained to my local 'greengrocer'. Who was actually, well, green.

'With your soldier for the Blue Moon,' he guessed correctly and smiled with green apple cheeks. It was a pleasant smile, despite the odd colour, and his eyes, though yellow, sparkled with kindness.

'Indeed,' I replied. 'I hope it will be a good moon for us tonight.' It was hard to guess what the residents of Spektor thought of my liaison with the deceased second lieutenant, but it seems they all knew about it, and they knew either by gossip or a knowledge of magick I myself barely understood, that the full moon created a special opportunity for us. 'I would like to purchase some candles, and perhaps some more of your homemade apple cider?'

'I do have some, if you like. Would he also be liking a Splitting Headache, or perhaps he would care to try Asses' Milk this time? The weather is turning warmer.'

Despite the odd names, I knew what Harold meant. These were drinks from the days of the Civil War. I'd researched what was popular at the time, to help Luke feel more at home.

'Asses' Milk,' I said, one finger at my lips. 'Is that the one with rum and lemonade?'

'It is. I do have lemonade at the moment, and a good rum.'

'Lovely. I'll take some of each.' The cider was best served warm, and Harold was right about the weather. 'And do you have some cheese and biscuits perhaps?'

'A tasting plate? How appropriate,' Harold agreed, and set about collecting the goods I'd requested. I wanted tonight to be particularly special. There were a number of reasons for this, and the one I was trying to put aside in my mind was the thought that this might be one of the last truly free nights I would experience before, well, before the Revolution and whatever might come of it.

I took the time to walk around the store while I waited, noticing the old-style packets of Puss'n Boots cat food, White King fabric softener and Rit color and dye, and packages of powdered sugar and other odd items. It wasn't the first time I'd noticed that a lot of what Harold carried wasn't, how could I put it, *current*. I supposed it was probably that way because his clients weren't current either. Then I came across something I really was not expecting.

'Excuse me, Harold?'

'Yes?' he called back as he filled a brown grocery bag with

my items. He bent over again, disappearing except for his green hair, floating like seaweed underwater, just above the countertop.

I stared at the small carved figure, wide-eyed. It was of a human figure, but wrapped like a mummy, and as I looked upon it the pendant around my neck had seemed to warm. Yes, it was warming, I confirmed, touching it with the fingers of one hand. I had thought from a distance that this might be an Egyptian figure of Osiris, ancient Egypt's god of the dead, sitting right here in Harold's Grocer when it looked like it should be behind glass at the Met, but on closer inspection I saw that it did not have the traditional crook and flail, nor the Atef crown of the well-known deity.

'Is this a … a shabti?' I bit my lip. 'Is this a shabti you have here, or a ushabti?' There were a few spellings. Hadn't my mother mentioned a shabti when she spoke of what Carter had found in KV20?

'An answerer?' he said, understanding. 'Ah, you have found it.' He stood up from behind the counter.

Shabtis were 'answerers' in the times of ancient Egypt. They would answer to do chores of many kinds, particularly manual labour, and Egyptians – well, those who could afford them – were buried with one for each day of the year, so they wouldn't have to work in the afterlife.

'You know what they are? How did you get this one?'

'Your great-aunt – what a woman she is,' he said, distracted for a moment with thoughts of her. 'She gave me some advance notice you might be wanting one.'

'She did? She gave you notice?' I hadn't known for sure

that I would want one but it had crossed my mind. How could Celia have known?

He nodded, his green hair floating strangely.

'Oh,' I replied. How puzzling, I thought, but then it *was* Celia. My thoughts were not private with her in the house.

'You would like some shabtis then, Miss Pandora?'

'Some?'

His brows pinched for a moment. 'Well, yes. They usually come in groups. Or would you like only the one? I only put one out.'

Good point. Was it about quality or quantity? I wondered. I supposed that shabtis were never really meant to work alone.

'I'd like … seven,' I said, deciding not to be too greedy. My great-aunt insisted on paying the tab at Harold's and I couldn't imagine a 2500-year-old relic would come cheap. I'd have to speak to her about this. 'Seven will be just fine … if you think you can get that many?'

His eyes became wide for a moment. 'How appropriate,' he remarked. 'Seven shabtis for The Seventh. I will get them for you. Any preferences?'

'Preferences?'

'Materials? Inscriptions? Dynasty? Would you like new shabtis to be carved for you or would you like the ancient ones?'

Oh boy. I hadn't thought of any of that.

Harold cocked his head, waiting. I wondered about the effectiveness of a shabti in the modern, living world. They were meant for the Underworld. They were meant for their ancient masters.

'I guess I need them to be for me.'

'So they do not serve anyone else.'

'Yes,' I said. 'That seems best.'

'Indeed. Very good,' he said.

'But . . .' I began. 'I suppose they need to be made by those who know how to . . .'

'How to make an answerer. Yes, don't worry about that, Miss Pandora.'

'Okay. Yes.'

'Very good. Seven shabtis. They will be authentic and only for you, Pandora English.'

'And I do have a bit of time pressure. It may not be possible but I hoped I could have them for this weekend. Is that possible?'

'You shall have your shabtis in time for the weekend.'

I shall? 'How do you do that?' I asked. 'I mean, where do you get such things?'

'If it can be made I can acquire it,' he replied simply. Of course, like everyone else in this supernatural realm, Harold did not like to answer questions. Requests, well, any request was welcomed, except requests for answers.

'Thank you, Harold. When shall I come back?'

'Saturday, any time after one,' he said matter-of-factly, as if I might have ordered a turkey or a special cake.

'Well, thank you.'

'I will put it all on the tab. Here you go,' he said in his usual, jovial way, and handed me the bag.

When I arrived in the penthouse Celia was not there. Enjoying the thought of having added privacy for the evening, I put my groceries in the kitchen, and immediately decided to make my way to the roof of the mansion – the very roof I had flown from with Deus the night before.

I stood and felt the wind in my hair, and turned from one direction to the next. The horizon to the south over Manhattan looked … normal. And beautiful. Likewise to the north, east and west. Sunset was fast approaching, the clouds turning different colours – crimson and gold, with tinges of mauve and purple. I was heartened to see that none of those colours was green. Reassured somewhat, I went back inside and began to plan for the evening ahead.

Chapter Seven

Some things are only possible after dark.

As day turned to night and the sunny skies gave over to the darkness, I could feel the anticipation building inside me. The atmosphere was changing subtly, the moon coming into its fullest glory, the air growing electric. I needed it to be dark enough for the moon to really take over the sky, really shine, for it was the moon that I needed this night, the Blue Moon – the last full moon of spring. Since moving to Spektor I'd come to better understand the moon's pull and power, so even with everything else going on, I'd been looking forward to this night all month. I'd been yearning for it. And if my conversation with Harold was anything to go by, all of Spektor knew about it.

Once in a Blue Moon …

I opened my windows and let the night air in. Spektor and the Manhattan skyline beyond looked beautiful tonight, buildings and lampposts haloed in soft white mist. The moon in the dark sky was bright, and there was still no green tinge, not that I could see. I wanted this bit of respite, so even if walls of upside down supernatural green fog had sprung up everywhere, perhaps I couldn't see it because I didn't want to? And the house – I thought I heard it shifting again on its foundations. Or had that been my imagination? I should check the portal again tomorrow, just to be sure nothing had changed. But for now, I would continue my preparations for the evening. I had waited eagerly for this full moon and the magick hours it afforded us. I wanted nothing to ruin it.

I bathed and dressed in my favourite vintage shirtwaist dress and made up one small jug of Asses' Milk and one of straight lemonade. I looked at them both, sitting on old-fashioned doilies next to a couple of tumblers and considered pouring a glass, but wasn't sure which he'd prefer. The cheese was sitting out next to some biscuits and a small knife. I noticed one slice of cheese was off-centre compared with the rest, and adjusted it by a few millimetres.

Stop fussing.

Taking a breath to steady myself, I got on my knees on the hardwood floor of my room and reached under my bed, where I found Lieutenant Luke's cavalry sword waiting. It was the physical sword itself, a piece of his former life as a soldier in the Lincoln Cavalry, wrapped lovingly in velvet. I pulled the sword out and gently unwrapped it. It was tapered and curved, and bore his initials – LT.

Four moons ago we had discovered Lieutenant Luke's cavalry sword in a storage trunk in the mansion. As it had been buried with him, the physical sword had probably been exhumed along with Luke's corpse (Gulp, I couldn't imagine Luke having a corpse) by Dr Edmund Barrett – the architect, famed psychical scientist and founding member of the Global Society for Psychical Research who designed and had previously lived in the mansion at Number One Addams

Avenue, and worked in the laboratory in the bowels of the building.

It was due to Barrett that the mansion had many of its peculiarities. He'd had a keen interest in communicating with the departed (an interest that was arguably aided by his current, non-living state as a ghostly necromancer). But while Barrett had tried to raise the spirit of the Civil War soldier, perhaps leading to his being trapped in this house so many miles from the place of his birth, returning Luke's long-lost sword to him had broken the curse that kept his spirit trapped. Now, of course, he was able to travel outside the mansion, as many other spirits commonly could, and when the correct elements came together on a full moon, Luke and I were able to achieve something quite beyond. As an item of importance from his living days, Luke's sword seemed to work as a talisman of sorts for him, and this combination – sword and moon – along with my obsidian ring (and perhaps my own unspecified powers?) appeared to make a miracle possible.

Taking another deep breath, and marvelling again at the hefty weight of the sword, I held up the sabre by the grip and summoned my beloved:

'Lieutenant Luke. Come to me,' I declared with purpose.

Having done this only a few times before, I still naturally harboured some doubt that the man of my dreams could actually arrive, flesh and blood, in my bedroom, but after a heart-stopping few seconds the familiar chill descended and the obsidian ring on my finger began to grow hot. Slowly a white figure formed before me, spectral hands taking shape around the grip of the cavalry sword. And there it was, the sudden shocking flash of heat and light passing from the ring through me, and bringing with it the most extraordinary phenomenon. *My Lieutenant Luke. Whole. Flesh.* His warm, human hands encased mine, the two of us finding ourselves holding his sword together, bodies just inches apart.

'Luke,' I said, looking into his beautiful face.

'Miss Pandora,' he replied. 'Are you all right?'

Lieutenant Luke frequently asked this, and usually he materialised in his spirit form when I was in distress. This was not one of those occasions, however. I was not distressed and he was not in spirit form. This feeling was something else entirely.

'I'm okay,' I said. 'Happier for clapping eyes on you.'

'Your mother has visited you,' he said, somehow knowing. 'Did seeing her comfort you?' He tilted his head.

'I guess so,' I said. 'Yes. Not comfort perhaps, but something like it. It meant a lot to me.'

We were still holding the sword together, lost in each other's eyes.

He broke from our intense gazing and cast his eyes downward. 'You have the Babel Pendant. It is good that you should have this,' he said, looking at the glowing stone. Again, he seemed to know things that were or had been beyond my knowledge. This was what drew so many necromancers to try to raise the dead – to try to discover secrets only they knew.

'My mom said it would help me to understand things,' I said, letting go of his sword, which he now brought to his side. I sure felt like I needed to understand things better. 'She warned me about this exhibition at the Met not being a coincidence.'

I'd hoped it would be a nice opportunity to take my friend Morticia somewhere interesting – a bit of normal life – but now I was worried. But I didn't want to dwell on that. Not right now. This was the night of the full moon, and I didn't know how many of these we would have. Many, I hoped. But if the Revolution was coming . . .

I shook off my fears and moved to the assortment of refreshments. 'I have some Asses' Milk for you, Luke, if you care to try it?' He could only drink or eat when he was in human form like this. If I were him I would be so hungry and eager to experience those physical pleasures again, after over a century and a half caught as a spirit in this house. And though I was underage, according to American law, he was quite legal to drink and like most soldiers he would have imbibed many times before his death at just twenty-five on the battlefield. (Was there just six years difference between us, or over a hundred and fifty six?) *I'm not legal, you're not living,* I thought, considering the madness of it all. And then I remembered I *was* drinking these days. Drinking blood. I didn't see that one coming back in Gretchenville.

'Rum and lemonade?' I suggested. 'I'm not sure if I've made it to your liking, but–'

'The moon is powerful tonight,' Luke said, looking out the window at the light streaming down, then holding up his human left hand and examining it.

'It is,' I said and abandoned my arranged table of treats. I stepped towards him and, two flesh and blood humans, we stood close to each other, frozen in place for a moment. Then Luke gently slid his sabre into the metal sheath hanging from his leather belt, and I stepped back again and took him in, from the top of the deep-blue Union soldier cap to the rest of the neat dress uniform he had been buried in, right down to his leather boots. The gleaming buttons of his frock coat were done up to the neck, and without delay I began unbuttoning them while he stood watching me, the vulnerability in his blue eyes melting a special place in my heart. I helped him take off his heavy frock coat, placing it on my bed covers and leaving him in the white shirt he'd brought from home when he joined the Lincoln Cavalry. (Uniforms back then had not been all that, well, uniform – at least not underneath.)

I tilted my head up to his and reached my arms around his neck. We kissed. His lips were warm and tender, his flesh against mine a delight to behold. Warm. Solid. Here, magically, was a body for Luke, thrumming with veins and blood and sensations. I leaned into him, pulled him in to me, feeling a heart beating against me. His mouth was liquid and hot, our passionate coming together quite unlike the misty kisses that thrilled me on other nights.

When we came up for air, he said, 'Miss Pandora, I'd wondered if you would call on me.' He admitted these doubts as if it were a confession.

'Of course, Luke! It is the full moon. Of course I would call on you,' I exclaimed, and kissed him again on his soft, human lips.

I only ever got to experience him in his carnate form in these special moments. It was up to the moon and its magick. But as for what I did have control over – I knew what I wanted. I'd made my decision, and this was the time. Tonight was the night. What better night than the full Blue Moon to have this long-awaited first?

'After the other night ...' He trailed off, brows pulled up forlornly in the middle.

'You mean a couple of nights ago when I had to go and work at the museum shoot? I am sorry about how we parted. Perhaps I didn't express myself well, but I'm not good at mixing my human work life and my, well, this private life of mine. They don't sit well together.'

'Miss Pandora, I know it is difficult for you. You are a living woman, a young woman, and you deserve a real man ... a living man.' He'd seen me coming home with Jay late at night from the Met. Of course that would make him think I'd been out with him, rather than surprised by him on the shoot.

'Don't start with that again,' I said and shook my head. 'You are a "real man". There's nothing I want that you lack. Luke, I have summoned you so that we can be together ... and to tell you something important,' I explained.

'Miss Pandora. I mean it about Jay. I understand completely–'

'To the contrary, dear Luke, clearly you do not understand. I have been thinking hard on this and I will not be seeing Jay Rockwell again. Not romantically, anyway. I want you. I only want you.'

'But Miss Pandora, he is an eligible match for you.' *According to mortals*, he seemed ready to add. 'He is mortal and living.' It sounded a bit painful for him to admit this, like it was a flaw of his to not need oxygen.

'Those things don't mean much to me anymore.' I placed my hands on his strong shoulders and sat Luke down on the edge of my bed, looking into those bright blue eyes and marvelling at the solid feel of him under my fingers. 'And I've already told Jay it's over. He took it pretty well, actually.' That might be in part because he didn't even remember some of the time we dated, on account of his being 'erased'. Anyway, it didn't matter now. We'd had some good times together but it was over, and looking at Luke on the edge of my bed, I had absolutely no regrets whatsoever. 'Jay and I won't be dating anymore,' I said firmly.

'And Deus?' Luke responded.

Now this threw me. I instinctively withdrew, taking a step back. The conversation about Jay had been one I expected, but Deus? I flushed terribly, and my cheeks stung. 'Ah, you would have seen me flying with him last night,' I said aloud, realising.

'He has been in your room often. I thought perhaps –'

Often. Deus has been in my room often. Gulp. 'You thought perhaps what?' I dared to ask.

'Please understand, Miss Pandora, your time is your own and I do not wish to spy, but because I am your spirit guide I am often aware of your movements, in case you are in peril or require me. It sometimes makes me aware of other things, however. I have no claim on you and I would never assume to, but when I knew a vampire was coming into your room, I was worried for you.'

Luke did not trust Sanguine. I can't say I blamed him for that. He'd even helped me escape the clutches of the Sanguine Fledgling Samantha when I'd first arrived in Spektor and hadn't even known vampires existed outside folk myth and popular culture. 'And . . .?' I prompted.

'Well, once I knew you were not in peril I allowed you your privacy,' he told me, head bowed. 'I am sorry to have brought it up. It was not the right thing. I am sorry, Miss Pandora.'

'No, no, Luke, it is good that we clear the air. You have given me a chance to correct your misconceptions. It's not what you think.'

'In my day to have a gentleman in a lady's bedroom meant …'

'No, Luke, we aren't sleeping together. I'm not sleeping with anyone, well, except you when we hold each other at night sometimes. No, he is coming to my room because I am simply drinking his blood,' I explained. The words sounded quite mad when I said them, but it was true. 'It's strictly a blood thing,' I said with emphasis. 'I promise you.'

Confused, he stood up from the bed and stared.

'I know it sounds crazy but apparently I am strengthening myself for what is to come. That is all. And it makes me feel unexplainable … *sensations* sometimes, sure, and that's confusing, but it's just a blood thing. Strictly. Cross my heart.' I did a little move with my fingers, crossing over my left breast.

'Miss Pandora, it is not my business. I apologise,' he went on, clearly confused and embarrassed. He was standing stiffly now, as was I. Oh, this was going all wrong, not at all as I'd intended.

'Please don't apologise,' I said. 'I'm glad you know. It's not like that. I'm not in love with Deus.'

So, Luke had kept his distance over the past two days, after our parting in the lift, thinking I didn't want him around and would rather spend time with Deus? I searched his face. He looked humble, forlorn, confused, yes, but not angry. No jealousy. No possessiveness. That was Lieutenant Luke for you. I wondered if he'd been like this in life as well, or if these were traits he had acquired after death. There weren't that many living guys who were like that, from what I gathered. Jay was always saying I made him jealous with the tiniest things, and that didn't seem healthy.

'I'm in love with you, Luke. I won't deny it.'

He'd been looking down at his tall, polished boots, and now he looked up. 'I am in love with you, Miss Pandora.'

'Then that works well,' I murmured as I leaned in and pressed my lips to his. Maybe talking wasn't the best way forward right now, I thought, and kissed him again. Oh, the feeling of him in carnate form was something I was unused to, and it thrilled me. It was a different bodily experience, a different aspect of him.

'Would you like to stay the night with me tonight?' I whispered huskily in his ear. 'Even with what I have told you?' I added.

'If you want me,' he replied, though he still seemed uncertain of my feelings about the vampire.

In answer I sat him down again and removed his white shirt, peeling it off his broad shoulders and down over his tanned arms while he sat motionless on my bed. He was still in his pants and boots, and I realised his cap was on. 'May I?' I asked, and gently took off his Union cap, freeing a lock of sandy hair that fell down across one eye. I placed it on the night table with care, and returned to my soldier. That vulnerable look was still in his eyes, but now he seemed somewhat less uncertain about my feelings. He looked expectant, aroused.

Good goddess, he looked so human, so alive, so flesh and blood. The spirit I loved, here with me as a whole man by the magick bestowed on him, by the magick of the moon and whatever fate it was that had united us. His arms were tanned and muscled, with fine blond hairs on the forearm. I saw veins in his wrists that seemed to pump blood. His chest and stomach were lean and strong.

I pulled my dress up over my knees and straddled his thighs. 'Luke Thomas, I want to make love,' I said. 'I want to make love with you. If you want me, too.'

I'd often dreamed of uttering those words. I never had, until now.

Luke had reached one arm around me, his hand cradling my back, about to bring me in for a kiss, and at my words he let go and sat back, leaning on his strong arms, looking serious and a touch startled, blue eyes large. 'Miss Pandora, are you sure?' he said, his tanned face etched with worry. We'd spent nights together in the past two months, holding each other tight. But this was different. A milestone. And he was flesh tonight. We could, well, we could do what billions of lovers have done before us. I had waited long enough. I was ready. I ran my hands over the sculpture of his body – his shoulders and arms, his triceps and the fine muscles of his wrists and hands. I noticed little scars on his skin that I hadn't seen before, or were not as visible when he was in spirit form, and one by one I kissed them – what had once been a cut at his shoulder, the little marks on his side that might have been buckshot.

I took my time, felt my body responding. I was sure. Yes, I was.

I pulled Luke back up to me, face to face, and pressed my lips against his. Our mouths melted together as we kissed deeply.

'Do I seem sure?' I said.

'Anything you want, Miss Pandora. You know that I am yours, always.'

'You want this, too?' I asked. I felt him rise beneath me, his breeches growing tight. 'I feel like that's a yes,' I whispered in his ear.

'Yes, Miss Pandora, I do want to be with you also,' he said softly, in his formal way. 'I … I feel that I should ask for your hand.'

'You *have* my hand,' I responded, placing my right hand in his, though I knew what he meant. 'Luke, we are bonded more strongly now than any ceremony devised by men could achieve,' I whispered. 'Besides, much has changed since … well, since you were a young man. We need not have a ceremony officiated by a stranger to be united. I am Pandora English,' I added, touching my chest, 'and you are Second Lieutenant Luke Thomas, my spirit guide, and we are bonded.' I placed my hand over his heart, and felt it beating beneath his warm chest.

Watching my face for further consent, Lieutenant Luke stroked my back with one hand, and with the other, he pulled at the buttons of my shirtdress and it opened up. One shoulder at a time, I slipped out of it and then stood before him so it could fall to the floor. Standing naked in front of Luke, in front of a whole, fully formed flesh-and-blood man, was exhilarating, exciting, yet I felt safe, and I closed my eyes as Luke reached out for me and ran a hand over my belly, tenderly, tracing the curve of my hip and my pubic bone, and sending shivers of pleasure through me.

He stood to meet me, his shirt off and his bare chest pressing against mine. I reached down and helped him with his leather belt, which was heavy with his sabre, and he placed it on the bed and removed his breeches and boots as I watched, feeling the moonlight on my naked back.

My curtains and window were open to receive the night air, and moonlight streamed into my bedroom. Luke looked perfect in the moonlight. Just perfect. Like a hero on celluloid come to life in the room with me. Sandy hair, chiselled face, tanned skin and a soft, warm mouth. The hairs on his chest were soft and light, and beneath that chest I could feel his heart beating. It was beautiful to kiss him when he was in spirit form – otherworldly – but this was something else. His body felt warm, his mouth wet and hungry.

By morning he would be spirit again. But we had tonight. And I wanted this. I really did.

In that first breath after I opened my eyes in the morning I expected to find him there next to me, but my Civil War hero was gone – of course – replaced by rays of late spring sunshine streaming across the crumpled linen of my four-poster bed, and a new sense of myself.

Lieutenant Luke.

With a touch of reluctance I sat up, rubbed my eyes and swung my legs out from under the sheets. As my bare feet slid down, making for the hardwood floor, my left big toe touched on hard metal, and I broke into a broad smile. I knew what it was without even looking – the tip of Luke's cavalry sword. Though he was long since dead, Lieutenant Luke had not been a figment of my imagination, exactly. He had been here, full-bodied and beautiful, even if he was spirit again today. He had been my companion through the night, my lover at last, and his sword was always there, under my bed for protection.

The Blue Moon had brought me treasure and respite. It was Friday now, I recalled with a jolt. Again, I had woken just minutes before my alarm and it was time to get ready for work. Today I would speak with Morticia. Tomorrow was the opening of HATSHEPSUT.

And I was a new woman.

'Race you!'

Right on noon, Morticia and I half speed walked, half ran the four blocks to our lunch together, laughing as we went, hands over our heads as we were rained upon by a light spring shower. When we sprinted under the big Fanelli Café neon sign on the corner of Mercer and Prince we were damp with fresh rain and a touch breathless.

'Quick! I see a free table,' I said, and we went inside and threw ourselves into the wooden seats at the one available table. We found menus already on the red-and-white chequered tablecloth. 'We don't have that long, but I think they serve pretty fast here.' The bar seats were filling fast for lunch. Soon a line would start at the door.

Though I had not eaten at Fanelli's before, I'd seen the sign many times, even before I'd first set foot in New York. It was a bit famous, not because their pub food was so different or extraordinary, good as it was, but because they had been serving customers since 1847. My lover Lieutenant Luke had died in 1861. That meant that had he been in New York he might even have had a beer here – a truly surreal thought. The bar inside was carved of magnificently aged dark wood and decorated with countless bottles, the walls covered in ageing images, framed and placed one next to the other to take up nearly every available inch of space. Fans spun above our heads, dangling from a pressed tin ceiling, wooden chairs creaked and the place buzzed with conversation – as it had, I supposed, for nearly one hundred and seventy-five years. This café had survived Manhattan life for nearly two centuries. Did these walls recall the last Revolution of the Dead?

How much longer would Manhattan life survive? Perhaps Fanelli's would still be around when the dead walked freely on the streets outside and pulled beers on tap.

'Cool,' Morticia said, breaking my unexpectedly morbid train of thought. She was looking at the table in front of her as if she might be the only person in New York who hadn't eaten in a restaurant all year. Come to think of it, that made two of us. Well, apart from precious few dates with Jay, but that was its own story. My life involved a lot of eating alone, I realised. The ability to actually ingest food had undeniably been a mark in Jay's favour. That and being visible to others. But that was over now and somehow I didn't feel sad about it in the slightest. No, that had been a necessary step to take, I'd decided. I'd shed any last lingering ideas about a 'human' romance, and the space that had opened in my heart had allowed something quite extraordinary in. Luke. All of Luke. I felt warm thinking of him and our night entwined on my bed sheets.

'This place is so famous. It's been around forever,' Morticia told me. 'It used to have a brothel upstairs apparently, and it was a speakeasy during Prohibition. And the Beat poets gathered here in the fifties. How cool, right? If the walls could talk,' she exclaimed.

Gee, I hoped they wouldn't. I already had enough going on.

We hailed a waiter and hastily ordered a grilled chicken club sandwich to share, as they were apparently huge (and 'fancy' Morticia said). I ordered a soda while Morticia ordered table waters. Tap. The waiter – a young man with a goatee – frowned at this, surely seeing that a big tip was unlikely for our table, but it hardly mattered. I took a sip of my water and drank in the atmosphere, the aged photographs of boxers and historic bar licences crowding the walls.

'You look so great today,' my companion told me. 'Is something different? Your hair, or ...?'

Luke ...

A little tingle went up my spine as I thought of him again, of our night together in my room with the moonlight streaming in. I smiled, I couldn't help it. Something in that smile gave it away.

Morticia noticed the look on my face. She tilted her head, and uttered a long *oooooh* sound. '*Really?*' she said. '*Did you?*'

She knew I was a virgin – or had been. Don't ask me how she knew but it seemed like everyone did, Celia and Deus included. *Pandora English, nineteen-year-old virgin no more.*

'Roses Guy?' she guessed with her wide eyes even wider than usual. Roses Guy was how she often referred to Jay, on account of the expensive bouquet he'd sent me at work.

I shook my head. Not Roses Guy.

'Really? Who?' She looked positively fascinated. 'Anyone I know? Who is this mystery guy? Or girl?'

I avoided her question, still smiling. 'Lunch is on me, I should have mentioned,' I said, feeling happy about my likely upcoming raise, among other developments. 'So if you want more than water and a shared sandwich, really just order what you like.'

'That will be plenty,' she insisted, though I knew she was pretty broke and that would have factored into her choice. 'The sandwich will be enough. I do hope you'll tell me about this mystery lover. But more importantly, *how was it?*'

I smiled again, feeling a bit happy with myself. 'Well, if you really want to know, it was great. Really great. But I'm not here to talk about that right now.'

'Oh, of course,' she said, perhaps chastened, then added with a mischievous glint in her eye, 'I hope it's not like the movies and some masked boogeyman comes after you now. Ha ha. Or your hot boyfriend loses his soul or something. Because, you know, like, that's what happens in every movie ever. Why do they always make losing your virginity so bad for women?'

I laughed along, if a little uneasily. Luke had become

possessed in the past, though not by a demon. Necromancers were an issue.

'Ah yes, eighties and nineties cinema,' I said, sounding a bit less casual than intended. 'And *Buffy*. That really was a trope, hey?' Yes, the perils of losing one's virginity seemed quite something, if popular culture was anything to go by. And if your boyfriend didn't turn into a demon, or you weren't stabbed to death by a serial killer, you could always have your powers taken away by 'the gods', like Jane Seymour's fortune-telling priestess in *Live and Let Die*. Would that happen to me? I didn't think so.

For my part, I felt powerful. Yes, somehow I felt powerful, and I wondered why we always couched women's first experiences in terms of 'losing' virginity rather than gaining something.

Oh Luke. I couldn't wait to see him after work.

I looked at my watch. 'I want to tell you something about myself,' I told Morticia, changing the conversation, because if I really got started on Luke I wasn't going to be able to get back on track. I'd thought long and hard in the past day about how to begin this conversation. It would have to be the first of several, if it went okay. 'Morticia, I want you to know that since I was a kid, I have been able to see ghosts.' I spoke in a low voice, saying what I'd practised. It was weird to tell her but I figured if anyone at the office would understand, she would. I watched her face for a reaction.

'Really? Real ghosts?' Those eyes of hers were huge, but delighted.

I nodded. 'Yes. It's been a rather, well, big part of my life.'

Understatement.

'How cool,' she responded. 'I try to contact ghosts sometimes. I'm not sure, though, if I have. I got a Ouija board a while back. And well, I think I saw a ghost once at this cemetery in the Bronx. At Woodland. It wasn't Miles Davis or anything, but it was this figure of a man.'

'Oh. Interesting.'

'My parents thought I was being foolish, and didn't understand why I wanted to hang about in a cemetery anyway. But death is part of life,' she said. 'You know?'

'It is,' I agreed. Well, this first part was easy. But the rest ...

'Is that what you wanted to tell me?' Morticia asked.

'Part of it, yes. And this is just for you to know. I don't really want the whole office talking about how I see the departed all the time.'

'Of course not! I understand. And I think it's cool you see ghosts,' she added in a low voice. 'I wish I did.'

Careful what you wish for.

Well, that was good. We both believed in ghosts, and that made her different than most. That was progress, of a kind. I had guessed as much after our previous conversations, and her comment about the Met ghost tour, but there was believing in ghosts and then there was *living with ghosts,* and that wasn't quite the same thing.

I absentmindedly scratched my neck, and that brought to mind Deus. Should I tell her about the Sanguine? No. Too soon. Besides, it was the rising up of the dead, not the undead that she needed to be warned about. I would take this one step at a time. Telling her I'd spent the night with a Civil War soldier was probably not a good move for right now either.

'Since we are going to the Met together tomorrow I wanted to let you know about this … ability of mine. To see ghosts, I mean. I think I saw some on the shoot, and I just, well, I just want you to be prepared in case I see any spirits there when we go tomorrow night.'

Now I had Morticia's attention, I could see her face change. She came over serious, thinking on that. Perhaps this was getting uncomfortable. Just then our sandwich arrived with two plates and some cutlery. The waiter placed it all on our table and retreated without a word. I looked around me. No one was staring. No one was overhearing me. This was going okay. This was a start.

'I don't mean to scare you,' I whispered when the waiter left, then cut our sandwich in half with an overly blunt knife. It made a bit of a mess, but I put the nicer looking half on a plate for her and pushed it across. 'Morticia, I just felt I needed to let you know. I think that's what the green blurs and things were on the photographs. I think they were ghosts.'

Now Morticia's face became animated again. She seemed to have found a comfortable frame of reference for our discussion. 'Oh, that is so cool! You think that's what it was?'

'Yes. I think that's what it was. Spirits of some kind.'

'That's great.'

Great wasn't quite how I'd put it.

We tucked into our food, and I thought on what to say next.

'You won't look at me different at work?' I asked my companion before we continued.

'Of course not! You are, like, my only friend in New York.

And I think it's cool you can see spirits. I've always believed they are there.'

'Thanks,' I said, and touched her hand. I took another bite, and when I swallowed I thought I would broach the next part of the subject. 'I don't know if I've mentioned this, but I live in Spektor. It's a suburb that's kind of in Upper Manhattan, north of Central Park. It's a bit of an odd place.'

'Yeah, I think you mentioned the reception is terrible there. And that you are on Addams Avenue? So funny, with my name being Morticia, after the Charles Addams creation!'

'Yeah.' *Too soon to tell her about Charles Addams? Yes, too soon.* 'There's a lot of ghost activity up there. A lot of supernatural activity,' I explained.

'Seriously?'

'Seriously. I know we don't have much time today, and we'll have to sprint back to work soon, but I just wanted to take this opportunity to let you know this stuff about me.' I caught her eye. 'It's a ... well, a big part of my life. I appreciate how well you've taken it.'

'Are you kidding me? I think it's awesome.'

'So, you still want to go to the Met tomorrow? Even though I potentially saw ghosts there?'

She nodded enthusiastically. 'Hell yeah I do. That just makes it more awesome. But, um, I should let you know my phone isn't working?' She held it up. 'Out of credit for the month. But just let me know where to meet you and I will be there with bells on! It's going to be so awesome.'

I hoped that would be the case. I really did.

CHAPTER EIGHT

After work I took the subway home and I entered Celia's penthouse, excited to be back in Spektor and closer to Luke and the night. Unlike the evening before, my great-aunt was in her usual reading nook, waiting.

'And how are you this evening?' came her voice.

'Hi, Great-Aunt Celia. I'm well, thank you.' I had found myself grinning all day, and I tried but failed to keep my smile at bay. Certainly that smile had given me away to Morticia.

'You put in your order with Harold, I hear?'

'For the shabtis? Yes, I did. How did you know?'

My great-aunt leaned forward and raised an eyebrow in response. Oh, she did prefer to be opaque. 'Harold is a very clever man,' she said. 'He can get nearly anything, in my experience. Do you know what you intend to do with these shabtis?'

I shrugged. 'Honestly, I'm not sure. But …'

She nodded and I wondered what was going on behind those veiled, ageless eyes.

'Um, about the other night,' I began. We hadn't spoken since I came across her drinking Deus's blood.

'Oh yes, was it all you'd dreamed?' she asked, grinning. Beneath her veil, those eyes of hers sparkled. I got her meaning immediately. She was talking about last night. It was my grin, no doubt. Oh, and the fact that she could read my mind as clearly as a living person could read time (the dead apparently couldn't, Luke had explained), and there was but one thing my mind kept focusing on today.

I blushed like a beet at the thought of Lieutenant Luke. 'Oh, yes. So you know.' I paused. 'Of course you know. You know everything.' I ran a hand absentmindedly across my collarbone, and Celia's eyes followed it. It was a sensual gesture, I realised, little goosebumps coming up across my chest. I really was an open book, wasn't I? Even without her powers of mind-reading she'd have me pegged. 'It was . . .' I stopped. 'Well, honestly it was indescribable. Wonderful and utterly indescribable.'

Celia nodded. 'As it should be.'

I was still blushing. I could feel it, and I knew Celia could see it, and I knew Celia knew that I knew she could see it. But really, I shouldn't be embarrassed. I was nearly twenty years old, a woman, and I'd made love with someone I cared deeply for. I had longed for him and it had been magickal, literally and figuratively, and who could ask for more than that?

I cleared my throat. 'Great-Aunt Celia, what I'd wanted to ask about was what happened the other night. You know, on Wednesday when I came across you and Deus, and you were drinking . . .'

'Yes, Pandora.' Her tone was even.

'First of all, thank you. Thank you for your patience. I was quite . . .'

'Yes, you were.' One eyebrow was raised.

'I am sorry for that. I perhaps didn't handle it well.'

Celia crossed one leg over the other, her silk stockings rustling. 'You handled it fine, all things considered, Pandora. Though I'd thank you not to insult Deus's blood again any time soon, and certainly not when he is right here with us.'

'Gosh, I am sorry. I hadn't known he was there, and in any case you're right.' When would I, um, summon him again? I wondered. To drink? Was it a weekly thing? Every couple of days? Luke had said Deus was in my room quite frequently. Just how frequently? 'Anyway ...' I took a breath. 'Great-Aunt Celia, you muttered "Hesiod" at some point and it has stuck in my mind, like it may be important. I wondered why you mentioned him?'

'Hesiod? Oh yes, dear, foolish Hesiod.' For a second she sneered with her crimson-painted lips, then they fell back into even lines again.

'Foolish?' I repeated back, surprised. Hesiod was one of the earliest Greek poets, known as the father of Greek didactic poetry. (As usual, there was no acknowledged 'mother', of poetry or mathematics, medicine, science, architecture ... the list went on. Though there was always 'invention' – not a discipline or a profession, but something life couldn't exist without.)

My great-aunt sat up and adjusted her veil. 'Well, as I recollect, you were at the time lamenting that all the women in the old origin tales were bringers of evil, pestilence, pain, destroyers of the world and so on. Pandora, Eve, Medea,' she explained.

I'd thought that, yes. But I hadn't said it, I recalled. She'd been reading my mind.

'If I muttered Hesiod's name then, it was no doubt with frustration, because the man was hellbent on twisting Pandora's glorious tale as a powerful goddess or demigoddess, giver of life, "giver of gifts" and "gifted one" into something quite different – "one who brought all the evil into the world". It was quite unfair of him, and just because they found his writings and not those of someone else, his uneducated, patriarchal view holds as some kind of authentic origin story. I assure you it is not.'

I was gobsmacked. 'It isn't?'

'Good goddess, no. Pandora, you are not named for the bringer of all evil – some silly woman who couldn't help but open a box brimming with everything awful, thereby cursing the entire world. I mean *really*. Does such a tale seem realistic to you? This is not her true origin story, which dates back much further than Hesiod's telling. Pandora was a figure of feminine power, not a cursed and weak girl in some cautionary tale about the need for male control. That's just propaganda for later Athens, when the balance of the sexes shifted and we plunged deeply into patriarchy. Think about it. It's absurd. Her name literally means "all gifted" and "giver of gifts". It does not mean wretched girl, bringer of evil, impulsive fool. That Hesiod's version is taken as some kind of authority . . .' At this she shook her head, clearly disgusted.

My jaw must have hung open for some time. I'd spent my whole life up to that point lamenting my parents' choice of name for me. All this time, all these years, I had not realised what my name meant. Yes, Celia had said my name translated as 'gifted', but it had not hit home that the entire backstory to it was twisted. I quietly collapsed back into my seat, blinking as if the world had shifted before my eyes.

'You were not bestowed with this name as some kind of cruelty, Pandora,' my great-aunt assured me. 'Quite the contrary. Had your mother lived longer, you might have talked about it, and she would have dispelled your misconceptions.'

I brought a hand to my mouth. *Mom.* Tears welled up in the corners of my eyes, my sight blurring.

'She would not do such a thing to you, her only daughter, her only child, naming you for someone cursed. No. She did explain many of the myths to you as a child though, did she not?' my great-aunt said.

'Yes, she did. I even … I even have some of the books now. I just, well, I was so young that I can't recall exactly what she said, and I've been teased about my name for so long. I kept hearing the other version. They only teach the other version.'

'But that wouldn't have been from her.'

'Possibly not,' I recalled, screwing up my forehead and trying to think back. I'd heard the other version so often I suppose I came to believe it, like everyone else. I hadn't questioned it.

'Fools. Those who teased you and told you this other version are fools. They haven't any idea of your power, or your gifts, Pandora.'

And perhaps I didn't, either. But that was changing. I had the power of a medium for speaking with ghosts – always had done whether I wanted to or not – and according to Deus I had the power of necromancy. I took this as meaning I could communicate with the dead, which was clear enough and an important gift for The Seventh. By now I could not doubt that

I also possessed the power of telekinesis, or mind movement. I could control the physical world with my mind to a degree, but under what circumstances? What other gifts did I have at my fingertips without even knowing?

I was quiet in contemplation for some time, considering all this, and then I turned and looked out the tall windows again. The moon was bright.

'Do you think there is . . .?' I began.

'Sufficient strength in the moon tonight? Perhaps,' my great-aunt offered.

A thrill ran through my body at the thought. *Luke.*

'You will see him tonight. That is good. And I believe you've been thinking about the portal, also?'

I'd been putting off descending into the unpleasant lower regions of the mansion and checking. The last time Celia had been there with me things had been rather dark and dire, no doubt about it. I had returned to put a bolt on a broken door in Barrett's study and after that had been happy to keep my distance while I could. Certainly I had not wanted to go down there last night, when the full Blue Moon was at its most glorious, not when there were other things on my mind. But Celia was right, I should make time tonight. She did tend to be right about things, my wise old aunt.

'Yes, you have been thinking on it, for good reason, I believe. It's not a half bad idea, Pandora darling, though I dare say it may not be pleasant to return to that place.'

This was a place like no other.

Celia's mansion in Spektor had not always been hers. It was built in the late 1800s, decades before her birth, by the infamous psychical scientist Edmund Barrett. He'd been a genius, albeit one of mixed reputation in his day. The experiments in his later career and his death by spontaneous combustion had always been surrounded in mystery, and what was even less known about him was that in those later years he'd built a secret laboratory in the bowels of this mansion in Spektor, having chosen the spot to be right at one of the hidden entrances to the Underworld. (Just imagine the real estate ad for that one: 'Large Victorian mansion with oodles of character. Fixer upper. Great views of the mist. Location, location, location . . .' No wonder Celia had gone for it.)

Where better to conduct Barrett's experiments as a psychical researcher than right at a portal to the Underworld? There were rumoured to be many entrances, and though I knew not where with any certainty, there had been tales over the centuries involving the Hekla volcano in Iceland, the Actun Tunichil Muknal cave in Belize, Pluto's Gate in Turkey, the Cave of Sibyl in Italy, the Cape Matapan Caves in Greece and more, as well as places of infamy the ancient Celts knew of. These portals were shrouded in mystery, and it was difficult to find real information on them. True portals for the dead did not like to be found by the living, and, of course, the living did tend to enjoy entertaining ghost stories as long as they weren't too 'real', so how many of these rumoured places were legitimate gates to the Underworld and how many were mere legend, I could not say. I thought the eight hells of Beppu in Japan, for example, though magnificent, were likely too heavily touristed to be operating for spirits. But who knew? The Chinoike Jigoku – or Blood Pond Hell – seemed quite compelling.

But this one, right here in Upper Manhattan, was absolutely legit, as I knew all too well, and it accounted for why the suburb was invisible to most. Portals to the Underworld do not like to be found by anyone but the dead and the psychopomps (the guides for the souls). The dead liked their secrets.

And now, holding a sabre from a second lieutenant in the Lincoln Cavalry, I summoned my own spirit guide. 'Lieutenant Luke Thomas,' I declared with purpose, and my obsidian ring warmed, along with my pendant, and the familiar misty cool descended. Soon Luke was holding my hands over his sword, and to my delight I found that he was flesh. Perhaps we had one more night of the moon's strength to enjoy.

'Luke.'

'Miss Pandora.' He took his sword and slid it into its sheath. 'Are you okay?'

'I am.' I grinned at the sight of him.

'You feel okay after …?'

'I do,' I told him and pressed my lips to his. He leaned into me and embraced me, feeling warm and alive, his leather boots creaking and clothes shifting in ways I did not notice when he was in spirit form. In his passionate embrace I was lifted slightly off the floor. 'I don't think I've ever felt better, actually,' I whispered, stroking the warm skin on his neck and the barely detectable stubble at his clean-shaven jaw.

'I am so pleased you are, uh, flesh tonight,' I said, though my words made me blush a touch. Making him flesh the day after or before did not always work, as it depended on the strength of that particular full moon. While a 'full' moon really was only a moment in time, the moon's strength and visible brightness lasted before and after that moment, sometimes for a day or so on either side. Some strength was evidently left.

I explained our task of checking on the portal beneath the mansion and, apprehensive, we took the small lift down to the lobby level. I used the skeleton key to open the hidden door beneath the curving mezzanine stairs and we walked the narrow, dark corridor that led to the secret side of the great mansion, the side where Dr Barrett's laboratory was. Neither of us wanted to be there after what had played out on our previous visit, yet as we neared the portal I felt a kind of charge. Not just the adrenaline of fear, but something else. Power? Was I feeling a kind of power?

'I can feel the Agitation,' Luke told me, and I held his hand tightly.

'What does it feel like?' I asked. 'I feel something too.'

'It feels like I'm being … pulled,' he said, and I felt a fresh stab of concern.

'How do you mean, exactly?' I asked. Would he be pulled two ways? In the Revolution, would he be the ally I expected, even though he was … dead? And I was alive?

'Miss Pandora, I don't think I can explain, exactly.'

I frowned. We stood in Dr Barrett's lab for a moment, and I tried not to look at the steel table and the terrifying chair with its leather straps. This place made me uneasy. I knew my way around now, having been down more than once, and

I wasted no time entering Barrett's old study – a charred place chaotic with papers and books, and evidence of the fire that had consumed him in life. It had a dark feeling about it, possibly even worse than the fascinating but eerie lab it was attached to, but this was not my final destination. I walked up and paused near the last door, still holding Luke's hand. It was a small door, secured with a bolt and lock I had put on it myself. There was some reassurance seeing that was locked, but of course that was a false reassurance.

'I need to check the portal now,' I told Luke, feeling excited and on edge as I unlocked the bolt. 'Do you think you can accompany me? If you feel you can't I will understand. I can go in alone.'

'I will accompany you,' my soldier told me, jaw clenched. 'Miss Pandora, I will do anything I can to assist you. As your spirit guide I wish I could do more. If there is something wrong beyond this door, some fresh danger, I'll not have you face it alone.'

Biting my lip, I opened the door and we carefully stepped through. The smell of sulphur hit my nose immediately, and despite having been in this place before, my eyes widened at the sight before me.

The vast space beyond the small door was awe-inspiring, both chilling and beautiful, and it was something few living mortals ever did or could see. The supernatural world preferred its secrets, and something of this magnitude would never be willingly offered up for view to the living, for seeing this space, seeing *this*, left little doubt of the existence of an Otherworld or a mighty world for the dead.

Before us were twenty-five broad stone steps leading down through a giant, echoing chamber of natural rock and disappearing into a pool of dark water. This was spectacular enough, but it was what was beyond it that really chilled the soul – some thirty feet in was an immense, flat rock wall, carved into which was a circular portal surrounded by some kind of runes. The entire chamber was lit by torches that seemed never to go out. Stalactites hung from the ceiling, stalagmites reaching up from the cavern floor, and on either side of the portal were stacks of bones – human bones it seemed, though I had never hung around long enough to check – and on either side were towering stone statues of muscled gods – one female, one male – each with fearsome death heads and a gold staff in their colossal hands. The sight of them chilled me to my core, and yet I felt a kind of power within me building.

Today the cavernous space seemed quiet, the giant wrought-iron torches glowing with their ever-lit red flames. Not green, but red like common flames. This was a relief. I'd seen these dark shallow waters filling with the dead, corpses risen from the graves of Manhattan, from the streets themselves. But for now the space was still. It appeared the portal was closed.

My shoulders dropped. So there was time yet.

'Luke, we should –' I began, but when I turned to my companion I stopped short. Lieutenant Luke had come over strange, his normally bright blue eyes black in the firelight of the cavern. On instinct I leaped away from him, my heart thumping in my chest. I'd seen his eyes change colour before and it had not been good. This, though, seemed different. He was not green-eyed as he'd been when the necromancer had controlled him and he'd been set on me. What did this mean exactly? 'Luke?' I ventured. 'Luke, are you okay?' I was backing up towards the door. Oh, I really should not have brought him into the cavern. It was too close to the portal. This had been a mistake …

'Beware, Pandora English, The Seventh,' he announced in a deep, formal tone, his voice sounding distant and warped. 'The Cobra Queen has come. Tomorrow, she wakes.'

The Cobra Queen? I thought, and my mind hit upon fragments of my nightmares, the hissing snakes, the glowing green serpents I'd seen in the mist about the Met. 'Who is she? Luke?'

At the sound of my voice Luke, my spirit guide, seemed to awaken from the trance. 'What did I say?' he asked me, frowning, face etched with concern. 'I believe I conveyed a message. What was it I said, Miss Pandora?'

My shoulders slumped. 'You do not recall?' I stopped backing away and stood my ground. Searching his eyes, I found them blue once more. He was back. For now. 'Well, Luke, you said the Cobra Queen wakes tomorrow.'

Tomorrow, the day of the Met launch. I thought of the exhibition my mother had cryptically warned me about. Hatshepsut had not primarily been queen but a king – a pharaoh. It was one of the most unique things about her. But she had been a queen also. And the cobra reference was not clear. What would she have to do with cobras?

'Does the name mean anything to you?' I asked. 'A Cobra Queen?'

He shook his head and frowned. 'I do not know the villain who comes.'

'Well, that's helpful,' I snapped, my frustration peaking. I had already faced the worst creatures to come to Spektor and Manhattan and it wasn't over yet. Vampires, thousands of spiders, the roaming dead. *My mother can tell me that I am The Seventh but she can't tell me what I need to do. The Revolution of the Dead is coming soon, but no one can say when. And now the Cobra Queen is here, or coming tomorrow, and we don't know who she is or where? Come on!*

I could see I'd hurt Lieutenant Luke's feelings. He held his hands in front of his body, head bowed. 'I am sorry,' I said and embraced him. 'I'm just under a lot of pressure and feeling pretty lost with all this. Perhaps we should leave here. I have seen what I needed to, and I feel . . . strange. The portal is closed. Let's go.'

'Miss Pandora, I am sorry I cannot tell you more,' he said. 'I feel strange here, also. If you are satisfied the portal is closed, perhaps you are right and we should make haste to leave this place. May I wait on you tonight? Perhaps provide you with some sustenance?'

His old-fashioned way of talking often amused me, and it was sweet. (Perhaps that was how my colleagues had regarded my small town way of speaking when I'd first arrived from Gretchenville?) I took his hand and we left the cavern and the late Dr Barrett's study and laboratory. I was feeling unsettled and unsure of what I could do to prepare for the next day. Being The Seventh was very strange. I was the youngest of those in my circle, in some cases by several centuries, yet everyone was counting on me. It felt backwards, somehow. In so many ways they ultimately could not help me, either, or inform me. Not my mother. Not Celia. Not my spirit guide. It really was going to be up to me in the end. What had Deus said? That they would all rely on me? My mother had essentially mirrored the same words after a lifetime spent trying to deny the truth of what her daughter would need to do.

I was terrified of what was to come. Absolutely terrified. And this Cobra Queen? Whatever or whoever she was, she was sure to be unaffected by rice. I was going to need to learn some new tricks.

Chapter Nine

The second night we made love was somehow more magical than the first.

We'd returned from the cavern unsettled, but once I had Luke in Celia's penthouse I found myself wanting to draw him into my room. I'd near leaped on the poor soldier once I'd closed the door, and our lovemaking had been unbridled, utterly instinctual, our initial caution tossed aside. Now, in the aftermath, I lay flat on my back on top of the bed covers, body warm and tingling, one arm reaching over to touch Luke's naked form, which was dewy with light perspiration. His warm chest rose and fell, heart still beating fast. So hurried had I been, that I'd not even pulled the bed covers back, and our clothes were strewn across the hardwood floor. My lover was without a stitch of clothing – I'd seen to that – and somehow my bra had remained on, though only just. I sat up slightly to pull it the rest of the way off, and lay back dreamily, opening my body to the night air coming in through the open window. What a deeply satisfying feeling of sensuality this was. Foreign. Exciting. Free.

Luke turned his head to look at me once more, his wonderfully human face alight with passion, cheeks rosy, blue eyes soft and admiring, and I raised my hand to caress his lightly stubbled cheek. If this was it, if the Revolution started tomorrow, at least I'd had this moment. At least I knew the love of this man, this ghost, this soldier, this spirit guide. Wherever Luke's allegiances would ultimately be, when pushed by these forces we faced, at least I knew this. There was no lie in his touch, his passion. His heart was true.

'Luke ... thank you for coming with me into the cavern,' I said then, my mind turning back inevitably to the issues at hand.

Luke remained still, his gaze turning to the ceiling as he spoke. 'It is good that the portal remains closed, Miss Pandora, though I feel a strong pull down there. And the house is beginning to speak once more.'

The rumblings from below the basement. Yes, I'd heard it too.

'It troubles me when you change like that ... like you did down in the cavern,' I said, rolling on to one unclothed hip. He had done it before. That last time we'd been in the cavern and Luke had not been himself was still something of a sore spot. He'd tried to kill me. 'You scared me.'

At this Luke sat up abruptly and slid his legs over the opposite side of the bed. 'I am so sorry,' he said. 'I shall leave you, Miss Pandora. I am sorry to have troubled you.' He began gathering his things, sliding his breeches on and pulling on his socks and boots.

'Hold it right there,' I replied, sitting up and taking him by his still firm and human waist, just as he finished buckling his leather belt. 'I'm not asking you to leave, I am just telling you I find it troubling when you aren't quite yourself. Though this time it seemed it was a warning you were delivering.' I curled my body around him. 'Don't go, please. I didn't mean it like that.'

'I did not harm you?' Lieutenant Luke said, turning to look at me, his strong jaw tense and his eyes wide with concern. 'I could not live with myself, Miss Pandora, if I found I had harmed you.' He ran a gentle finger over my face, and down the delicate skin of my neck to the clavicle. I shivered.

'Just now? No, you did not hurt me. Far from it. And down in the cavern you only spoke. Your eyes weren't . . . green.' *But perhaps still a little terrifying.*

'I wish I could control these things,' he said, casting his gaze to the floor, his magnificent shoulders slumping forward.

A sound at the window distracted me, and I turned. 'Oh!' I exclaimed suddenly and moved so fast I was a blur. In seconds I was standing at the end of the bed, wearing Luke's Union soldier frock coat to cover my nakedness, having buttoned it hastily at the waist so it wouldn't open too far. I held it around myself with both arms crossed over my chest. I could move fast when I needed to. Supernaturally fast.

It was Deus, the ancient Sanguine. He was hanging upside down at my open window, pale face seeming almost to glow in the low light.

'I am so sorry to surprise you, Pandora English, The Seventh,' he said. 'You called me to you.'

How awkward. 'You are mistaken,' I said, blushing like a beet.

Deus turned himself in the air, a thoroughly odd movement, and came to rest, right way up, on my windowsill. He wore his neat black suit, hair slicked down. 'You must feed, to prepare for what is to come tomorrow,' he said sensibly. 'You will need your strength.'

I flicked my eyes to my lover, and found him on his feet, hands balled into fists. His blue eyes blazed with anger and protectiveness. The sight of him shirtless was arousing, the proximity of Deus and his magnetic blood, confusing. Oh, this was not good. The timing was terrible. Luke was not good with vampires, not good at all. He deeply distrusted them, and not without reason.

'This isn't a convenient time,' I managed in a voice that sounded much smaller than intended. Dear me, I did feel confused. My body was pulled two ways, and my mind in many others – *I want to stay here with Luke, but I probably should feed? Though I couldn't do that in front of Luke, yet I don't want him to leave. And I have never been conscious of drinking Deus's blood, so could I even do it now, consciously? But if I was already doing it in the night and I needed to do it for everyone's good then what was the harm in doing it again?...*

'You are not welcome here, *vampire*,' Lieutenant Luke said in a low voice brimming with anger that shocked me out of my tangle of thoughts. 'Miss Pandora told you it is not a convenient time. She does not want you here.' He almost seemed to growl.

Oh, I had said that, hadn't I? I bit my lip.

'I see you are a *man* tonight,' Deus said, putting emphasis on the word in his deep, ancient accent, grinning as always. That bloody grin. He was by now standing on the hardwood floor of my room, about a foot inside from the window, not far from where my clothes lay, and the tensions were rising between these two men in my room, one undead, one dead (though temporarily not deceased?). Deus had moved closer, somehow imperceptibly. It was so curious how he was able to do that.

'Yes, I am a man and Miss Pandora does not want you here,' Luke told him, and walked towards him, spine straight with a military bearing, ready to fight for me.

Oh hell.

'You have consummated your human form,' Deus said impassively, still smiling that eternal Kathakano smile and standing the ground he had gained.

At this reference to our consummation, Lieutenant Luke, usually so gentle, took his sword from the floor and flew threateningly at the grinning vampire, blue eyes ablaze.

'Luke, stop!' I shouted, and at my words he stopped just short of Deus, who had not so much as flinched, and his sword dropped to the ground with a loud clang.

He had . . . disappeared? I flitted my eyes around the room. Luke had vanished. *No!*

'My goddess! What happened? Where did he go?' I cried, running forward in a panic, Luke's still solid frock coat flying behind me. I stood next to Deus and looked around me, wide-eyed. 'Luke! Luke, where are you?' I said. I lifted the heavy sword from the ground and held it by the hilt. 'Luke?'

The air grew cool around us and a nebulous shape emerged a few feet away, misty and then more solid until Second Lieutenant Luke Thomas returned to us, again in human form. Only he wasn't holding his hand over mine this time. The obsidian ring on my finger had not grown hot. We weren't holding the sword together. I stood holding it and he appeared again in his uniform, his discarded clothing on my floor fading until it vanished. We exchanged a look, both appearing confused.

'Oh goddess!' I yelped and sprinted to the ensuite bathroom, suddenly finding myself naked. Luke's Union frock coat no longer covered me, it was back on him, just as it always was when he first appeared.

Still blushing vigorously but somewhat more composed, I emerged from the bathroom a few minutes later, wearing a carefully wrapped towel for lack of clothing options. I'd moved so fast I'd not even realised I was still holding the sword, and I approached them, with sword and towel, wearing as even an expression as I could muster. 'Excuse me, gentlemen,' I said, slowly approaching my uniformed soldier and my Sanguine blood supplier. 'Can someone please explain just what is going on?' I placed Luke's sword carefully on the ground, out of the immediate reach of both of them, not wanting to hand it to its owner while he was still giving Deus the side-eye.

'He has consummated his human form,' Deus repeated calmly. He was grinning of course, though this time I detected some genuine amusement.

I folded my arms again. 'I heard you say that before. Can you perhaps explain precisely what you mean?' I replied, doing my level best to speak in a normal, even-tempered tone.

'As you can see, you have bestowed powers upon your spirit guide, Pandora English, The Seventh. He may now be flesh at will.'

I shook my head. 'No, no, you misunderstand. That's

the moon,' I explained, gesturing to my open window. 'We discovered that a few months ago, after we discovered Luke's sabre.'

'The moon is not so strong now, Pandora English, The Seventh,' Deus said, and indeed it was presently hiding behind the clouds, I saw. 'The full Blue Moon was yesterday.'

'I know. But when the moon is full and there is enough strength to it, sometimes the day either side, for a spell, and if I hold his sword and I wear my ring . . .' I said and trailed off, frowning.

Luke had stopped glaring at the vampire and was looking at his hands as if he'd not seen them before, even though he had seen them many times. He squinted slightly and just like that, he disappeared.

My jaw dropped.

A few seconds later the misty form returned and Luke was standing in place again, renewed in his fully human form, his dress uniform complete. I hadn't said a word. My ring had not grown hot. He had not touched his sword and neither had I. It still lay on the floor where I'd placed it.

'Yes, it is as I thought. The soldier's powers have been bestowed on him by The Seventh, who has now freed him to change into ghost or human at will, all the better to fulfil his role as the spirit guide,' Deus pronounced.

I blinked, and a small indecipherable sound escaped me.

'Now, Pandora English, The Seventh, you must feed,' Deus declared, having evidently decided that the mystery was solved, and he had other pressing engagements this night, which he doubtless did.

I exchanged looks with my spirit guide. 'I think perhaps I need some privacy.'

'As you wish, Miss Pandora,' Luke said, bowing at the waist, though I could feel his internal struggle, leaving me alone with a Sanguine predator. 'I will wait just beyond your door. If you need me, call my name and I will be here,' he said, and instead of opening the door and walking away, he faded into his misty ghost form and slid through the wall while I watched, mouth agape.

I have given him the power to change forms, from spirit to man and back again, I thought. *It's really true.*

Drinking from Deus was not at all the difficult task I had feared.

He made it easier for me, as I supposed he did for my great-aunt, by slitting his own wrist (which still made me wince) and filling a wine glass for me. If I really wanted to, I could almost pretend I was trying a Cabernet for the first time, or a Merlot. That was a normal thing that humans did, and as I had not partaken before I could pretend the taste was almost right. Almost. But *boy* was it intoxicating, that blood of his. So much more than I imagined a single glass of wine could be. (Too young for alcohol but drinking blood was evidently my thing now.) While Deus watched, I sat on the edge of my bed and I drank every drop, head swimming with pleasure, and when I was finished he bowed courteously, placed the empty glass on my table and slipped away into the night through my open window. I flopped back against my sheets and stayed in place for a while, legs dangling over the edge and body thrumming with an oddly invigorating feeling of deep contentedness.

After a time I rose. Trying my best to be conscientious, I brushed my teeth before going back and opening my bedroom door. My soldier was in human form at his post, standing like a sentinel just outside my room.

'You are unharmed, Miss Pandora?' Lieutenant Luke asked me, jaw tense.

'I am unharmed,' I assured him, and leaned in to kiss his mouth. He hesitated at first, and then accepted my lips, his body – real and human – relaxing into me. 'See? It's strictly a blood thing with Deus,' I explained. We kissed again, and it felt wonderful, turning my insides to honey. It must have had a similar effect on Luke because his worried and tense expression melted away.

Reassured, I led him to my room and closed the door behind us.

On the morning of the Met exhibition opening I woke late, and alone. No Civil War soldiers, living or dead. No ancient Sanguine. Just me. The shining light of the day was streaming in, warming my sheets like it was already high summer.

I swung my legs out of my bed, yawning and shaking my head at the memories of the previous night's events. Go figure. Making love for the first time had not altered my powers in any way I could detect, but it had meant I bestowed new powers on my beautiful ghostly lover. Again, the opposite of every pop culture warning I'd been fed as a girl.

I walked past my little table on the way to the ensuite bathroom, seeing the emptied wine glass where Deus had left it, my gaze stopping on my mother's books. There it was, the triskele, right on the cover of the book on top. I shivered at the sight of it and crossed my arms over myself, thinking of the great, moving pattern in the sky over Manhattan – neat, interlocked Archimedean spirals of glowing green swirling mist, with Spektor at its epicentre. True, I had not seen green flames and mist by the portal, but I was sure that pattern was still there, gathering strength across the island, and I could only surmise that this 'necromancy' Deus spoke of and that we both could see in the assembling mist, was the necromancy of *raising* or even controlling the dead, not simply communicating with them. Even after my run-in with the necromancer months ago – a necromancer whose dark magick caused the same kind of eerie green mist to accumulate – I could honestly say this current pattern of necromancer's magick was far larger and more widespread than anything I'd witnessed before. But others must have seen it in the past? Perhaps even Archimedes had been inspired by the Agitation, back in ancient Syracuse, when he recorded those famed interlocking Archimedean spirals.

If so much was up to me, I had to get my fears under control. And what of tonight?

The Cobra Queen wakes, this day. And the Hatshepsut exhibition would open. Could it be a coincidence? Perhaps. But I did not much believe in coincidences, and if what my mother had alluded to was correct, my concern was not entirely irrational. And in addiction to Luke's warning, there was that swirling mist. Should I still try to go and do my job at the Met as my human, mortal employer expected me to? In the past I would have felt lucky that I'd scored a ticket for Morticia and myself, and that we could go to such a big event in New York. It wasn't every day that I could attend such a thing, let alone bring a friend. And yet . . .

Now, after so many years I was to rediscover the ancient world my mother had been involved with. It made me feel closer to her, which was simultaneously reassuring and difficult, particularly considering the revelation about my parents' deaths at Hatshepsut's tomb. I'd come to believe in many things since moving to Spektor. Did I believe in ancient curses? Well, yes. Quite possibly I did. With everything else I'd seen, why not? And my mother's books had spelled some of them out:

> *Any person . . . who shall enter this [tomb] and do something therein which is evil . . . it is the crocodile, the hippopotamus or the lion which shall consume them.*

What would an ancient pharaoh consider 'evil'? Removing their possessions? Putting them on display for a foreign public across the world? Time would tell if that curse was to come true, I supposed.

And time was nearly upon us.

Morticia!

With a jolt I thought again of Morticia, the mortal friend who was to accompany me to the launch. I'd begun the process of easing her into knowledge of the supernatural, but how could I walk Morticia into the Met with so little preparation? What if the Cobra Queen was tied to Hatshepsut and the exhibition? What if everything went wrong? What if something happened to my only real human friend in New York, because of me?

I got myself dressed and went out for a walk, leaving Spektor's circle of mist and finding a spot in Central Park where there was reception for my phone.

It wasn't until I called her twice and left a message on her mobile that I realised my error.

Morticia's phone was not working. She was out of credit.

CHAPTER TEN

Hours before the glamorous Met museum launch I stood at the entry to the Underworld, floors beneath my bedroom in Spektor, wearing old jeans, ballet flats and a T-shirt. I'd tried reaching Morticia several times, to no avail. She would be dressing up for tonight by now, expecting me to meet her in my great-aunt's chauffeured car.

Contemplating the moment, I stood at the edge of the dark, quiet waters of the subterranean cavern, watching the closed portal to the world of the dead. My stomach felt cold, as it often did in the presence of the dead or the supernatural. What I hoped to see, I did not know. The air smelled of sulphur and the stalactites and stalagmites around me glittered in the light of the red torch flames. Around the portal the piles of bones were stacked eerily like double helixes, and these made my stomach feel yet colder. When my gaze fell upon the giant skull heads atop the colossal statues that flanked the portal, the ice in my stomach was almost painful. These statues were like gods. Or protectors? Or both? They were powerful and still, the vast space deathly calm around them. And yet I felt anything but calm.

What do I do?

I had even more pressing responsibilities than Morticia's

safety, one could argue, and yet I would feel responsible if anything happened to her, having invited her to the event. I had explained that I'd seen spirits at the museum, but I had left a lot out, and since talking with her at Fanelli's I'd learned so much more. But what if I stood her up, and everything at the launch was normal? After brushing her off so many times, our friendship would be unlikely to survive.

I shifted on my feet, then slipped off my right shoe and dipped my foot gently into the cool water. It was not painful, not poisonous, only cold. For a moment I felt a pull into the water, an instinct to step in. How curious.

Perhaps I needed to stop thinking of my attempts at human friendship and concentrate on being The Seventh, whatever that meant. What would The Seventh do? Well, she would go to the museum, right? She would do so fearlessly, and in the knowledge that she was supposed to be there, if those misty, swirling green snakes above the museum were anything to go by – a cryptic invitation.

Between calling Morticia's mobile to no avail and coming down to the portal, I had picked up the seven shabtis from Harold's Grocer, still unsure of their use, but now, if I was to go, it was time for me to get ready. This was the big moment of decision, my two worlds crashing together once more. I couldn't prevent the launch from going ahead, and I did not have solid proof that it shouldn't. Would the launch happen with or without me? Would it be better for the living world if Pandora English was there, or wasn't?

I gazed again at the unnerving statues on either side of the portals. All was still and silent, like the calm before a storm.

The torches glowed red, not green. It was time to go, and face what the evening would bring, outside of this cavern, outside of Spektor. And I'd have to look the part and play my role, but which role would it be? *Pandora*, assistant to the editor? Writer of bit pieces in Pandora magazine? Or Pandora, The Seventh?

When I returned to my bedroom I found a gleaming, three-quarter-length, navy-blue dress hanging from the old antique wardrobe. I ran up to it and gaped, admiring the fine, luminous silk.

My great-aunt appeared at the door behind me. 'I think it will suit you well, if you care to wear it tonight.'

'If I *care* to wear it? Great-Aunt Celia, it's too much! It's incredible.'

'There's no use having it collect dust in the cupboard,' she said casually. 'Hedy Lamarr would be pleased to have you wear it, I think.'

'This was one of Hedy Lamarr's dresses?'

Celia nodded, the fine mesh of her veil shifting slightly. Hedy Lamarr had been a remarkable actress – as intelligent as she was beautiful. Though better known for her film roles and her arresting beauty, she had been a great mathematician and had co-invented an early form of wireless communication. Celia designed a number of dresses for her in the forties and fifties, and they'd struck up a friendship, from what Celia had told me.

'Well, you'd better get ready. There's not much time left, and it will be a big night tonight,' my great-aunt commented, and I couldn't tell if it was a barely detectable smile on her face, or a look of friendly concern. 'You did take your time down there,' she commented.

So she knew where I'd been. Of course she knew.

Celia was right about the time. I had to hustle if I was to meet Morticia and get to the exhibition. I'd thought long and hard about it and I just couldn't bring myself to leave her there by the subway, all dressed up and stood up.

I showered quickly, careful not to wet my hair as I had no time to dry it again. After towelling off I walked briskly back into my bedroom to gaze again at the vintage dress hanging from the wardrobe. Celia was impossibly generous sometimes. I held my breath, wondering if it could really fit me, took it gently off the hanger and stepped into it. With ease, I pulled it up and slid my arms through the sleeves. Celia's dress – or should I say Hedy's – felt positively luxurious on my skin. It was in amazing condition considering its age. (A bit like my great-aunt, one could say.) The lining was intact, the silk showing only the tiniest hint of wear, just enough to add character. I reached behind my back and closed the couple of buttons I could manage to reach, and then looked in the mirror to see how it fit. *Wow.* I exhaled and smiled. Incredibly – the dress fit like a glove, as all of Celia's clothes seemed to, yet it had enough give and movement through the bottom to allow a good stride. I stood before the mirror on the old wooden wardrobe and marvelled at the flattering cut. Subtle shoulder pads and short cap sleeves gave it that true 1940s period look, and the draping fabric fell across the bust and down from the waistline gracefully, the hem falling just at the bottom of the calf. Ah, it was split at the back, to just above the knee. That accounted for the freedom of movement. Perfect. I couldn't wait to show it off to my great-aunt, and I sprinted out into the lounge room barefoot to do just that.

'What do you think?' I asked, and took a spin, letting the bottom of the dress flare out a touch.

Celia was at her reading nook and now she stood and looked me up and down. As usual, her appraisal was what you would expect of a former fashion designer. She took in the dress, the hemline, the fit, the fall of pleats, the line of every seam. She stepped up to me and did up the last of the buttons, finishing with a clasp at the nape of my neck. 'Very fitting for a night at the museum,' she said. 'You look lovely.' With a designer like Great-Aunt Celia in my life, I never had to worry about arriving at an event in the same dress as someone else.

'You have forgotten something, though,' Celia added.

'I have?'

'The Babel Pendant.'

'Of course!' I ran back to my room, put on my mother's pendant and sprinted over to Celia again. I had my leather satchel with me, which made her raise an eyebrow, but there was no use in bringing something more dainty and vintage-looking. I had things I needed to carry. As least it was an unobtrusive black.

'Very sensible, Pandora,' she said, giving her approval.

I smiled. 'Thanks. And thank you so much for lending me

this dress,' I said, and thought, *And I can run and kick in it too. No Morticia shuffle for me …*

Oh, Morticia.

'No use having it in the cupboard,' Celia repeated. 'Wear the Mary Janes tonight.'

'What?' I said, my thoughts having been caught up with my companion for the evening and what I should do about her. 'Of course,' I replied. My plain ballet flats wouldn't do. She meant I should wear the Mary Jane shoes she'd given me. They were crimson and sparkling, with a strap across the instep and a sturdy heel. There was almost a sense of magick about them, I thought. I suspect they'd seen a few dance floors in their day. Considering the clock, I wasted no time pulling them from the wardrobe, slipping them on and fastening the glittering clasp across the arch of my foot. I added a slick of red lipstick to match the shoes and the sense of 1940s' style (when every woman seemed to favour a strong red lip), and figured I looked ready enough. I wasn't one for a lot of makeup or fussing about. As the event was black tie, I would look suitably elegant, without stealing the show, I thought. I hoped, well, I hoped nothing too out of the ordinary stole the show tonight.

'Oh, I wouldn't be so sure that you won't steal the show,' my great-aunt said slyly as I walked back out to the lounge room.

She knew I'd figured out one of her little secrets – that she was a telepathic witch, though she hated labels, of course. And a blood-drinking one, as I now knew. I thought I detected something else in her eyes, too. Was it her usual sense of mischief showing, or was that concern I detected?

'I do wish you were coming,' I told Celia sincerely, and she said nothing.

I had been living with my great-aunt for a few months now, and it was beginning to feel strange that we never went out as a pair. I gathered she did not like crowds and I knew she was, well, *light-sensitive*, so daylight was not her favourite thing. The event tonight was after dark but, again, *crowds*.

'Oh, I'm sure I'll hear about it,' she said softly.

I hesitated. 'Great-Aunt Celia, I am ... worried.'

'What are you worried about? The portal is closed, yes?'

I nodded. 'It is. But I am worried about tonight anyway. Deus showed me the Agitation, and there was a lot of activity over the museum.'

Celia nodded, her face inscrutable. 'You have overcome many challenges since coming here, yes?'

I nodded.

'And if fresh challenges present themselves, I know no one else more capable of handling them.'

I swallowed. There was that sense of responsibility again. How could I live up to that?

'Do not forget, Pandora, you are the most powerful person in New York. It is right that you will be there.'

I did not know how to respond to that. 'Most powerful person in New York' seemed rather a stretch.

'Vlad is waiting downstairs,' my wise great-aunt reminded me.

She was right. I'd already made my decision. I needed to hurry so we didn't leave Morticia waiting at the subway station alone. Heart pounding, I bid my great-aunt goodnight, and rushed down.

When Vlad pulled up the car at the subway entrance, I spotted Morticia immediately. She was wearing head-to-toe black, and for once she had eschewed the striped goth tights in favour of fishnets, and her usual Doc Martens had been replaced by a pair of cute kitten-heeled ankle boots. She'd piled her hair on top of her head in a loose beehive. A sort of eighties does sixties nostalgia glam. She looked sharp.

'Hi, Morticia!' I called out as I opened the door. I wanted to open it before Vlad did, because he'd probably terrify her. 'You look great,' I said as she swung herself inside. In seconds she'd buckled herself in and patted her dress down. She seemed pretty nervous, I thought. 'Are you okay?' I asked.

Her anxiety made me feel on edge again. There was no turning back now. We were headed to one of the biggest events in town, and that wasn't even the part I was worried about. There would be no backing out.

'This is such a nice car,' Morticia remarked, and I got the feeling the big car intimidated her. She knew my great-aunt was a touch eccentric and had a chauffeur. But knowing a thing and experiencing it were different.

'Yeah. I know,' I said, and shrugged. There was no explaining it away. 'That's my great-aunt's driver, Vlad. He doesn't talk much,' I said, and she looked towards the front seat of the long car. I didn't want her to look too closely, or she might get scared. 'I, um, mean it about your outfit,' I said hastily. 'You really do look great.'

'Thanks,' she said shyly, looking in her lap. 'I found it in an thrift store. It's sixties, I think.'

'Yes, and very cool. Hey, how big is your handbag?' I asked casually, trying to keep a normal expression on my face.

'What?'

'I have something for you,' I said, smiling and trying not to freak out. 'It's a little, well, shabti; it's Egyptian and I want you to have it.' I handed her one of the small figures.

The look of the figure seemed to transfix my friend. 'Wow! This is amazing! Is it a souvenir or something?'

'More like a ... like a ...' I searched for a way to frame it. 'A good-luck charm. And here's another one. Have them both,' I pushed a second figure into her hands. 'Can you fit a third one in your bag?'

'What? No. One is fine.' She tried to hand one back. 'Really.'

'I want you to have them,' I said, pushing the figures back towards her. 'For protection,' I admitted.

She cocked her head as she looked at me, and some recognition passed behind her eyes. 'The spirits at the Met, right?'

'Yes. The spirits. Please will you hang on to them? For me?'

Morticia accepted them, looking touched. 'This is sweet of you.'

We arrived at the steps of the Met just on time, with Vlad pulling up smoothly at the kerb right on the hour. A valet opened the door for us and I showed our invitation card while Morticia struggled to fit two of the shabti figures into her handbag. A third simply would not fit, so she handed it back and I tucked it in my satchel. She still seemed quite nervous, fidgeting and breathing a touch quickly. It might have been Vlad – who didn't seem to breathe at all – or it might have been the prospect of going to the big exhibition opening.

'Are you okay?' I asked.

She nodded, though it was unconvincing. 'I'm fine, thanks. Thank you so much for bringing me with you.'

'Let's do this,' I said, and linked my arm with hers.

Chapter Eleven

I walked through the main doors of the Met with Morticia at my side, and when we saw some of the crowd moving through, assembling for the Hatshepsut exhibition opening, Morticia audibly gasped.

This was a well-heeled crowd. Some women wore ankle-length gowns, one or two even with an elaborate train to grab photographers' eyes. I was glad to be in a calf-length gown, and one that was pre-loved by the likes of Hedy Lamarr, no less, but Morticia needn't have worried. She'd chosen her vintage ensemble well and there were plenty of women in cocktail length dresses and shorter, as well as men in everything from tuxedos to the common slick jeans and suit jacket combination that had become popular in the past decade – though few pulled that off particularly well, in my view. A photo wall was set up with a red carpet in front of it, flanked by paparazzi and celebrity photographers with large flashbulbs. They were shouting, flashes going, but certainly not for us, and we scuttled past with our heads down, me dragging Morticia behind me. After a few months in New York at these kinds of things, I knew the drill by now. We ended up ducking all the way through the media throng and the assembled fake pyramid entry to the exhibition, giggling.

'That was wild!' Morticia exclaimed, panting a little.

Now that they had finished setting up the exhibition, the space looked spectacular. The always-extensive Egyptian wing had been reorganised, with temporary, decorative walls erected so that the focus was on a single time period, a single ruler. On both sides of us were rows of statues of all sizes, some several metres high, each of pharaohs wearing the distinctive Nemes striped headdress and false beard of the kings of ancient Egypt. But again, something was different about these statues – they had the plump cheeks, high cheekbones and feminine facial features of a young woman – Hatshepsut, the female pharaoh. In glass cases were countless artefacts relating to her reign – tools and implements, small figures and funerary equipment.

'Wow.'

'Indeed,' I replied.

Many of the statues were heavily worn and damaged, in ways that could not solely be accounted for by the immense stretch of time that had passed since their construction around 1478 BC. 'A lot of Hatshepsut's monuments were defaced, seemingly to try to erase her era of female power,' I told Morticia.

'So, she was really a female pharaoh,' she remarked. 'So badass.'

'Well, she started out as a queen. Actually, she started out as a princess – the daughter of a king – but then came to power when her father and her husband had both died, and her stepson was too young to rule. After a few years as regent she declared herself pharaoh.'

'Ballsy,' she said.

'So to speak,' I responded, and she laughed.

Morticia and I moved with the crowd into the Sackler Wing, near the Temple of Dendur. Though the temple was not part of Hatshepsut's reign, it did take pride of place in the Met's most spectacular and spacious area within their Egyptian Wing, the same area they used for the famous annual Met Gala, and I saw that they had assembled a number of key pieces from the exhibition here, along with a microphone, some staging and a few chairs for speakers. We passed the shimmering reflecting pool and joined the well-dressed throng, waiting for the speeches to begin, while I balanced my satchel and my pad of paper and pen. Behind us was a spectacular sphinx, with Hatshepsut's distinctively feminine features, atop a lion's powerful body. The museum's floodlights illuminated the space magnificently, further enhanced by hundreds of glowing tea lights in rows along the floor and flanking the steps to the temple. The overall effect was quite magical, and in that moment I realised how glad I was to share this with my friend. Most of all, though, I was glad I hadn't left her standing outside the subway, all dressed up and alone.

'Look, it's her sarcophagus,' Morticia said, and I spun around.

A few metres away was a large rectangular reddish stone box inscribed with Egyptian hieroglyphs. They had indeed listed it as Hatshepsut's sarcophagus, recut for her father Tutmosis I, I saw. It was one of three quartzite sarcophagi made for Hatshepsut during her time, this one brought to New York from a museum in Boston. Another, similar-looking sarcophagus could be seen a few feet away. The third was not in view. Where was it? I wondered. Had they brought it from the Valley of the Kings? I wondered if my mother had seen these at some point or had even been there when they were excavated. She would have loved this exhibition. She belonged here more than I.

'Beautiful, isn't it?' a man said. I raised my eyes and found myself faced with Jay Rockwell.

'Yes, it is beautiful. Hi,' I managed. Jay towered over us, clean-shaven, hair tidy, wearing a classic tuxedo. He had a date with him, I noticed. *Fair enough,* I thought. *Fair enough.* It did feel peculiar, seeing him there with another woman so soon after he'd asked me to go with him, but it wasn't jealousy I felt, that much I was sure of. Being sure on that was a relief, even if this was an undeniably awkward social encounter. Inevitable, perhaps, but awkward just the same.

Morticia, sensing the moment, was watching me with widened eyes. Her gaze moved to Jay and then to his attractive date, and then back to me again, as if watching a kind of silent, invisible, social ping pong.

'Funny they should call it that,' I remarked then, standing tall and reading the information plaque.

'What do you mean?' Jay asked, as his date loitered next to him, trying to read the moment. She was slim and blonde, not too dissimilar to Pepper in appearance and style. I wondered when I would see my boss.

'A sarcophagus. It is common terminology,' I said. 'But the word is from the Greek *sarkophagos* or "flesh-eater", referring to a stone coffin that devoured its occupant. Knowing how the ancient Egyptians regarded their bodies after death and the lengths they went to for mummification, they would not have wanted to be buried in a flesh-eater,' I told my assembled listeners. 'In fact they were very particular about preserving their bodies and keeping them from being disturbed in any way, let alone eaten, so to speak.'

Morticia did a little wiggly dance, flicking her fingers as if to show she was grossed out. Then she went back to staring at Jay. I could hardly blame her. It was an awkward thing, and he did look pretty good in his tuxedo. But I had expected this.

'Well, aren't you full of interesting facts,' Jay said dryly.

'Thank you,' I responded, deciding to pretend it was a compliment. This tendency of mine to spout facts, often on topics considered unsavoury, rarely won me favour. But no matter.

'Jennifer, this is Pandora. Pandora, Jennifer.' He ignored Morticia and her stare, and I shook hands with his date, keeping an unfaltering smile on my face. I moved to introduce my friend but was cut off. 'Look, the speeches are about the begin,' Jay then said, turning to walk away, conveniently saving us from hearing any more from me. 'Have a good night.'

'You, too, Jay and Jennifer,' I called back, deciding they sounded like one of those celebrity couples. Perhaps they would be *Jaynnifer*? Or *Jennay*?

Now Morticia was looking at me with a wicked expression and her mouth pulled over to one side. 'Awkward,' she whispered, and I shrugged.

'Bound to happen,' I said.

We swept around the exhibition, taking it in, and when the crowd moved into place we took our positions near the front of the standing crowd, behind a few people who Jay or

Jennifer appeared to know. He was taller than both of us, so Morticia and I had to jostle a bit to get a view.

'I thought that was really interesting about the sarcophagus,' Morticia whispered to me. 'Gross but cool.'

'Thanks,' I said softly, appreciating her solidarity.

Now the director of the Met took centre stage in the gallery, and I held my pad of paper up and began to jot down my observations, making a mental note to also ask some of the more elaborately dressed guests who they were wearing once the formalities were over.

'For the first time, we have gathered together nearly every known fragment of Hatshepsut's funerary belongings,' the director said, 'including this, the most complete of the famous granite sphinxes of Hatshepsut's mortuary temple at Deir el-Bahri, excavated by the Met and pieced together from fragments, and weighing more than seven tons,' he said, motioning to the impressive sphinx. 'We have her three sarcophagi,' he went on, and again I had a flash in my mind of the unsettling meaning of sarcophagus, and wondered where the third was. 'We have on display two known shabti figures of brown-black basalt, or diorite, belonging to Hatshepsut, brought from museum collections at Rijksmuseum Meermanno-Westreenianum in the Hague and Musée d'Aquitaine in Bordeaux, and two shabtis of blue faience also thought to be hers, brought here from the City Museum of Bristol.'

The shabtis, I thought, and almost felt a touch silly for bringing my satchel heavy with the things. But then, the night was young.

'For the first time under one roof are the famous female pharaoh's shabtis, her Canopic jars and their contents, several ancient tributes to her – many with the faces hacked off in antiquity in the famous campaign that aimed to remove her from the history books – and finally, we also have the pharaoh herself.'

I swallowed. Had the director said 'the pharaoh herself'?

Ahead of us, Jay leaned in to his date and joked, 'Lordy, he makes it sound like she's going to waltz in and say a few words.'

My mouth had gone terribly dry and that familiar cold feeling was growing in my belly, the feeling that I often got around the presence of the dead. Perhaps it was only the mummies and other ancient artefacts in the exhibition; their spirits were surely here – I had not lied to Morticia about that. But the director had said, 'the pharaoh herself' and I wondered what exactly that meant. Could it mean what I thought it did? And now I noticed a white-draped rectangle on the stage behind the director. Was that a table? No, there was nothing on it. It was not entirely flat.

And then I knew. It was the third sarcophagus. The one, it seemed, that would be displaying the mummy of Hatshepsut herself.

'Are you okay?' Morticia whispered, having noticed the shift in my mood.

I nodded, though I was not really okay. My heart had sped up and that awful feeling in my belly was intensifying. I'd thought on the possibility, of course, but it had still seemed a stretch that the Egyptian Ministry of Antiquities would allow the prized, recently identified mummy to travel, and with everything going on I hadn't focused much on the possibility, or what it might mean. But now here we were, in the museum, at the launch, and evidently close to Hatshepsut's mummified remains, and I found the idea of an unveiling deeply troubling.

But why? Hatshepsut's body was hardly the first mummy to be publicly displayed. There was something a touch unsavoury about groups of people looking at a dead body when the person who had once occupied it had not consented to it being on display, but this was standard in my mother's field of work, had been standard for centuries. No pharaohs had donated their bodies to science, yet they had become disinterred specimens for scientific, historical and cultural study, and much had been learned in the process. Like other Egyptians of her time, Hatshepsut would have felt that the sanctity of her body and royal tomb were important to the success of her afterlife. Despite her wishes, her tomb and mummy had been defiled in antiquity, and now the discovered pieces of her life and her body were on display – photographed, probed, autopsied – thousands of years after her death. The dead pharaoh might rightly be angry. Perhaps that was where these rumours of curses came from – not from ancient texts as much as our own guilt for defiling the dead for our own knowledge, curiosity and commercial gain.

What did the dead think of this? What did my own mother think of this, having been one of the archaeologists forever searching for answers in artefacts of the past, with so many of those being funerary artefacts?

'Are you sure you're okay?' Morticia asked again, having noticed my notepad was shaking.

You are fine. This is all fine, I reassured myself. How ridiculous it would be to fall apart at the idea of seeing a mummy in a museum, after having faced hundreds of reanimated corpses on the streets of Manhattan?

'This is indeed a historic occasion,' the museum director continued, and I took notes. 'And this evening we have the man responsible for this great exhibition – the head of antiquities in Egypt, the archaeologist responsible for solving one of Egyptology's greatest mysteries – positively identifying the mummy of Hatshepsut herself, Dr Zahi Gamal. We are honoured to have him.'

What a find, I thought. This is the man who positively identified possibly the greatest female ruler in ancient Egypt. And all because of a tooth. This was the kind of discovery my mother would have hoped for her whole career.

The sound system squealed with feedback for a moment. I looked to Morticia. She was riveted by the displays and the prospect of what was to come, her hands held together in front of her, as if she might applaud at any moment.

We watched as, having been introduced, the esteemed archaeologist Dr Gamal stepped forward, wearing a slightly crumpled shirt and slacks, his corduroy jacket fixed with the suede arm patches of the archetypal professor. His mouth was held open slightly, set in a barely contained grin, as if he did not wish to seem too eager or unprofessional but his enthusiasm was getting the better of him. I waited with the crowd to hear what he would say of his successes and the significance of the new exhibition, and wondered fleetingly if my mother had ever met him. The archaeological community was small enough that it was just possible.

The doctor's barely perceptible grin stayed in place as he adjusted the microphone to his height. He surveyed the crowd with a brief glance, seeming to gather his thoughts. Then he opened his mouth to begin.

And nothing came out.

His lips closed and then parted again, and he blinked, brows pulling together. A choking sound echoed through the room as he strained to speak. His face reddened. Next to him the director's eyebrows shot up. There was a brief confusion, and in seconds one of the staff arrived with a glass of water and handed it to the stricken archaeologist. There was a nod of thanks before he eagerly gulped it down.

I crossed my arms and frowned.

Something.

Something wasn't right. That cold feeling had settled in the pit of my stomach. I exchanged a glance with Jay, who had turned around to look at me despite his date standing by, and somehow he did not seem particularly perturbed by the scene. If anything he seemed mildly amused. No doubt he had given a few speeches or presentations over the years. A dry mouth was probably not so unusual. And yet …

The doctor had finished his water and now the glass was whisked away. He gave an embarrassed shrug to the director and approached the microphone again. What an awkward start, I thought. The archaeologist opened his mouth to speak to the well-dressed crowd, and again, the horrible choking sound came out. He looked startled and perplexed. He held his throat and for one sickening moment I had the sense that he might not be able to breathe. He tried again to form words and failed, and then with the entire crowd murmuring uneasily and shifting impatiently from foot to foot, the director stepped in and pulled his star speaker aside.

How odd, I thought. And a line popped into my head – something I had learned from my mother's books many years ago. It might even be in one of the books sent to me in the box I'd recently received. A curse:

> *Every workman, every stonemason, or every man who shall [do] evil things to the tomb of mine of eternity by tearing out bricks or stones from it, no voice shall be given to him in the sight of any god or any man.*

'What is it?' Morticia said and touched my elbow.

'I'm not sure,' I replied, 'but it can't be good.' Whose tomb had been protected by that curse? Was it Seti the first? Ramesses? I couldn't recall. 'Just keep an eye out, okay?' I said.

'Is it the spirits?' my friend asked in a low voice, sticking close.

'Yes, I think it is the spirits,' I told her. 'And they are not happy.'

No voice shall be given to him ... In the sight of any man.

My stomach grew yet colder.

Evidently an executive decision was made to move on with the program, and perhaps reintroduce the archaeologist later in the evening when he was recovered. 'Without further ado,

I'd like to introduce Professor Lotfia Sabahi, from our department for fashion and culture ...' Having been announced, a woman with short, wavy, silver hair and a sleek suit took to the stage.

'Ancient Egypt was a time of unsurpassed artistic beauty,' she began, speaking without difficulty. She spoke engagingly for several minutes about the merits of the works on display, and their cultural and historical significance. When the professor finished, there was some discussion among the speakers and Dr Gamal. The crowd was tense and silent, sensing that things were still not going to plan, and after a time the museum's director again took to the microphone.

'It is my pleasure this evening to reveal, for the first time in the USA and in our museum, the pharaoh Hatshepsut, the mummy that baffled scientists and remained a mystery for centuries ...'

Doctor Gamal, evidently still unable or now unwilling to speak, pulled the white sheet away on this cue, to reveal the third sarcophagus. It was without a lid, and was beautiful if quite plain – a heavy rectangular coffin with ancient, intricate hieroglyphs across it. It would have been a disappointment, perhaps, to anyone expecting the famous gold death mask of King Tut, but this was riveting nonetheless, and now I sensed this was the focal point of my feelings of unease. From our vantage point, we could not see inside the sarcophagus, except to note that there was a Perspex box or shield covering it, to protect the ancient artefact and its precious inhabitant. This was it. This was why my stomach was so filled with cold dread.

'Wow, they really have her mummy in there,' Morticia commented, shifting forward in an attempt to better see, but thwarted by the crowd. 'I have always wanted to see a mummy.'

Again, there was some muffled interaction between the speakers, and the director returned to the microphone. 'For now, we invite you to take a look around the exhibition and enjoy refreshments and canapés, and we will be back shortly with a continuation of the speeches and formali–' the director began, but was cut short when there was a quick electrical flash and the room fell into sudden darkness, causing gasps of surprise.

'What's happening?'

Is this part of the presentation? I wondered fleetingly as the gathering waited uneasily, murmuring and whispering. No. No, this is wrong, all wrong. My eyes slowly adjusted to the low light and I observed the moon far above, through the slanted glass. It was dazzling and haunting, still bright after the full Blue Moon, and no longer hiding behind the clouds. Morticia and I exchanged worried looks in the near blackness. Before long, the museum's emergency lights came on, throwing the space into a strange, greenish hue. I frowned. Did it have to be green? Of all colours? First the speeches, now this. All the while, that cold foreboding in my stomach told me to beware. I felt I needed to prepare for something. But what precisely?

The Cobra Queen has come ...

'Stick close to me, okay, Morticia?' I whispered, and we stood back to back, looking around us at the strange scene, holding hands.

'What is that noise?' I heard a woman near me say.

'It must be some part of the show. I think there's going to be a show,' her companion replied.

A noise? There was a strange, sibilant sound rising up from the front of the gallery. Perhaps it was part of a show, but something about it caused my throat to constrict and again, the pit of my stomach was as cold as frost on an icicle. What was that noise, exactly? It sounded like a kind of *hissing*...? The faint noise grew louder, until it was a din that dominated the large gallery. Suddenly I knew why it troubled me so.

My nightmares. It was the sound from my nightmares.

'Oh god!' someone yelled.

'Help!'

The first shriek came from the front, near the podium where the speakers were. It was quickly followed by loud gasps and another scream, and the crowd at the front, closest to the stage split off suddenly, running from something that, at first, I could not see. And then my eyes grew wide. Though surely they must be deceiving me? Because I could swear that a river was moving towards us across the floor of the museum – a dark, seething mass of water, perhaps one or two feet high.

'Snakes!' someone yelled.

They were right. This was not water. Snakes. Thousands of them.

'This way,' I said, and pulled Morticia through the gallery as best I could in the tight crowd, away from where I thought the noise was coming from.

The gallery around us was chaos. The crowd had bolted in all directions, tuxedo-clad men slamming straight into one another in the panic, women falling over long dresses and landing on their knees, handbags flying through the air. I saw a man slide right under a woman's broad ball gown. Guests fell over into the Pool of Reflection with a splash. Morticia was hanging on to my dress as if I was her life raft. I'd heard about crushing crowds like these. Someone would surely be trampled underfoot.

'Let's get up off the floor,' I shouted to Morticia. 'There, quick!' We scurried to the colossal Hatshepsut sphinx, and before any thought of preservation for the ancient relic took hold, we hurled ourselves on top of the lion-like body on its pedestal, holding on to her human-shaped head and the sides of the Nemes headdress she wore, like two women clinging to an elephant by the ears. From our new vantage point I could see the terrifying flood of serpents, writhing and hissing across the floor of the gallery, some rearing up to show the distinctive heads of poisonous cobras, their hoods sitting out. I dropped my notebook and didn't care, instead holding my pen like a dagger and looking this way and that. 'Oh my goddess,' I whispered, horrified and wishing I could somehow be lifted away, by Deus or Lieutenant Luke, who might by now, as it was after dark, sense my disquiet and panic, as our bond seemed to allow him to. And yet I knew there was no way I was about to be magically whisked away by anyone. This felt personal, like destiny. Otherwise why the nightmares? The premonition?

The serpents were slithering over fallen guests and storming after others, striking angrily. *The Cobra Queen has come,* I thought. Lieutenant Luke had given me the message. Now I had to be prepared.

'How on earth!? Where have they all come from?' Morticia asked in a shaky voice. This was clearly not a natural event, no matter who was seeing it. First the mute archaeologist. Then the electricity. Now this. 'Is it the spirits?' she asked.

'It is, but I don't know what kind of spirits, exactly,' I admitted.

Time passed strangely in the darkened gallery and the screaming crowd went quiet, their movements slowing until they swayed in place where they stood. The phantom serpents who had attacked them disappeared as suddenly and mysteriously as they'd arrived, vanishing to some unknown realm, but in their wake, the guests at the Met had changed. How strange that they had grown so quiet, the mass panic of the crowd having subsided. How strange that they swayed like this, as if in a group waltz. Morticia and I hung on to the Hatshepsut sphinx and watched the eerie scene.

'Are they okay?'

'I don't know,' I said. I thought not. 'Something has happened to them.'

'Where have all the snakes gone?'

I shook my head, and we continued to cling tensely to the giant sphinx of the female pharaoh as each of the guests, swaying quietly on their feet, began to swoon. One by one they fell sideways or collapsed straight down on to the hard flooring, as if fainting or rather too suddenly dropping to their knees and crumpling into a ball. Down went one. Then another, and another, their bodies making soft thudding sounds as they hit the ground, and within less than a minute all of the guests, perhaps two hundred of them, were down. Some appeared to curl up to sleep on the hard floors, though their eyes remained open. The speakers, the director and professor, and Dr Gamal were all down on their sides, though they seemed to have fallen into unconsciousness, like the others, their eyes were open, staring forward. Further back behind us, some servers had fallen, their trays of canapés clattering loudly. None had uttered a word or so much as a pained grunt as they hit the ground.

The well-heeled crowd of guests were quiet now, sprawled out in their tuxedos and designer gowns in what was a strange spectacle of glamorous slumber in the darkened gallery of the Met; body upon body, eyes open but seemingly oblivious to the supernatural forces surrounding them. At least I *hoped* they were only unconscious. It was like a kind of collective trance. Mass sedation.

All of the guests but *us*.

I spotted Jay a few metres away, and on instinct I climbed down from the sphinx and ran over, bobbing and weaving around the bodies of fallen guests. I cocked my head and regarded my ex-boyfriend, who seemingly slept on his side, one strong arm curled under his head. I watched him closely and saw his chest rise and fall, barely perceptibly. Yes, he was breathing. Was he sleeping?

'Jay, are you okay? Were you bitten?' I asked him and crouched down.

As I expected, he did not respond.

His hazel eyes were staring forward, glazed. I'd seen this look before, when Deus had erased dozens of people on the street. It was something like the vague look I'd seen on his face in Spektor, when he was driving me home, only this was more intense, the face less soft. I looked to one guest's face and then another. I spotted Jennifer nearby. Each face was blank, staring forward, bodies limp, each making soft breathing sounds. I checked for a pulse at Jay's neck. His heart was beating slowly, he was breathing. He was there and yet not there. And then I followed his line of sight. He was staring towards the sarcophagus in the centre of the room. I looked to my left and right and saw that they all were, each set of staring eyes looking towards the revealed mummy of the pharaoh.

'Jay, if you can hear me, I will try my best to get you out of this. You may never remember it, but I will try. And your friend Jennifer too. I will try,' I promised him, and stood, surveying the scene and trying to decide what to do next.

This mass exercise in paranormal erasure, if that's what it was, could only mean that something big was set to happen, something that was not the business of the mortal living world. I looked to Morticia, still clinging to the statue, eyes as big as saucers. How odd that she would be untouched, I thought, when everyone else was stricken by this strange sedation. Had it only been the chance of rising above the sea of serpents in time by climbing the sphinx? They had all been bitten, hadn't they? And sent into this weird trance? But not Morticia. Puzzled, I took a few steps forward and stared at her on the sphinx, my head inclined to one side. It looked like there was some kind of dark arc on her pale face, I thought, though it was only partly visible under her shaggy bangs.

'What is it?' she asked, eyes wide with fear. 'What?'

'Nothing.' Possibly my imagination.

Morticia climbed down off the sphinx, staring at the scene around her with her mouth open. We were close to the presentation stage now, where the director had been speaking, and I turned and noticed again, with a sense of unease, that third and central sarcophagus of the pharaoh Hatshepsut, housing the pharaoh's shipped remains. Something made me take Morticia by the hand and lead her away from it.

'I have a feeling,' I said. 'Don't look on the mummy. She does not wish to be seen,' I said.

Oh boy.

Morticia was not untouched, I realised. It had not been my imagination. There was, in fact, something on her face.

'Morticia, are you feeling okay? Is there something … on your face?' I asked gently, and just as the words left my lips an inky teardrop appeared to fall sideways from the outside corner of her eye, sweeping out like a kind of cat eye flick.

'Push your hair back! Now!' I demanded. I spoke so brusquely that she went rigid as a statue and obeyed me, looking quite terrified as she pulled her dyed-black hair back with both hands in a kind of double salute, hands shaking.

I blinked at what I saw. My friend now had one eye tattoo that trailed from the inner and outer corners of her right eye. 'What is that on your–' I began to ask, but my words left me as the inside corner of her other eye began to bleed with the same inky blood, like a teardrop splitting into two lines, with one dropping straight down and stopping about one inch from her inner eye and the other sweeping in a trail across her cheekbone and up under her lashes in a decorative curl. I knew this ancient symbol.

The Eye of Wadjet.

'Something is happening! What's happening to me?!' Morticia wailed and covered her eyes, stepping backwards and tripping over the body of a sleeping man in a tuxedo.

I grabbed her hands away and pushed her shaggy hair back as she lay back, terrified, over the man's body. *My goddess.* When I saw clearly the twin marks etched on her face – horizontal lines curving around her upper eyelid into a wing shape and the twin tear drops and curved tails – I leaped backwards in horror. It was the symbol. She wore the symbol over both of her eyes.

'What is it?' Morticia said, beginning to shake. 'Tell me, Pandora!' She curled forward and stood unsteadily. 'Tell me what's happening!'

'The Eye . . . You have the Eye of Horus,' I told her, memories wheeling through my head as I tried desperately to make sense of what I was seeing. 'Or they call it the Wadjet Eye.'

This is the hour of Wadjet, the Cobra Queen, the Queen of Vengeance, The Goddess of Protection.

'The eye is . . . It's a symbol of Wadjet,' I said stupidly, trying to find my memories and my words. 'It's a royal symbol like . . .' *Come on brain, you know this stuff. You must remember!*

To ancient Egyptians, the eye was not a passive organ but an agent of action, of wrath.

'The Eye of Horus or Eye of Wadjet is an eye of protection and wrath. When Set and Horus were fighting for the throne Set gouged out Horus's eye and it was eventually recovered. He offered it to Osiris, the King of the Dead or the Underworld, and the eye became associated with resurrection and sacrifice.'

Why did Morticia have this symbol on her face? The symbol

of Wadjet, the Queen of Vengeance and Royal Protection? The symbol of Horus?

Morticia was looking at me, bewildered and panicked. I pulled more facts out of the vault of my memories, but none of them quite made sense. 'Wadjet is a patron goddess … um, she is a protector of pharaohs, usually depicted as a snake-headed woman or an Egyptian cobra …'

Oh boy. The Cobra Queen.

'I don't understand. Why is this happening to me?' She rubbed her eyes and face and the marks did not budge. She was not marked with anything so temporary as charcoal or makeup.

I had no answer to her question. But whatever the reason, it seemed unlikely to be good. I looked around me at the slack faces of the many fallen visitors. They were not marked. Why were we unaffected by whatever magick kept the rest of them passive, and why was only Morticia marked? I was The Seventh, but what was she?

'Now think carefully, Morticia. Can you think of any reason, any reason at all, why an ancient queen or goddess or other being would want to … mark you?'

Her eyes were as big as dinner plates now. She looked like she might faint from panic and I didn't seem to be helping much. 'No!' She threw her hands in the air. 'No!' She grabbed at her face again, trying to rub the symbols off, and when she looked at her hands they were unmarked. 'Oh god, oh god!'

'Have you ever dabbled in magick?' I said, trying to make sense of it. 'Or tried contacting spirits?'

'I …' At this she faltered.

Oh boy. Morticia had dabbled in something. Something

deadly serious, and during the Agitation there was no telling what could happen. Hadn't I been told that the Agitation changed things? Even the simplest wishes and rituals or games could spawn real paranormal activity?

'Tell me. Tell me now,' I pressed.

My friend turned a whiter shade of pale before turning a deep, embarrassed crimson. Even with all those colour changes, the black marks around her eyes did not budge. 'I've been, you know, reading books on witchcraft,' she explained guiltily. 'It's no big deal. Lots of people do it. So I lit some candles and tried some stuff. Who cares? It didn't do anything,' she said. Though her words were casual and she was quite right – lots of people tried a spell or two when the whim took them and it very rarely did anything, unless it was the likes of my Great-Aunt Celia doing the spell-casting – I could tell that Morticia was unconvinced. She was very afraid that something *had* happened. And, well, in that moment I could not blame her.

'The thing you tried … Did it involve any Egyptian gods? Horus? Or Thoth, by chance?'

She covered her mouth suddenly, recognising the name. Morticia nodded.

'Thoth. With the head of an ibis?'

Again a nod. 'There was a … an invocation written in the book.'

As a god of magick, Thoth was a common subject for occult rituals. And that's what she'd done. She'd read an invocation to the Egyptian god of magick just as we were set to come to an exhibition filled with Egyptian antiquities. The ancient Egyptian god of magick, knowledge and wisdom – one of the most important deities in the ancient Egyptian pantheon. He was the scribe to the gods and in some tellings, the actual keeper of the universe. He was often depicted as a man with the head of an ibis, holding a staff of power in one hand and an ankh – the key of the Nile, the symbol of life – in the other. In later history he was strongly associated with judgement of the dead.

Oh boy.

'But I prayed to all kinds of gods and goddesses and nothing happened!'

'Well, I think this one may have heard you. Thoth was said to have restored Horus's eye.'

'Holy ... holy hell!' she shrieked and covered her face with both hands.

'No such thing,' I said of hell. Then thought, *I hope.* I would have believed just about anything at that moment. 'Look, Morticia ... I think you have been chosen for some reason, to wear this Wadjet Eye or Eye of Horus.' It seemed a near-impossible coincidence that she could have been dabbling in the occult, calling Thoth just as the Agitation was happening, without knowing. I had not told her about the Agitation and the Revolution of the Dead. She would have thought I was crazy, I'd believed, but now, of course, I'd have to tell her everything if we got through this alive. But could it be a coincidence? No. Had something or someone led her, suggested it to her in her dreams, influenced her in some way so she would invoke an Egyptian god of magick, and so I would invite her to this event, everything conspiring to bring us to this moment?

'Chosen for what?' she said, her voice high-pitched.

'That, I do not know,' I said, and I was scared for her – both of us, really, though I had at least a slightly better idea of what I was chosen for. 'Can you remember what you were doing? What you might have said, specifically?' I looked to the exits, both of which seemed miles away across the strewn and resting bodies of the hundreds of guests. Maybe I could get her out of here before …

Breaking glass diverted my attention and I looked back as four shabti figures, two of them made of blue faience and two of brown-black basalt, broke from their display cases in the exhibition and began to swell dramatically in size, outgrowing their carved bodies and mummification wrappings and shedding the faience and basalt like snake skins. In seconds they were ten feet tall and standing strong in the big gallery.

Holy hell on wheels. Or not hell exactly. Wrong mythology.

The shabtis! Of course. This must have been some kind of premonition. Remembering my own, I fidgeted with my bag. Morticia was past the point of motion, standing in terrified silence and gaping at the huge figures.

There was a deep rumble that shook the sandstone foundations of the Temple of Dendur, and several patrons moaned or fidgeted in their supernaturally induced sedation, perhaps distantly aware of the terror to come. It seemed the forces that be, whatever forces were at work, were ready for their moment. Morticia was as white as I'd ever seen her, and now she stood behind me and held on to my arm.

Here we go.

I pulled out my five shabtis and instructed her to remove the two from her bag. Morticia still could not move, petrified as she was, and I took her bag from her and placed the seven shabtis at our feet and willed them to grow large. 'Obey me,' I whispered. 'Please ...' They did not. *Come on ... come on ... do something ...* 'Shabtis, I call on you,' I whispered urgently. Still nothing.

Now there was movement, something rising up and taking shape from within the sarcophagus I dared not peer into. A creature was materialising. Or several. No, it was one creature, unmistakably an Egyptian goddess of the old world, and she rose and took form until she filled the space above me, perhaps thirty feet high, taller even than the great gate of the Temple of Dendur behind her, bent and peering angrily down at me.

Gulp.

The goddess was swathed in the traditional kilt and headdress of a pharaoh, a striped Nemes headdress falling just above her bare human-like breasts. But this creature, though unmistakably female, was not human. Above her neck was not a woman's head, but that of a lion with its terrible lips parted to display pointed feline teeth. And above the striped headdress were two fiercely hissing cobras, their hoods flared. They spat and hissed, as wrathful as the mysterious supernatural serpents who had put the other guests into their unnatural slumber.

Yes, Wadjet. I knew her from my mother's books. This was one of the physical forms of Wadjet, protector of the pharaohs. And she was not happy.

I gaped, unable to take my eyes off the twin snakes that sat like second and third heads above her headdress, emitting a terrible sibilant noise at a frequency that seemed to shake the brain in my skull. I was shocked and yet I had expected this, had known somehow that something would happen at this launch, though I'd known not what. Whatever the reason, this lion-headed woman had risen from Hatshepsut's sarcophagus and she wanted my attention. Her two large feline eyes and four smaller serpent ones focused directly on me with a kind of steady, barely contained rage. Finally the bone-rattling hiss subsided, and I heard a booming voice. Though this powerful and menacing being – *Or is she a collection of beings?* I thought – was not visibly speaking, and had no human mouth, I could hear her clearly. She spoke with long pauses between each word:

I am Wadjet, the Cobra Queen.

I am the Queen of Vengeance, the Protector of Kings, sworn to protect my Pharaoh for all time.

The great pharaoh has been defiled. Now she will rise.

Prepare for your destruction.

I swallowed and backed up, nearly causing Morticia to trip over behind me. Destruction? Because of the pharaoh Hatshepsut? But her tomb was defiled centuries before!

'Wait,' I said, holding up my hands, and my gaze passed over the shabtis at my feet, sitting as uselessly as little toy soldiers. 'Great Goddess Wadjet, Cobra Queen, respectfully, you've made a mistake. We are not responsible for this. We did not defile the mighty pharaoh,' I said in a loud but placating tone, with my hands still in the air, as if a great cannon were trained on me. The cobras on her head shifted back and forth in the air, ready to strike out. Morticia had moved to crouch down behind my back, unsuccessfully hiding. The marks on her face had not budged. This was not good. None of this was good.

'What mistake?' Morticia said quietly into the backs of my legs. She could not hear the creature's booming voice, I realised, but I was quite sure she could see it, or at the very least feel the malevolent magick at work, as she was shaking like a leaf.

I held up my hands further in surrender and didn't so much as twitch for fear of prompting a swift and violent attack. I spoke very softly. 'This is Wadjet, the protector of the pharaohs,' I explained in a low voice to my terrified friend behind me. 'She thinks it was us who defiled the resting place of Hatshepsut. I think.'

'Us? But we just came to a launch at the museum!' Morticia shrieked, and the cobras atop Wadjet's head darted forward, spitting something green and acrid into the air between us. I dodged to one side and Morticia shrieked and fell to the ground, covering her head. The green spit of the Cobra Queen narrowly missed us, and I noticed with a shiver that it bubbled and hissed on the floor next to us, as if eating away at the stone.

Launches seemed like increasingly dangerous propositions, I decided. The first one I had ever attended ended in a confrontation with a 400-year-old dead noblewoman with a penchant for virgin blood, and this time it was an acid-spitting lion-headed goddess with cobras for hair. This new big-city lifestyle wasn't all it was cracked up to be.

'Great goddess, great Protector Wadjet, respectfully, it wasn't us,' I told Hatshepsut's ancient protector. 'We are here only as guests of the exhibition. We are not the ones responsible for the exhibition, or the removal of her body from her tomb. I swear this to you.'

The lion-headed creature moved forward, narrowing her huge cat eyes. I swallowed heavily.

'The Great Pharaoh Hatshepsut has been defiled,' she announced with a pause between each word. 'There must be a sacrifice. You are the representative of your people.' She pointed at me accusingly with one long, human-like finger. Hatshepsut's four great shabtis came to stand on either side of the sarcophagus and the giant, looming figure of Wadjet.

'I am? The representative of which people?' This was a thing to do with being The Seventh, no doubt about it. It was always down to me, wasn't it? These countesses and queens and goddesses always wanted answers from me, but I didn't have any! It hardly seemed fair that I'd have to answer for grave robbers and the actions of archaeologists who explored the Valley of the Kings more than a century before I was even born.

'Hatshepsut's grave was desecrated in antiquity,' I said as calmly as I could in the face of the titanic creature. 'I was not responsible. In fact no one here was responsible.' *Directly*, I thought. 'I was not even born then, I can assure you. We have ...' I began, thinking. 'We have gathered your great pharaoh's funerary belongings together in one place,' I said, stretching my arms out to gesture to the gallery, 'so ... um, so your great and wise pharaoh may be whole again and rest in eternity.'

I wasn't sure what made me say it, but for once so many of Hatshepsut's belongings were in one place and I thought it might appease this great creature whose job was to protect her beloved pharaoh. The cobras continued to watch me, writhing and hissing, and Wadjet's lion eyes drilled into me as she thought this over. Hatshepsut's mummy had been moved out of her tomb and damaged, along with most of the statues and reliefs of her. It was all thought by most academics to be part of a campaign of Tutmosis III to discredit the female pharaoh after her death. So why didn't this Cobra Queen go after him? Or Howard Carter? Or any of the other number of archaeologists who had been to her tomb and taken things? Surely a mighty being like this would have got the memo? But now it was all here in New York and it was the Agitation and here we were. How about that for luck?

I looked down and frowned. Blasted shabtis!

'The great pharaoh was stolen, and lain in the tomb of her wet nurse.' At least that's what I'd read. 'She was hidden away, but not by us. She is now recognised as the great pharaoh she is, and –'

The hissing and spitting serpents grew still, eyes on me, and in that great voice Wadjet spoke. 'The pharaoh must have her sacrifice, and she has chosen.'

'Whoa. Look. With respect, Cobra Queen or Wadjet, or whatever you would best like me to call you, I feel like you haven't listened to a word I said –'

'Most wise one, Thoth, has brought her sacrifice here. We shall begin,' the Cobra Queen said, dismissing my words, and to my horror Morticia began to shift along the ground towards the sarcophagus. But her feet weren't moving; she was being pulled along by some force, and now the giant shabtis were reaching for her and lifting her up above their heads. Poor Morticia was positively stricken with terror, struggling but unable even to scream, her strength no match for the ten-foot-tall, supernaturally animated figures of ancient workers.

No, Thoth did not bring her here! That was me. And Vlad. *Hell.* I really should have left her heartbroken outside the subway. Anything but this.

'No, no, no . . .!' I shouted. 'Put her down! Put her down now!' I demanded, but the pharaoh's shabtis did not listen to me. Neither did mine.

'No!' I screamed, and the air grew cold and misty around me, and in seconds the form of Lieutenant Luke materialised, stepping forward and standing between the giant creature and me in his fully human form, uniform impeccable, his cavalry sword raised.

'Luke!' I gasped, relieved to see him.

The great creature before me turned to notice him, and her eyes fixed on his face. 'I see you have a servant willing to sacrifice himself.'

I looked to Luke and back to the giant swaying goddess. 'No one is sacrificing anybody!' I shouted.

I couldn't lose Luke. Not now that we finally had each other. I stepped forward and placed a hand on his uniformed shoulder. 'Don't leave me,' I said. We could battle this thing together, I reasoned.

Luke raised his sword. 'I will not let you harm her!'

'Very well,' the goddess said and behind us glass broke again. Canopic jars flew past.

'What's happening?' Morticia cried as she was shifted in the air, and with relief I saw that she was being gently lowered to the ground by the shabtis. She was being released!

'Thank you,' I said, relieved, but when Luke turned I saw confusion etched across his handsome features, and worse, I saw that his eyes were changing. They were not turning green again, nor black, this was something else, something worse. Ink ran from the inside corners of his bright blue eyes, the symbols forming as if drawn by invisible hands. He was marked, as Morticia had been.

In moments he fell, thudding to the floor as so many of the guests had done, his Union cap rolling to my feet, and cavalry sword clattering to the floor

'Good goddess,' I said aloud as Luke, his face now marked with the Eye of Horus, was pulled forward across the ground, out of my reach, and then picked up by the giant shabtis (not mine, which remained frustratingly inert), his beautiful human form heartbreakingly limp and vulnerable. An ancient brain hook went flying across the gallery to the centre of the Temple of Dendur, where I could see he was being taken. Now I understood.

This was the place my lover would be sacrificed for the resurrection of Hatshepsut. The Cobra Queen was going to resurrect Hatshepsut so she could avenge those who defiled her tomb, but something was missing.

'They want a brain. A brain for their pharaoh . . .' I whispered in horror.

'They what?' Morticia said. I saw that the lines on her face had disappeared. She had been released and was safe now, or as safe as she could be in this chaotic wing of the Met before a colossal serpent goddess, an angry mummified pharaoh and her giant shabti workers. Luke had presented himself at just the right – or wrong – moment. It was to be him, now. The sacrifice was to be him. I just couldn't let that happen.

'Great Pharaoh Hatshepsut,' I called, summoning the spirit of the ancient king. 'I call on you now!' I had my mother's interpreter jewel, the Babel Pendant, around my neck. Thank goddess I brought it. I did not speak the pharaoh's language.

The serpent goddess, who had been overseeing the preparations for the sacrifice of my lover, turned and hissed at me with her double cobra heads, blocking my path to the temple. 'How dare you call on my mistress!' she bellowed, and I outstretched my arms and closed my eyes, filled with fury. There would be no swaying this protector. I had to go to the source.

'I am The Seventh. *She will hear me!*' I declared with authority. The Cobra Queen had to let me pass, and I had to convince Hatshepsut this sacrifice could not go ahead, that the shabtis should cease their mission. This was madness. 'Your mistress will hear me now!'

There was a moment of silence, and then the sarcophagus began to emit a keening sound I had never heard before, and I felt my throat seize up. *Stay strong, Pandora. Stay strong. You have the power. You are The Seventh.*

'I am The Seventh!' I declared again, this time stronger and with yet more fury, thinking of Luke's human form and his vulnerable state, and I lifted from the floor of the gallery, actually lifted into the air. Beneath me, my seven shabti figures burst to life, growing in size until they were ten feet tall and standing at my sides, as I was suspended in the air. 'I am The Seventh! Hear me now!'

My shabti figures lumbered towards the centre of the temple, where Luke lay helpless, set on their task of stopping the ritual. There was a tussle between the pharaoh's shabtis and mine, who, at seven, thankfully outnumbered them, and I winced as part of the Temple of Dendur was broken, puffs of dust rising into the air, as reanimated shabti smashed against its ancient walls. I hoped it was not too late to stop the gruesome ritual happening within.

'Your Pharaoh Hatshepsut will hear me! Now!' I demanded, and finally the Cobra Queen relented. As if dismissed by her unseen mistress she began to dematerialise, shrinking down again until she was back inside the sarcophagus from whence she came, and out of the sarcophagus something else rose …

Someone else …

Soon a ghastly figure was revealed, standing upright from within the heavy sarcophagus. There was no doubt as to her identity. Hatshepsut's mummified body had been greatly damaged by time and by those who would defile her, ribs showing through where her brown, leathery skin did not cover her. Her nose was stuffed with cloths, one ear had sunk into her head. Her eyes were leathery and without eyeballs, the sockets stuffed with wrapped cloths, as big as bugs' eyes. The pharaoh's wrath was great, and perhaps justified, but I would not let her sacrifice my spirit guide, my Luke.

'I am the Pharaoh Hatshepsut. Who dares to call on me!' the mummy demanded, her lips unmoving but her voice loud within my skull.

I could hear the Egyptian tongue in my own language, clear as day. Her voice, and the rage behind it, chilled me.

'Do not take his brain, Great Pharaoh!' I shouted, walking towards her floating, mummified corpse and bowing my head before her. 'Take mine!'

She placed one withered and skeletal hand on my head, and I returned the gesture, touching her dry, bald skull, and an extraordinary flash of light overcame me.

I was no longer in the museum in New York, I was flying through constellations, through spinning colours and shapes and now I was in ancient Egypt, I was a child, a princess, and I could see the world through her young eyes, and now she was older, a young wife and mother, and then regent for her stepson, and there was Punt, where she led a peaceful expedition, and there she was negotiating and ruling, wearing a false beard and the clothes of men to ensure her authority, and then she was older and dying and her body was growing weak with disease and age, and I witnessed her deathbed, and finally her embalming and mummification, performed gently, with care and reverence, and her body laid to rest in its proper place, in her sarcophagus – one she had commissioned to be fit for the pharaoh she became – and there was such peace, such a sense of wonder in the great Elysian Fields, the Field of Reeds with her people. She was next to join the gods, it was her turn to rise and take her place, and just as she was to rise she was ripped away, torn from her burial place by thieves, criminals sent by Tutmosis, and her spirit was back in her withered and damaged body, trapped on the dirty floor of a cave deep underground – no shoes, no crown, no burial goods to accompany her. Her rightful ascension had been taken from her, and she was doomed to lie there for centuries without rest, unnamed, with only her anger and grief to accompany her.

'You are The Seventh,' she said, her mummified face showing awe. She released her hand, and I released mine, feeling great empathy, as if this woman were someone I knew intimately. 'Without you, The Seventh, the living world will fall,' she said. 'The balance will be undone.' And then I could see her, the woman herself, not the corpse, her living visage sitting out from her withered remains like a misty white projection. It was beautiful, almost angelic. Hatshepsut was a noble-looking older woman, heavyset and proud, wearing crisp, ceremonial robes and a stunning, elaborate headdress. She had those rounded, high cheekbones from the statues that surrounded us.

There was something wet and glittering on her face. Tears. Tears that came from the round, mummified, cloth-plugged holes that had once been her eyes, but which also came from her ethereal ghostly visage, and I realised I was the same, my cheeks also damp as I wept. 'I cannot let it happen,' I told her. 'I must save the living world,' I said, though I knew not how I would do it.

'The defiling of my tomb demanded a sacrifice, a tribute. It has already been given, Pandora English, The Seventh,' she said.

'It has?'

'Your sacrifices have been given,' the pharaoh said gravely, and in a flash I was given a vision of my mother and father, reaching out for me with open arms, suitcases on the ground next to them, having arrived home to Gretchenville to retrieve me from my Aunt Georgia's, another reality in which they survived the trip to Egypt. In this reality my eleven-year-old self was swept up into my mother's arms, smiling, and she was here still, by my side to guide me and help me understand my powers. The feeling of this reality filled me for a moment with an almost painful love and contentment, for I knew it wasn't to be. And then their loving, outstretched arms were pulled away, the vision of them and our future potential together unravelling, and I was left with the image in my mind of their fatal embrace beneath the sands of the Valley of the Kings, where they had been trapped, holding on to each other as their lives drained away like the sands in an hourglass, arms linked, together to the last.

Predestiny.

The interconnectedness of time, and of all things.

I was struck with a profound sense of knowledge then, a weighty recognition of something ineffable and so much bigger than myself, so vast and all-encompassing and mind-altering that for the moment I could not speak.

'Your sacrifices have been made. The Great Protector Goddess Wadjet is appeased,' Hatshepsut said. 'My belongings are returned, and I can be at rest once again with my people in the Field of Reeds, soon to ascend. Go in peace, Pandora English, The Seventh. The living world depends upon you.'

And with that she crumbled into sand before my eyes, along with her sarcophagus and the Canopic jars her shabtis had assembled, and soon all of her belongings, her shabtis, her funerary goods, each part of the exhibition and displays turned to sand and were gone, returned, somehow to their rightful place, somewhere many miles from the confines of the museum, in some place that would not be found again by the living. I reached out to the space where she had been, and found I was alone, except for my friend, Morticia.

The pharaoh Hatshepsut and her protector had left us.

My sacrifices have been made?

I was deeply uneasy about what that meant. Had the deaths of my parents so many years ago been a consequence of this moment? Some kind of predestined trade? Surely not? Would they have died if I was never going to meet Hatshepsut, was never going to have to face the Agitation or the Revolution of the Dead? If I wasn't needed as The Seventh?

Sacrifices …

Luke.

Without hesitation, the Cobra Queen no longer blocking me, I left Morticia to run towards the Temple of Dendur, finding great sections of the temple smashed, lying on the ground. My seven shabtis, which had been mighty and tall, lay like tiny, insignificant fragments among the ruins, I noticed. But Luke, where was my Luke? I found the broken entry and stepped inside the confines of the temple.

Luke was there, and when I saw him, a gasp escaped me. He was in the centre of the temple, on the floor, unmoving. I ran to him and knelt at his side. 'Luke? Luke are you okay? Luke, I got her. The Cobra Queen is gone now. The pharaoh is at rest …'

He did not respond. I leaned over him and felt for a pulse – a disorienting thing to do after knowing him so long as a ghost. Shifting his wrist made his head fall to one side, blood trickling from his right nostril. Beside him was an open Canopic jar, I noticed with horror. It was not empty. *Oh good goddess, it was not empty.* Tears sprung from my eyes afresh. Could it be? Could they really have done this to Luke?

'Pandora?' It was Morticia's voice. 'There is someone here. He says his name is Deus?' I heard her say, and heard her approaching footsteps on the rubble.

Deus. Of course. This wasn't his battle, but he would help us get home.

'Oh!' she said, with a kind of shock, and I knew she'd stepped into the temple and could see where Lieutenant Luke lay.

I was holding his head in my hands. 'He's gone, Morticia,' I said, weeping despite myself. 'He's gone. The Cobra Queen took his … she took his brain for her pharaoh. I was too late to stop it. The shabtis were too late.'

Morticia brought a hand to her mouth. 'Who was he?' she said, her words muffled. Of course she could see him. Luke had made himself human, living, for us, so we could carry on.

Who was Second Lieutenant Luke Thomas? My throat was so tight I almost could not speak. 'He was my lover, Morticia. My spirit guide and friend. He was … the only man I've loved. And he loved me.'

Chapter Twelve

The Cobra Queen and the great Pharaoh Hatshepsut came to New York, but New York did not remember. There would be some explanation, no doubt, for the destruction in the gallery. A pipe had burst. There was a gas leak. A terrorist attack. Headlines would be made and the launch guests – who had begun to wake as we made our exit – would not remember what happened in the Egyptian wing of the Met.

I certainly remembered. And there was not much chance my friend Morticia would forget the night her brain was nearly sacrificed to an ancient pharaoh and her serpent queen of vengeance – but then, the supernatural world had its way of assuring secrecy. Humans had a way of forgetting or being entirely blind to the most extraordinary things, like those swirling green clouds in the sky Deus had showed me. But not Morticia, I thought. No, I had a feeling my friend would not wake erased. She was different.

With a heavy heart I looked over to Celia's luxurious velvet Victorian settee to see my friend sleeping soundly, a pillow tucked under her arm and one gangly leg hanging out from under a plush blanket, the leg cased in torn tights. My great-aunt had helped me move her favourite settee from her lounge room to the corner of my bedroom, to give Morticia somewhere safe to sleep the night off. (She'd insisted I not give up my own bed.) I watched my friend, wondering what she would think when she came to. Her face was thankfully without the mark now. That mark had fallen on Luke. He had given himself. Was that what he'd intended? Or had he come to fight? He'd appeared so suddenly, so heroically, and now . . .

Now his dead body lay under a velvet cloth in Celia's antechamber. I'd hoped it would somehow disappear at daybreak, like so many horrors of that night. That he would be renewed in his ghostly form, the form he had taken for over a century. But he was there in his uniform. Human. Lifeless.

I ran a hand over my face. Sacrifices.

And what about my friend here? Would Morticia remember anything? *Everything?* The Wadjet Eye and the Cobra Queen and the shabtis with their brain hook and the grisly sacrifice of that beautiful Civil War soldier who had appeared seemingly from nowhere? The supernatural serpents had chosen not to bite her, and there were no Sanguine here, erasing her memories, and Deus had not taken on that task. Would she have the kind of mind that closed off supernatural events, like my father, or like Jay Rockwell? Or would she be open? If she remembered I would have no choice but to try to explain the Agitation and the Revolution of the Dead. And, well, the haunted house in Spektor where she currently slept. It might take her a while to recover from it all, I reflected. Physically, but also in other ways. And even with everything else I'd been through in the preceding months, it would take some time for me to process everything that had transpired in one night at the Met.

Well, I had wanted to confide in her. Now there was no way to avoid it.

She *was* just sleeping, wasn't she?

I tiptoed up to Morticia and crouched down near her face. She was so still and so pale. I frowned. There was a makeup compact on the counter in the bathroom, I recalled, and I found myself jumping up to get it. When I came back to Morticia she had not stirred, and I held the open compact up to her mouth and watched the mirror carefully.

Phew.

It fogged up with her barely detectable breathing. My shoulders dropped. I was relieved. On top of everything else, I couldn't have anything happen to my only real girlfriend in New York – not on my watch.

When my great-aunt knocked on my bedroom door, it was late evening, the moon high, and I had never felt so blue. I got the feeling she sensed my misery radiating through her beloved penthouse.

I invited her in, my voice barely loud enough to be heard through the door, and she found me sitting on the edge of my bed, gripping the bedpost, my gaze locked on the wedding photograph of my parents. I'd been there for some time, unable to move, thinking on my parents, thinking on Luke, and wondering what, if anything, I could have done to save them. For a moment Great-Aunt Celia said nothing, but it didn't take a lot of imagination to guess what I was thinking about.

'I made some tea, darling,' she said from the doorway. I looked up and saw that she had her mesh veil on, and her red silk jacket and skirt ensemble. As usual, she wore silk stockings and her feet were in glamorous marabou slippers. I wondered if Deus was back, if they had had another of their 'dates' and what he had told her of the night before at the Met. True, he'd been helpful in getting us swiftly out as the guests had begun to come out of their trance, but he'd not been much help when I was faced with a several-storeys-high cobra-cum-lion goddess creature with ideas of resurrection and sacrifice. I could have used a hand.

'Great-Aunt Celia, do you think they died because of me – my parents?' Maybe it wasn't a simple accident that killed them, nor an ancient mummy's curse for disturbing her tomb, because ultimately Hatshepsut had not been at her tomb, no mummy had been, as they'd been moved in antiquity. If it wasn't a curse from a tomb, was it *me*? Was it Pandora, their child? Was I the reason they were dead?

'Am I the reason they died? Luke died because of me,' I added.

'Darling Pandora, your Civil War friend died many years before you were born,' Celia replied, sounding a touch more blasé about it than I appreciated.

I looked at the floor, feeling fragile. Celia's certainty and wisdom was something I usually cherished, but in that moment I just couldn't take her calm in the face of my fresh loss. 'You know what I mean.'

'There's no point in being morose, darling. Your friend Morticia is eating now but she will doubtless want to talk with you tonight. And I think you ought to check on the portal,' she said simply. 'Once you've had some tea.'

The portal? I had been thinking on it, feeling it in the deep bowels of this mansion, hearing the house shifting, but I hadn't had the will to rise and go down there, not when I'd been with Luke the last time I checked on the entry to the Underworld, and now Luke, my first lover, my spirit guide, was lost to me.

'Come. Have tea,' Celia beckoned, and I did.

Half an hour later I took the elevator down to the lobby, somewhat restored by my great-aunt's tea and the company of her and my friend Morticia (who was only just coming to her senses, and would no doubt soon have many questions). I stepped out and found myself alone, pleased the lobby was free of Sanguine. But there was something in the air that wasn't right. Or more specifically, something in the earth.

Beneath my ballet flats the lobby tiles were cracked. It seemed to me the cracks had grown a little more, pulled further apart somehow. Where once the cracks were hairline, I now fancied I could lose a marble in the gaps across the floor. Yes. The cracks were larger. I was sure of it. I'd noticed it on the way in, but Vlad had been carrying Morticia, and Deus had been carrying the fallen body of my lover (Luke would not have liked that, I guessed) and there had been much else to distract me.

Still, I'd known for days that things were afoot, the house shifting and speaking.

Feeling the prickle of the tiny hairs on my neck standing on end, I used the skeleton key to open the hidden passage which led to the other side of the house and to Dr Edmund Barrett's laboratory. By the time I reached the laboratory door, and then Barrett's study, my stomach was as cold as a winter's day in Moscow. I felt a foreboding like none I had experienced before, (and that was really saying something), and as I unbolted the lock that would lead me to the great cavern and portal to the Underworld or Otherworld I felt a rumble. There was movement.

No.

I stepped out the other side and saw that the vast cavern was alight. The runes were glowing green. *GLOWING.*

And I was not alone. A white figure was floating just above the waterline of the deep sulphurous lake that stretched through the cavern to the glowing portal. A nebulous figure, a uniformed figure, familiar, his back turned.

'*Luke!*' I cried out. 'Lieutenant Luke!'

The figure turned and began to walk across the dark water towards me. It was Luke, unmistakably, his face unreadable, eyes glowing blue.

'Luke, you're alive! Or, a ghost ... You aren't gone!' I was confused and relieved, so relieved.

After a minute he reached me, his face taking shape, his form solidifying into the ghostly shape I knew – the Union cap I'd last seen on the temple floor now at an angle on his long, sandy hair. 'With the night I am renewed, Miss Pandora,' he said, as he reached me, and we embraced.

I gaped, holding him. 'You knew?'

'It was taking some chance, but yes, Miss Pandora. I knew I would see you again.' He looked at me, his face close to mine.

I buried my head in his shoulder and held his ghostly form so hard I thought I would go through him, and then suddenly it changed, became solid under my hands, and I realised he had made himself human for me. I wrapped my eager arms around his uniformed, human body, the body that had made love to me only days before, the body I'd thought I'd lost, and closed my eyes as I felt him, his spirit coursing through me.

'Luke, I thought I'd lost you.'

'You are my beloved. I will always be there when you need me,' he said.

'I think you saved Morticia. And possibly me, as well.'

He pulled away, and looked at me with a degree of seriousness, his brow knitted. 'You are The Seventh, Miss Pandora. Never forget that. You are more powerful than you know. You did not need saving.'

I didn't know what to say to that. 'But I did appreciate the help,' I whispered into his ear, finally, and kissed his neck gently, breathing him in. For the moment his heavenly, human scent made me forget the sulphurous smell of the cavern and our unsettling surrounds, and I forgot the sight of him dead on the temple floor.

The earth shook again, so forcefully that we broke from our embrace. I turned and stepped down to the edge of the dark water, Luke trailing behind. The torch flames turned green around us, matching the green of the runes around the portal, and the fire reflected through the huge cavern, turning the water an eerie hue. Helplessly, I stood at the base of the stone staircase with my spirit guide by my side, and we watched as the giant portal opened, as if by invisible hands.

Or not so invisible hands. Hands that were on the other side of the portal.

Oh boy.

It's here.

It's now.

The Revolution of the Dead had begun.

ACKNOWLEDGEMENTS

The ongoing journey of my beloved Pandora English would not be possible without the support of her dedicated fans who would not give up on her, the wonderful Echo Publishing and author and editor Angela Meyer who got on board with her resurrection, and my own 'Great Aunt Celia', my dear Australian literary agent Selwa Anthony. Thank you for believing in Pandora, as I do.

Readers, I truly couldn't do this without you. Thank you.

I imagined Pandora and her world as an homage to classic mythology, old school horror tales and popular stories of the paranormal, but with a twist. Hers is a world where the witches aren't always evil, and for that matter, neither are the fanged undead (though to be fair, they aren't all that easy to live with either) and perhaps most importantly, the women aren't relegated to the role of victim, love interest or innocent young girl who needs saving. In Pandora's world, women are powerful and complex, if not always good. They are villains and heroes, but never one dimensional.

I owe some thanks to Bela Lugosi, my first dark crush age 6, Bram Stoker, who has 'a lot to answer for', and the real Elizabeth Bathory, whose story and subsequent mythology was the inspiration for The Blood Countess herself. I must also thank the Met, and of course Hatshepsut, the real life princess who became a pharaoh, for the inspiration for The Cobra Queen. For Hatshepsut's identification I would like to acknowledge the work of Dr Zahi Hawass and his team. (The names of the Egyptologists present at the ill-fated fictional launch of the exhibition in this novel are made up.) Thank you also to Wiccan goddess Fiona Horne for the obsidian and circle of protection, and the ethereal mists of the Blue Mountains where I wrote many of these books, for the supernatural mists of Spektor. The supernatural seems always to sit at the edges of the natural world.

To my precious family, Dad and Lou, Nik and Dorothy, Jacquelyn and Wayne, Annelies, Linda and Maureen, I love you. To my daughter Sapphira – who I was pregnant with as I wrote *The Blood Countess*, and I have now seen grow old enough to read these books to at bedtime – you are a loving, creative and precious human being. Thank you for making my life infinitely richer. To my dear husband Berndt, thank you for the patience, the love, the coffee, and so much more.

Mom, I never forget you.

www.taramoss.com